P9-DER-457

Premeditated Myrtle

THE MYRTLE HARDCASTLE MYSTERIES

Premeditated Myrtle

How to Get Away with Myrtle

Cold-Blooded Myrtle

ALSO BY ELIZABETH C. BUNCE

A Curse Dark as Gold

StarCrossed

Liar's Moon

Premeditated Myrtle

A MYRTLE HARDCASTLE MYSTERY

Elizabeth C. Bunce

ALGONQUIN YOUNG READERS 2021

Published by Algonquin Young Readers
an imprint of Algonquin Books of Chapel Hill
Post Office Box 2225
Chapel Hill, North Carolina 27515-2225

a division of Workman Publishing
225 Varick Street
New York, New York 10014

© 2020 by Stephanie Elizabeth Bunce.
All rights reserved.

First paperback edition, Algonquin Young Readers, September 2021.
Originally published in hardcover by Algonquin Young Readers in
September 2020.
Printed in the United States of America. Published simultaneously
in Canada by Thomas Allen & Son Limited.
Design by Carla Weise.

LIBRARY OF CONGRESS CATALOGING-IN-PUBLICATION DATA

Names: Bunce, Elizabeth C., author.
Title: Premeditated Myrtle / Elizabeth C. Bunce.
Description: First edition. | Chapel Hill :
Algonquin Young Readers, 2020. |
"A Myrtle Hardcastle mystery." | Audience: Ages 10 and up. |
Audience: Grades 4–6. | Summary: When twelve-year-old
aspiring detective Myrtle Hardcastle learns her neighbor in
quiet Swinburne, England, a breeder of rare flowers, has died,
she is certain it was murder and that she must find the killer.
Identifiers: LCCN 2019030590 | ISBN 9781616209186 (hardcover) |
ISBN 9781643750637 (ebook)
Subjects: CYAC: Mystery and detective stories. | Criminals–Fiction. |
Murder–Fiction. | Great Britain–History–Victoria, 1837–1901–Fiction.
Classification: LCC PZ7.B91505 Pre 2020 | DDC [Fic]–dc23
LC record available at https://lccn.loc.gov/2019030590

ISBN 978-1-64375-187-0 (PB)

10 9 8 7 6 5 4 3 2 1
First Paperback Edition

For Sophie:
look what you started.

1
CORPUS DELICTI

A true Investigator is a master of the art of Observation, paying keen attention to his surroundings. Even the least significant piece of evidence may prove the key to unraveling the truth.

–H. M. Hardcastle, *Principles of Detection: A Manual for the Amateur and Professional Investigator,* 1893

"Correct me if I'm wrong." My governess, Miss Judson, strolled into the schoolroom, her sharp bootheels clicking like a telegraph. "When I persuaded your father to order that telescope, it was with the express understanding it would be used for studying the night sky." She gave an altogether too cheery yank on the curtains, flooding the room with sun.

Adjusting the focus, I was rewarded with a clearer view of my target. *Morning, very fine,* I wrote beside my earlier notes. *Light rain overnight.* "I am Observing objects at a distance," I said. "Which is the purpose of this device." *Subjects: The residence (and residents) of 16 Gravesend Close, Swinburne. Commonly called Redgraves.*

Miss Judson bent over the casement beside me, chin nestled in her light brown hand. "Well. How foolish of me. Because it looks like you're spying on the neighbors."

"That, too. Look!" I pointed across the lane (with my own rather sallow hand), where a delicate blue butterfly had alit on the hedge. "*Celastrina argiolus.*"

"Don't try to distract me. Wait–" She straightened, a crease forming between her eyebrows. "Is that the police wagon?" The crease turned to a genuine scowl. "Myrtle?"

I covered the telescope with its special cloth. "Why do you always look at me like that? *I* didn't do anything!" I bit my lip. "Well, I may have summoned the police."

"To Miss Wodehouse's? What on earth for?" Miss Judson hurried to the schoolroom door, grabbing her cape on the way out.

"Are we going over there?" I scrambled off the window seat and gathered up my things: my notebook and bag, my magnifying lens, my gloves, and the little specimen collection kit with the tweezers, pins, and tiny sample jars.

"I think we'd better. Get your coat. And you can explain to me–so I can explain to your father–whatever could have compelled you to call the police on the gentle-woman next door!" Pausing in the doorway, she gave me a dubious look. "It's not the bit about her cat again."

"Of course not!" I scurried to catch up. Miss Judson in a hurry was a force to be reckoned with. "Well, mostly not. She started it."

She whirled on the stairs, hand on the polished banister. "Explain."

I had a lot of practice at this. "I didn't see her this morning," I began.

"Miss Wodehouse?"

"No, Peony—well, not Miss Wodehouse, either. And then Mr. Hamm didn't show up for his rounds." Mr. Hamm was the groundskeeper at Redgraves, and his 6:15 check of the fountains and birdbaths, Peony the cat at his heels, was his first order of business every morning. He tended the south lawn by 6:40 at the latest. Often he was supervised by Miss Wodehouse, earning nothing but scorn and criticism from the spry old lady. *Clean up those leaves. I don't want the delphiniums touching the daisies. And keep that cursed cat out of my sight!*

I may have Observed them once or twice.

"And then I saw something strange."

Miss Judson watched me expectantly, arms folded, fingers tapping the elbow of her neat tweed suit. This was the tricky bit to explain. I had aimed the telescope somewhere that was Strictly Off-Limits that morning, and I knew as much. But it *was* the cat's fault. When I didn't see Mr. Hamm, I did what any good Investigator would do. I looked for clues—and I found some.

"The pot on Miss Wodehouse's balcony was over-turned—that great heavy planter thing—and Peony was digging in it. You know how Miss Wodehouse hates it when the cat disturbs anything, especially her flowers, so I tried to shoo her away."

"Please tell me your attempt involved smoke signals, or perhaps telepathy."

"Now you're being ridiculous. I used my slingshot."

Miss Judson closed her eyes. "This tale gets better and better."

"I hit the French doors, and a pane broke—only a little one! I'll pay for it with my allowance. Mr. Hamm always keeps spares. But *nobody came out.*"

She leaned against the banister, looking ever so slightly relieved. And intrigued. "That is strange. Not even her maid?"

"Not for *ages.* And then she just poked her head round the door, and made sure it was closed and the curtains drawn. She looked nervous." The word I'd used in my notes was *furtive*, but Miss Judson occasionally accused me of getting carried away.

"And that's when you called the police."

I turned my toe against the rose on the carpet. "Not exactly. I thought they might all be sick—you remember the Holyrood arsenic poisoning last year—so I went over to check on them."

"Oh, dear Lord."

"That maid killed *six people*."

Miss Judson crouched beside me on the stairs. "Myrtle. This is really going too far. I'm starting to worry about you. You can't honestly think little Trudy—or anyone at Redgraves—did something so"—she groped for a word—"incredible."

"No." Although arsenic murders had been on the rise again lately. "But *something* was wrong over there. I knocked and knocked, and no one answered. Mr. Hamm wasn't home, either."

Miss Judson pursed her lips and gazed past my head. I could tell she was sorting through possible responses. "And it didn't occur to you to tell anyone?" she finally said, somewhat faintly.

She remembered as well as I did what had happened the other times I'd mentioned my concerns to adults, so I didn't bother answering.

"Very well." She rose briskly. "Let's go. Your father will be up soon, and we'd best be back for breakfast by then, so he can ship me straight back to French Guiana."

Redgraves was next door, but we had to cross our lawn and the lane, and then go down the street to reach the front of the great house, where the police carriage was parked. The constable with the coach tipped his helmet to us as he patted the horse's neck, but I didn't recognize him. Otherwise, Redgraves was eerily quiet.

"Where's the cat?" I hissed, and Miss Judson shushed me. Straightening her smart little hat, she marched up the massive stone front steps and rang the bell, which clanged through the quiet morning, disturbing a roost of pigeons in the portico. When no one answered the door, I wandered away, looking for Peony or any other evidence of last night's occurrences. A brick footpath flanked by bare earth twined through the flowers. Firmly impressed into the dirt were footprints leading around to the back of the house.

"Where are you going? Myrtle!"

The trail disappeared when the path turned into a well-manicured lawn, but I saw muddy scuffs on the brick terrace surrounding the conservatory.* The conservatory roof was Miss Wodehouse's balcony, which I could see from the schoolroom windows. I studied the scuffs, trying to determine what might have gone on here.

"Myrtle! Wait for me!" Miss Judson hastened to my side, careful not to disturb the mud. Or maybe just not step in it. "Oh, well done. Footprints!"

"Those are Mr. Hamm's." I pointed to the larger footprints, showing the horseshoe-shaped mark from the gardener's metal heel plates. But the other set—

"And those are Peony's!" Her voice was triumphant.

* a fancy name for a sort of sunporch

"Those are squirrel prints." I eyed her sidelong. "*You're* supposed to be teaching *me* biology."

"I got caught up in the moment. Well, those other ones aren't Miss Wodehouse's, or Trudy's, either. They're too big"—she hovered her own foot nearby for comparison, skirts held up—"and they look like a man's shoe."

"Did you bring your sketchbook?"

She blinked at me. "I didn't realize we'd be gathering evidence—oh, never mind. No."

I knelt down and got out my collection kit, using the tiny spatula to take a sample of the soil beside one of the prints. Miss Judson did produce something impressive: she handed over a retractable measuring tape, so I could take down the prints' dimensions. "I know you have one of these," she said, a hint of smugness in her voice. "If those prints are Mr. Hamm's, then he *was* out here. At some point."

"It rained last night," I said. "But the soil is too hard to take prints now." I stepped firmly in the nearby earth and left only the barest impression. "These must have been made hours and hours ago. Around midnight, I'd say."

"Is that right, little lady?" boomed a hearty voice behind me. Miss Judson and I stood up and whirled around. "Why, if it isn't young Myrtle, the lawyer's girl!"

"Good morning, Inspector Hardy," I said. My favorite policeman on the Swinburne constabulary,

Inspector Hardy was with the brand-new Detective Bureau, which I hoped to join when I was old enough. Assuming I didn't go to London and work for Scotland Yard. I gave a little curtsy. "Thank you for coming so swiftly." I'd had to run down to the telephone kiosk at the tram stand to contact the police, since Father didn't see the necessity of having service installed in our home. There was an entire *list* of modern things Father hadn't seen the need for, and Miss Judson repeatedly admonished me to be thankful that the Education of Young Ladies of Quality was not among them.

"You called us, then? Station desk said some little boy, playin' a prank."

I tugged on the hem of my dress, which was stubbornly refusing to grow too short for me. Before I could answer, Miss Judson spoke up.

"Yes, I'm sorry, Inspector. I think Myrtle saw something that concerned her, and she got carried away. We didn't mean to cause any trouble."

"Oh, you've not done, no worries." Inspector Hardy doffed his uniform hat and scratched his balding head. "We are having a bit of a go with the locals, though, if you know what I mean."

A young man about Miss Judson's age was lurking about the conservatory door, smoking a cigarillo.*

* a disgusting sort of small brown cigarette, about which the Author remains otherwise ignorant

I glanced about for dropped stubs. I couldn't see the man's feet, but he might have left the second set of footprints.

"You there! Are you just about done, then?" His voice was nasty and impatient. "I'd like to get this over with before the neighborhood gawkers come out in droves. Oh, I see the pack is closing in already." He turned on his—invisible—heel and slammed the door.

"Who was that?" I demanded.

"Oh, some nephew or something of the—" Inspector Hardy hesitated. "What was it you called about, then, Miss Myrtle?"

Nephew? I didn't know Miss Wodehouse had any relatives. Of course, if I had an aunt like Minerva Wodehouse,* I would make myself scarce as well. Returning my attention to Inspector Hardy, I delivered my first official report. "At approximately six forty-five this morning I suspected something was wrong at Redgraves. Miss Wodehouse and her groundskeeper, Mr. Llewellyn Hamm, typically work in the garden every morning, but neither appeared for work today."

"Nor the cat," Miss Judson murmured. She was glancing skyward beneath the brim of her hat, so it was quite impossible to guess what she was thinking.

"Eh? Cat?" asked Inspector Hardy.

* See page 83.

Miss Judson gave a tiny shake of her head and gestured for me to continue. I repeated the account I'd given Miss Judson (minus the Holyrood poisonings, but stressing the irregular routine at Redgraves that morning). "So I decided I ought to summon help."

"Again, I'm very sorry for all the bother," Miss Judson put in. "Will you tell Miss Wodehouse that *it won't happen again*?"

I nodded firmly. I'll admit the consequences of upsetting Miss Wodehouse had not been foremost in my mind. "Unless it's a matter of life and death," I vowed.

Inspector Hardy gave me a solemn look. "Well, then," he said, "it's a good thing you called us." Just then, the conservatory doors opened once more, and two more constables came out, carrying a litter. Miss Judson squeezed my hand, hard, as we saw what was borne on the stretcher. It looked like a body, completely covered in a black sheet.

"Aye," Inspector Hardy said. "It's the old lady, rest her soul. She died last night."

2
RED GRAVES

In the case of suspicious deaths, it is critical to examine
the crime scene, interview witnesses, and collect evidence
as swiftly as possible. Time is indeed of the essence.

–H. M. Hardcastle, *Principles of Detection*

We were late for breakfast. Inspector Hardy kept us
there a little longer, asking questions whilst skillfully
evading mine, though he did inform us that Miss
Gertrude Guildford, housemaid at Redgraves, had
discovered her mistress's body in the bathtub when
she went to rouse her that morning. I answered thoroughly (Inspector Hardy must have already had a
long day; he was looking rather weary by the end of
my account), but my mind was awhirl. Where was Mr.
Hamm? What had become of Peony? Who'd been
prowling about Redgraves in the middle of the night?
Where had this "nephew" come from? Why had Miss

Wodehouse taken a bath at night, when everyone knew that Trudy ran the bath for her at half past ten in the morning, after the gardening?

I'd have stayed to help with the investigation, but Miss Judson kept giving her watch pointed glances. Father wasn't as strict as some parents, but he would certainly expect his daughter and her governess to be at home for breakfast, not out consorting with police constables. Besides, I was eager to get home, not just to share the news of Miss Wodehouse's mysterious and sudden demise with Father, but because the morning meal was a critical part of my day. It was the one time Father, Miss Judson, and I were sure to be together, engaged in ordinary, domestic activity; making it my singular opportunity for Father to see the three of us as I did: as a family.

But Father was distracted, as usual, and didn't notice that Miss Judson and I were tardy, let alone that we'd already been out and about. He was hunched over the table, his plate surrounded by a sea of paperwork, a half-forgotten slice of toast dangling from his fingers.

"The new trial's starting today, isn't it, Father?" It was my favorite sort of case, a murder, although this one was not all that interesting, just some street thugs who'd got into a tavern brawl.

"And finishing, if all goes well," he answered, catching his toast a moment before it dropped jam on an affidavit.* "Why don't you come down for a visit? We'll have lunch after. Make an outing of it." He gave me a warm smile.

"Can I sit in the gallery and watch the proceedings?" Father rarely allowed me to come to court with him because the Magistrates and other Solicitors thought children were distracting. But I'd read every single word about his cases ever published in the *Swinburne Tribune*, as well as done my own studies of his law books, so I could discuss the finer points of jurisprudence with him. That hadn't actually happened—yet—but I was ready.

"I think Myrtle would enjoy that," Miss Judson put in. She was applying butter to her own toast with a practiced and efficient hand, not the least blob in danger of escaping.

"Mmm?" Watching Miss Judson, Father seemed to have forgotten the conversation that was taking place. "That's settled, then." He rose, gathered up his papers, and gave me a quick kiss atop my head. "Your hair's wet. Have you been out in the rain?"

I shot Miss Judson a look, but Father disappeared before either of us could reply. If Miss Judson let out a sigh of relief, it was a very subtle one.

Dear Reader, kindly permit me a pause to properly introduce one of the Key Players in this narrative, my

---

* a particular sort of legal document *not* to drop your breakfast on

governess and confidante, Miss Ada Eugénie Judson. As you will have already Observed, Miss Judson was an exceptionally composed individual, with a cool head in a crisis*—qualities certainly useful in the governess of an aspiring Investigator. The daughter of a French Guianese nurse and a Scottish minister, she was of average height, neat and practical in dress, with the deep complexion of her Caribbean heritage. Fearing that their daughter would fall afoul of some Dread Tropical Disease, her parents had sent young Ada off to boarding school in England. (I supposed no one had told Mr. and Mrs. Judson about typhus, smallpox, tuberculosis, and cholera. As well as occasional bouts of plague, not to mention the unmentionable afflictions I was not supposed to know about. As a Young Lady of Quality.)

⁓

With Father gone for the office, we had nearly two hours to get to work before we were due in court. While Miss Judson was still making her way through her extremely precise toast, I sprang from my seat and cleared my plate. Despite years attempting to imitate Miss Judson, I'm afraid I took after Father. My own place was a mess of crumbs, and I had somehow managed to get poached egg *inside* my stocking.

---

* The Alarming Snail Affair of 1890 was an excellent example, and would make a fascinating monograph one day, as it did demonstrate a number of heretofore unappreciated scientific principles. It does not, however, pertain to *this* account, so no more shall be said about it here.

"Where are you off to?" Miss Judson asked. "I've never seen you this eager for geography before."

"We have to find Peony," I said. "She saw what happened last night."

"Ah." Miss Judson rose, though her hand lingered near her teacup, as if she were contemplating refilling it. I stared at her impatiently. "I cannot wait to learn what method you've devised for extracting the testimony of a cat."

"Don't make fun of me."

"I would never," she said. "But, Myrtle, you have to admit that even for you, collecting a cat as a witness is a bit fanciful."

I hesitated. Adults tended to call me many things, the nicest being "precocious," "curious," and "irrepressible"—which I did not think was the compliment they pretended it to be—but compared to other children my age, I was not generally considered "fanciful." Miss Judson was an excellent judge of character, however, so if she suggested I was being anything but strictly rational, it gave me pause.

"Very well," I said carefully. "Perhaps we should go speak to Mr. Hamm. We'll need to know what to do about my botany lessons, anyway." The Redgraves groundskeeper had been tutoring me for the last two years. He was extremely knowledgeable, and Father approved because he thought it was "good for me to play outdoors" once in a while.

"Now that," Miss Judson said, "is a capital idea."

Fifteen minutes later, we were back at Redgraves, this time properly dressed for an outing in the gardens. Describing Redgraves's grounds as "gardens," however, does them a grave disservice. They were bigger than Gravesend Commons, the public park our neighborhood was built around. It used to be a cemetery before they built up all the houses,* but it had all once been private land belonging to the Wodehouse family. Redgraves, the ancestral home of the Wodehouses, was a gloomy redbrick affair, its slate rooftop studded with gables and turrets and chimney pots, with a downturned-mouth of a staircase out front. Compared to famous castles like Windsor or Highclere, Redgraves was just a cottage— a mere four stories and twenty-three rooms, including a nationally famous library and a locally famous modern bathroom. By Swinburne standards, though, it was a palace.

We approached Redgraves the usual way this time, through the hedge between our properties. But already we could see, or rather smell, that something was amiss.

---

* I was *certain* they moved all the graves first. There was a court order and massive amounts of paperwork, Father said; a small museum in a converted mausoleum displayed photographs of the disinterments. But Caroline Munjal insisted that some of the bodies were still there, their ghosts haunting the new houses. *See* fanciful, *above.*

"Is something burning?" Miss Judson said. "I hope it's not the house!"

That idea threw the morning's events into an even more dramatic and sinister light, but it turned out it was just Mr. Hamm, finally out at work. Mr. Hamm was the only groundskeeper at Redgraves, despite the gardens' size and reputation. In her eccentric way, Miss Wodehouse had whittled the staff down over the years until only the head gardener was left. He was tending a bonfire just outside the garden walls. I couldn't tell what was being burnt, as the fire had already reduced its contents to ash.

"Hullo, Mr. Hamm," I said, since "good morning" hardly seemed appropriate, given that he'd just lost his employer and potentially his livelihood.

He tipped his floppy hat to us, showing a red and sweaty face and damp black hair. "Aye, lass, Miss Ada. You heard the news, then?"

"Yes, terrible business." I could sense Miss Judson's approval of this response, that I'd remembered polite niceties and hadn't dived straight into interrogating the man.

"We've the flower show coming up," he said, voice creaky. "We were to exhibit her Black Tiger hybrid. A real beauty, took her four years to develop."

I nodded sympathetically, although I had not seen these flowers myself. Miss Wodehouse had forbidden our lessons to take place in her lily garden, and I had only glimpsed it briefly as I hastened past on other business. But Mr. Hamm talked of them often, and those lilies might have been the only thing at Redgraves that Miss Wodehouse was actually nice to. They were almost certainly the only thing she loved.

"You still can, surely?" Miss Judson said. "Even posthumously, in her honor?" There was prize money in a flower show, and Mr. Hamm might have been eligible for it if Miss Wodehouse's lilies did well.

Mr. Hamm shrugged. He wore a loose-fitting brown coat and oilcloth coveralls. I recognized his boots—the same ones with the horseshoe-shaped plates on the heels for walking through slick, muddy earth. "Doesn't seem right, somehow, without her." He raked mournfully at the fire, stirring up bitter embers.

"What are you burning?" I asked, trying to see through the smoke. August wasn't the usual season for bonfires.

Mr. Hamm was accustomed to my questions about his work, but he wasn't as forthcoming as usual this morning. "Debris," was all he said.

"From the storm last night?" I suggested, although there had only been the mildest of rain.

He gave another shrug and fanned the smoke with his hat.

I concealed my frown by shielding my eyes with my hand and squinting up at Miss Judson. "Do you know what happened to Miss Wodehouse?" I finally asked, after what seemed a respectful interval.

"Sommat about the bath, they say. Heard the news when I come down for work this morning."

"This morning? But I didn't see you."

"I was working on the beds north of the house."

I could see those beds from the schoolroom, and Mr. Hamm hadn't been there. Not this morning. "What about last night?"

"Myrtle." Miss Judson's voice was firm. "Mr. Hamm, Myrtle was concerned about the cat."

His expression softened. "I've not seen her this morn," he said. "Poor little kit. She's bound to be missing the Mistress, eh?"

I chewed on my finger to keep from saying something rude. "Can I look for her?"

Here he crinkled his face in an almost-smile. "Try the laburnum—you know how she likes the butterflies there. But watch out for that young fellow, the Mistress's nephew. If he gives you any guff, you tell him who you are, who your da' is, and that you've *my* permission to be here. End of." He gave the rake an emphatic shove, and a burst of sparks flurried into the air.

"Certainly, we'll do so. Thank you for the warning, Mr. Hamm." Before I could ask anything else, Miss Judson shuttled me off toward the gardens, past the bonfire and through the hedge.

"Ow! What's the hurry?" I said.

"The smoke smelled foul," she said. "Like it might be toxic."

"Smoke *is* toxic." I glanced back with a frown. "Do you think he's burning something poisonous?"

Miss Judson shooed me forward with her hand. "No, Myrtle Hardcastle, I'll not have you cooking up suspicions about that poor man."

"He lied about where he was this morning," I said.

She frowned. "I noticed that."

"But," I admitted, "that doesn't make it suspicious, necessarily. He could have been planning to burn that debris all along."

"It wasn't storm damage, though. He lied about that, too."

I scrunched my nose. "No, he didn't. I'm the one who mentioned storm damage. He just didn't correct me." Adults often *didn't* bother trying to correct me, since I was apt to argue with them. But only when I knew they were wrong! It wasn't for argument's own sake.

Miss Judson smoothed her skirts and straightened her gloves. She always looked composed, neat and smart and *ready*, as if she were expecting action at any moment, bicycling or lawn tennis or saving a runaway pram.

Or cat wrangling!

"There she is!" I cried, spotting the telltale slink of black-and-white fur sneaking through the tall grass by the western hedge.

"Are you sure?" Miss Judson was swift on my heels, boots dashing over the lawn like they were designed for racing, not merely conveying authority in the schoolroom. My own boots squelched, not unpleasantly, as I landed in a low spot still wet from the rain. Round the hedge we flew, straight into Forbidden Territory. Miss Judson grabbed my arm even as I skidded to a halt. There was no gate, no grand archway or signage announcing the entry into Hallowed Ground, but I felt Miss Judson's fingernails dig through my layers of sleeve, holding me back. This was a place I'd only seen from a respectful distance, and would scarcely even dare point my telescope toward, so trained were we to behold it with awe.

This was Miss Wodehouse's lily garden.

Or it had been. Something had gone terribly wrong. Knowing full well I was trespassing, I shook off Miss Judson's hand and took a step inside, and another, where the world-famous lilies were supposed to be. But all around me, the beds were empty, barren as winter.

The lilies were gone.

3

TRIAL BY JURY

An Investigator's life will not be an easy one. Be prepared
to deal with Obstructive Fellow Detectives, Reluctant
Witnesses, all manner of the Criminal Classes, and Family
Members with No Imagination.

–H. M. Hardcastle, *Principles of Detection*

"What happened here?" Miss Judson sounded breathless as she caught up to me. "Wait, I don't think we
should be in here."

"What does it matter now?" Miss Wodehouse was
dead, and her beloved lilies with her. Miss Judson
made a good point, though. This might be a crime
scene, and we should take care not to disturb it. I read-
ied my tools (magnifying glass, notebook, sample kit)
and crept through the lily garden, or erstwhile lily
garden, anyway. It looked like the whole Napoleonic
army had been through, razed the beds to the ground,

burned anything they hadn't mown over, and buried the rest.

I approached one of the workaday, wood-edged beds. Unlike the main gardens with their ornamental urns and pretty, twisted-willow fencing, the lily gardens were plain and serviceable—an experimental space, not a decorative one. I spotted a disturbance in the gravel. "Look," I called to Miss Judson, who was still standing in the verge, looking stupefied. "There are tracks here, like from someone rolling a cart through."

"A wheelbarrow, maybe?" She roused herself and crossed the garden, taking a path on the other side.

"And footprints." A scuff in the path revealed several smudged prints, and I could just make out the familiar impression of Mr. Hamm's boots—and as clear as a bloodstain, a single muddy print where someone else had stepped onto the wooden edging of the flower bed. "It's that other shoe print again," I said. "Just like the one near the terrace."

"Cigarillos?" she asked, flipping open her sketchbook to record the evidence.

"No such luck." Crouching low, I studied the impressions from Mr. Hamm's boots and the unfamiliar print on the ledge. "But what's happened to the flowers? Who could have done this—and why?"

"Mightn't it have been Miss Wodehouse?" she said. "Clearing out the beds for some other purpose?"

I squinted at the ruined plots, trying to imagine it. Those flowers had been worth hundreds of pounds. "Can you see miserly old Miss Wodehouse doing something like that?" The decades of research, all her experiments and specimens, not to mention all the bulbs—

"Look around," I said, with new urgency. "Did they dig everything up, or just destroy the plants?"

Miss Judson understood. She doffed her gloves (why was she wearing them, then? I didn't understand fashion, I really didn't) and plunged her hand into the freshly turned earth. "I can't feel anything," she said, "but it would take all day to search the whole place."

I dug through the loose soil in my own corner of the bed, trying not to get any on the footprint. My fingers found not the fleshy, turniplike bulb of a lily plant, but cold metal. I pulled it out and shook off the dirt. "What is this?" It was embossed silver, about the length of my thumb, with a round end like a spoon handle and a sort of springy lever built in. I held it up, noting a faint reddish smear on one side.

"Oh, good for you," Miss Judson said. "For not knowing, I mean. That is a cigar cutter. Is that blood?"

I frowned at it. "There's no way to tell. But it looks like it." I sat back on my heels, surveying the scene. The cat had disappeared again. "Mr. Hamm doesn't smoke cigars, and I doubt Miss Wodehouse did, either."

"Well, probably not while she was working. And Nephew Wodehouse doesn't need a cigar cutter for his cigarillos."

"Would someone smoke both?"

For a moment she looked torn. I recognized the expression—she was weighing the virtues of withholding information for my own good versus satisfying my thirst for knowledge. "No," she finally said. "Probably not."

"So there was another man here last night." I rose and tugged a handkerchief from my pinafore pocket. The cigar cutter was too big to fit in one of my specimen jars. I was reasonably certain the "bloodstain" wouldn't wipe off if I handled it carefully.

"How can you be sure it was last night?"

The cigar cutter safe in my bag, I recounted the evidence. "The stranger's footprint was left here sometime after the rain stopped, or it would have been washed off the ridge. But the ground was too dry by morning to leave prints."

"You don't know that the cigar cutter was dropped then, *or* that it belonged to your so-called 'stranger,'" she challenged.

"There was some kind of disturbance here." I gestured toward the ruined plants, the scuffed-up path. "And we know it was last night, because the plants were intact yesterday when I had my lesson with Mr. Hamm." I had seen enough through the gate to know that. "We know it's not *his* cigar cutter, because he doesn't smoke cigars, and he was the only other person Miss Wodehouse ever let in here."

"Perhaps it was an heirloom," she countered. "His father's."

I shook my head. "It's new—you saw how shiny it is, and the blade was barely used."

This was how we got on, and why I liked Miss Judson as a teacher so much. She let me figure things out on my own, asking challenging questions as I went.*

"Very well," she said. "Last night, someone dropped his cigar cutter into Miss Wodehouse's lily garden. What does that tell us?"

That was one question I had no answer for. Yet.

I wanted to search for more clues, but Miss Judson brushed off her hands on her apron. "I think we've done quite enough for one morning. Besides, we don't want to be late to court."

"If we leave now, they'll have time to get rid of any other evidence." Whoever "they" were.

Miss Judson did not look as sorrowful over this as she might have. "That is a risk we'll have to take. Home."

☙

We rode our bicycles to the courthouse. They were the most wondrous modern conveyances, tremendously

---

* a pedagogical technique known as the Socratic Method, named after the ancient Greek philosopher, which I understood was likewise popular with law schools. And vexed parents.

efficient, right down to the specialized attire they entailed. Miss Judson wore a suit with puffy bicycling bloomers,* although I only had a plain black split skirt. Pedaling past Swinburne traffic–what traffic there was, at any rate–felt deliciously urgent and dangerous.

We coasted down Swinburne's cobbled streets, out from Gravesend with its new brick houses and postage-stamp gardens, past the schoolhouse I had never attended, along the tram tracks into town. As we rode, I imagined we were the heroes of my favorite penny dreadful adventures, Billy Garrett, Boy Detective, and his "side-kick" Franz, chasing down suspects through the Wild West. I knew the stories were preposterous– Billy solved his cases through luck and flights of fancy that owed nothing to logical deduction–but I found them splendidly inspiring. Once or twice I'd even caught Father reading one, when he was supposed to be studying his legal briefs.

Miss Judson pulled up next to the courthouse, a grim stone building with tall windows, iron railings, and statues outside. There was nowhere to park the bicycles, so she gave a man at the cab stand sixpence to watch them for us.

"Do you think that's wise?" I asked as we made our way across the street. "Those bicycles cost twelve guineas apiece."

* **Thank Amelia Bloomer and Lucy Stone, two famous American suffragists, for promoting this practical innovation.**

"Who would steal a bicycle in front of the courthouse?"

"It's full of criminals," I pointed out.

We hadn't had a chance to talk on the journey over, so as we hastened up the mountainous courthouse steps, I peppered Miss Judson with conversation. "How do you suppose Miss Wodehouse died?"

I was half expecting the answer to be that it was none of our business, but Miss Judson slowed down and turned back. "Well, she was old," she said. "She may have simply passed away."

"She has to have died of *something*," I pressed. "There's always a cause."

"Mmm," she said. "But the cause need not be nefarious."

"Don't you think it's strange that she had her bath in the middle of the night?"

"Perhaps she was cold," Miss Judson suggested. "It did rain last night. She may have had achy bones."

That was logical, especially if she'd been out tearing up her own lilies. "Did she drown, then? Fall asleep in the tub and slip under the water?" Wouldn't she have woken the second her face hit the water and she tried to breathe? Coughing and sputtering and splashing should have alerted anyone, particularly Trudy the maid, who presumably had a room adjacent to her mistress's—so she could be at hand for peculiar requests like drawing hot baths at midnight. "Do you think the Coroner has had a chance to examine the body yet?"

"Myrtle!"

"In the case of suspicious death, any citizen has the right to demand that the Coroner perform an inquest."

All cheeriness left Miss Judson's face. "You will *not*," she said, voice severe. "I understand that you're curious about what happened, and I know you're not simply being morbid. But haven't we bothered that poor family enough? She only just died. Why can't you wait for the obituary like everyone else?"

I wasn't sure how to make her understand if she didn't already. She *should* understand; she was Miss Judson, after all—nobody in the world knew me better. "I just need to know what happened," I mumbled. "We're going to be late." And I shoved past her into the courthouse, and tried to content myself with a nice murder trial.

The proceedings had already started, but the bailiff recognized us and let us slip quietly into the public gallery overlooking the courtroom. Father looked splendid in his black robes and white wig, marching boldly before the Bench. Swinburne was exceptionally progressive in employing a professional Prosecuting Solicitor. Father would not be prosecuting the whole case, unfortunately. Murders were too important to be tried locally. This was just the initial stage, to determine if the case against the men had merit, and was worth committing them to the higher courts. Still, Father's role was significant, and it was a thrill to watch him work.

The defendants sat in the dock, a small boxlike room whose single door led straight into the jail cells. It was designed to give everyone in the courtroom a clear view of the occupants. The first man, whose name was Cobb, had a furious scowl, heavy eyebrows, and a lumpy nose which I suspected had been broken at least once.* The second, called Smythe, was younger. He was pale and sweating and kept yanking at his collar. I tried to picture them beating another man to death, and it seemed very pointless.

We had arrived at the best part: the Coroner was just starting to give his testimony. As the official in charge of everyone who died in Swinburne, he was regularly called on to testify in Father's cases. He didn't perform the post-mortem exams on murder victims—that job fell to the Police Surgeon—but he was otherwise extremely well versed in the Science of Death.

"I arrived at Bell's Tavern at half past eleven on the night of July eighth," the Coroner was saying. "There I found the body of the victim. It was clear that the

---

* Since he was charged with killing a man in a brawl, it seemed likely he had boxing experience—although my own efforts to study the art of pugilism had met with some difficulty, so I could not say for sure.

cause of death had been multiple blows about his head and face. A broken whiskey bottle lay in pieces beside the body."

"And what was your verdict, sir, regarding the cause of the victim's death?"

"Wilful murder."

Notebook in hand, I listened happily for the rest of the morning, my disagreement with Miss Judson temporarily forgotten. I didn't really intend to request an inquest into Miss Wodehouse's death, but I thought the Coroner might want to know the inconsistencies in what had happened last night. I wasn't convinced Inspector Hardy had conveyed my concerns in his report—plus he hadn't known about the lily garden. If anything nefarious *had* happened to Miss Wodehouse, shouldn't someone find out for sure?

Eventually Miss Judson shifted slightly, permitting a view of her sketchbook. She'd squeezed a small portrait of Father in his wig into her depiction of the trial. He looked very dashing, and she'd quite captured the strong corner of his jaw and the fierce way his eyes burned out over the courtroom. My heart swelled.*

As we observed, the opposing counsel began to build his defense, but Father knocked down every point he raised until the only thing left was the single inescapable conclusion: that the two accused had

---

* metaphorically, of course. Edema of the cardiac tissue would be an extremely serious medical condition.

wilfully murdered an innocent man. I found Father's work mesmerizing, the way he pieced together individual bits of evidence into a clear, undeniable picture. It was like the way the planets fit together in the heavens, or the sixty-six elements in the Periodic Table. A natural order to the universe, life and death, good and evil, law and order.

I turned my notebook to a fresh page. In a trial, the Prosecution is charged with lining up a *preponderance of the evidence*, an overwhelming impression that all clues point toward the suspects' guilt. I didn't have any suspects yet in Miss Wodehouse's death, and I couldn't prove anything, but I was starting to see a preponderance. The destruction of her lilies, mysterious men skulking about the gardens in the middle of the night dropping their bloody cigar cutters, the improbable timing of her bath, Mr. Hamm's bonfire of "debris" and his lies . . . Old ladies in good health didn't just suddenly drop dead in the middle of the night after the total destruction of their life's work. Maybe I couldn't call for an inquest, but I certainly found Miss Wodehouse's death suspicious. More than suspicious, in fact.

"It was murder!"

4
POST-MORTEM

The post-mortem examination, also called the autopsy, requires a skilled deductive mind to interpret both the medical and criminal evidence. The difference between a murder and a death from natural causes sometimes comes down to one stroke of the Coroner's pen.

–H. M. Hardcastle, *Principles of Detection*

That was *definitely* said with more enthusiasm than I'd intended, not to mention volume–right in the middle of the Defense Counsel's dramatic pause, when the entire courtroom was tense with heavy silence.

"What? What murder? Who's that?" snapped Mr. Justice Fox, who was quite elderly and somewhat hard of hearing. "That's the Prosecution's job, my good man!"

"I didn't say it," protested the counsel for the defense. "It came from the gallery."

I was on my feet by then, Miss Judson urgently trying to tug me back down, as all heads in the courtroom—including Defendant Cobb's lumpy one—swiveled my way. All heads but one: Father's was bent over, buried in his hand.

"I'm sorry, my lord," I said. "I didn't mean this murder. I meant a different one."

Justice Fox scowled at me, but he might have just been trying to see me clearly from the Bench, so I waved. I saw Father's back stiffen. "What's this about a murder, child? Who are you?"

"Myrtle Hardcastle, my lord," I answered promptly, with a very professional curtsy.

"Hardcastle? You don't mean—"

"Yes, sir," I said proudly. "My father's the Prosecuting Solicitor." For some reason, this made everyone laugh.

"Myrtle." It wasn't *technically* possible to hiss my name, but Miss Judson had made an art form out of fierce whispering.

The judge shifted on the Bench. "Miss Hardcastle, what is the meaning of this outburst?"

"I'm very sorry, sir. I was caught up in the proceedings. It won't happen again."

"No, it won't," said the judge. "But you plainly said, 'Not this murder, another murder.' Whose murder were you talking about, if not the one that concerns us here today?"

I flushed but held my ground. "My neighbor's, sir."

At this, Father finally broke free from the table. "I must apologize, sir. My daughter and her governess were *just leaving*. I assure you that–"

"Yes, yes." The judge waved an impatient hand. "But what in the world's she talking about? Are you on another case at the moment? Your neighbor?"

"If you let me come down, I can explain it to you," I volunteered. A judge could certainly call for an inquest.

The judge's lips twisted and it took him a long time to answer. "No, Miss Hardcastle, that won't be necessary. Mr. Hardcastle, we'll talk about this after court."

"Thank you, my lord. Very sorry, sir."

"Miss Hardcastle, if it's all right with you, can we continue with *this* murder?"

"Objection!" cried the Defense Counsel before I could answer.

"Overruled," said Judge Fox wearily. "Miss Hardcastle, what say you?"

"Oh, yes, my lord. Of course. You may proceed."

"Thank you," the judge said. "The Defense may call its next witness." The judge banged his gavel, and Miss Judson bundled everything up and fairly shoved me out of the gallery.

⁓

I was in disgrace. I knew that as soon as Miss Judson marched me from the courtroom and down the steps to the cab stand to reclaim our bicycles without so much as a word. I was a little afraid to look at her, but finally stole a glance as she was mounting her bicycle. Beneath her straw hat, her face was flushed scarlet. Was she embarrassed? Or angry?

"But the judge—" I said.

"Home." She pointed ominously in that direction. I pedaled silently back to Gravesend, trying to figure out why she was so upset. I hadn't intended to interrupt the trial, and it wasn't as if the judge had called *her* out. And what was I supposed to do, anyway, when he'd started asking me questions?

Father didn't come home until late. He sent word that he was dining at the club with another solicitor. It had been planned for days, but it still felt like an undeserved rebuke. I sulked through my cold supper in the kitchen, amid a scattered array of brass fixtures and loose pieces of the cast iron hob, which Cook, on a perpetual quest to improve its efficiency, had disassembled again. The hob seemed to be winning.

"I ruined Father's trial," I said.

Huffing like a steam engine, Cook extracted herself from the oven compartment, culminating in a grease-smeared and ruddy face. She looked like a chimney sweep. "Ruined? Fah. Don't exaggerate." She reached for her spanner and gave the unit a couple of alarming thwacks that could not possibly have been helpful.

Cook's Christian name was Harriet Stansberry, although I'd never heard her called anything but Cook. I was six years old before I realized she even had another name. Father's favorite dish was something we called Stansberry pie, and I had once suffered a week of botanical confusion trying to classify the elusive stansberry, which did not appear in any field guide, taxonomy, or recipe book that I could find.* Ongoing feud with the hob aside, Cook's pastries were unimpeachable, but her comfort was sometimes as cold as her suppers.

"Himself works late a lot," she said now. "Don't assume it's your fault."

"You weren't there," I said, poking glumly at my slab of cold ham. "You didn't see the judge."

When Father finally did return, long after I was supposed to be in bed, he summoned Miss Judson to his study immediately. That was very bad, indeed; when I was truly in trouble, it was Miss Judson who received the lecture. I had made the mistake before of interrupting to defend her, and knew better than to burst in and plead her case, so instead I eavesdropped anxiously from the water closet behind Father's office. The wall was conveniently (or inconveniently, depending on your perspective) thin, and with his voice raised to courtroom volume, it was all too easy to hear everything he said.

"What happened today was absolutely inexcusable," he began. Was he pacing, as he sometimes did

* It turned out to be a tart containing apple, strawberry, and rhubarb. It was rather good, particularly warm out of the oven, with cream.

in court? Or standing firm at his desk? "I shall spare you a description of the indignity of being dressed down by one of Her Majesty's judges for the behavior of *my daughter* in the courtroom."

"Oh, dear," Miss Judson said. I cringed in my hiding spot, grateful neither of them could see me. "Mr. Hardcastle, I'm sure Myrtle did not intend to disrupt the proceedings, much less embarrass you."

"It's never her intent!" Father exclaimed. "She just has a knack for it. I'm beginning to see it not as an isolated incident, but as a symptom of a larger problem."

"Oh, sir?" For a hopeful moment I thought perhaps she planned to Socratic Method Father, but that hope was swiftly dashed.

"Snooping about the neighborhood at the crack of dawn?" His sharp voice made me shrink even lower on the commode. "Disturbing a sleeping household on no more than the behavior of a cat? Then interrupting a trial! You don't see other girls doing such things! How do you explain this behavior, Miss Judson?"

Miss Judson's voice was as clear and authoritative as any barrister's. "First of all, Myrtle *isn't* other girls," she said. "She's a unique individual, and your daughter. I doubt you'd find another child of twelve with a keener, more eager mind." I sat a little straighter at this bolstering character evidence.

"But this preoccupation with death and murder—it can't be natural."

"Sir, I would urge you to look at that another way." Miss Judson's voice had softened a bit, and I had to press my ear against the paneling to hear. "She's a sensitive girl who was exposed to death at an early age. You yourself entered the field of prosecution shortly after the loss of Mrs. Hardcastle. Does it surprise you that Myrtle acted in kind?"

"Are you blaming *me* for her morbidity?"

"She's not morbid! She's curious about your work, and, if I may say, sir, her mother's medical studies. She has combined them into one singular passion, which is more than can be said for most young people. Did you know you wished to be a solicitor when you were twelve?"

I heard the thump of Father sitting heavily in his armchair. "I wasn't sure I wanted to be a solicitor at *thirty*," he admitted. "But girls Myrtle's age should be doing needlework and riding ponies and thinking about dresses—*not* dead neighbors. I expect you to put a stop to this immediately."

I imagined Miss Judson giving him her steely, unwavering glare, and I held my breath, waiting for her retort. But the silence from Father's office had gone so cold and *solid* that it hurt to listen to it. What was taking her so long?

"Well, sir, whatever you think best, of course," Miss Judson finally said. What did *that* mean? I heard Father's chair scrape back.

"Miss Judson, by tomorrow morning, I would like to see your revised lesson plan for Myrtle on my desk, as well as arrangements for her to spend more time with girls her own age. There is more to life than criminology, for heaven's sake. It's time she learns that."

∽

The next morning was pale and rainy, a gloomy drizzle ruining any remaining evidence in the lily gardens. Redgraves was locked up tight, no movement at all from any of the household still left. And no sign of Peony, who must be cold and starving. I paced before the window, restless and discontent.

The schoolroom door swung open, revealing Miss Judson with a breakfast tray. "There," she declared, dropping the tray unceremoniously on the counter. "The morning *Tribune*. Let this put an end to all this 'murder' business."

I scurried over to grab the paper.

"I should make you eat something first," she said. Breakfast in the schoolroom could only mean I must still be in trouble. Mindful of her lecture from Father, I picked up a piece of toast and sat dutifully at the workbench.

Once fortified with toast and tea, we read the paper together. There was nothing at all on the front page (which also thankfully failed to feature DISTURBANCE AT LOCAL MURDER TRIAL: PROSECUTOR HUMILIATED), so we flipped to the obituaries. And there we found a few sparse lines about Minerva Faye Wodehouse, 79, Swinburne, who:

> . . . died at home of natural causes Wednesday morning. Survived by her niece, Miss Priscilla Wodehouse, Boston, and a nephew, Mr. Giles Northcutt, Swinburne. Private funeral to be held this Saturday, 5 August, at St. Agnes Chapel. Condolences may be sent to the family home at 16 Gravesend Close. No flowers, please.

"That's it?" Miss Judson sounded sad. "No flowers?"

"Natural causes? What rubbish!"

"It doesn't even say anything about her gardens, or her life. They might as well have said 'Another spinster dies alone. Yawn.'"

"Miss! Focus, please! They're about to bury her," I said. "We have to do something before it's too late."

"Do what, exactly?"

"Prove it was murder, of course!" I waved my toast in frustration, scattering crumbs in an arc.

Miss Judson was still studying the obituary, her mouth pressed thin. "We'll need something stronger than the suspicions of a twelve-year-old girl and her governess, I'm afraid," she finally said.

"Then you believe me?"

She returned my gaze steadily. I decided she was considering her conversation last night with Father, which I wasn't supposed to know about. "Always."

I let out a breath. "We don't have much time," I said. "The first thing we'll need to do is get our hands on the Police Surgeon's report. The Coroner can't have written the death certificate without it."

"That's not going to be easy."

I tapped my fingers against the newspaper. "Oh, but I have a plan. One even Father will approve of."

5

ACTUS REUS

A crime requires two elements: *mens rea* (Latin for "a guilty mind") and *actus reus*, "the guilty act."

–H. M. Hardcastle, *Principles of Detection*

Later that day I Observed Trudy through the window, hanging the wash in the side yard. It wasn't Redgraves's normal laundry day, so I went down to see what she was up to.

"Mistress needs clothes for her funeral," Trudy explained with a teary sniff. I felt a stab of sympathy for the maid, doing this task by herself, so I dug in and pulled a damp nightie from the basket. The nightgown was trimmed in delicate white lace, with tiny pearl buttons and an *M* monogrammed in white.

"Oh, Trudy, this has a stain." There was also a small tear at the wrist, where some lace had torn free.

She glanced over, shaking out an armload of wet linen. "I can't get them out. I washed it twice with hot water and castile soap, but they won't budge."

There actually was something ominous that hot water would not wash out of a nightgown—but I didn't think this particular stain was blood. It was too pale, for one thing, with a distinct yellowish hue. "It's pollen," I said.

"Mmm," Trudy agreed. "It got on all her clothes."

"On her nightgowns, though?" I studied it more closely. The stains were all over, around the hem, on the cuffs, smeared across the back. I just hadn't noticed them at first, among the wrinkles and lace. It looked like Miss Wodehouse had been kneeling among the flowers.

Or like she'd been pushed—knocked to her hands and knees in the dirt. In the lily garden, in the middle of the night, in her nightgown.

"Was she wearing this on the night she died?"

She nodded. "It were allover mud, too, but that washed out. Like the bathroom."

She'd got ahead of me. "There was mud in the bathroom when—when you found the Mistress?"

Trudy gave another tragic sniff. "It took ages to mop up after."

I wanted to ask about the footprints, too, but the expression on her face was so doleful I was afraid she'd fall right to pieces. I held tight to the nightgown. "Can I keep this?" That sounded morbid. "Borrow it for a while, I mean? I want to study these stains, maybe show it to the police."

She looked shocked. "Oh, no, Miss Hardcastle! She'd never want that. Those common men touching her . . . personal things!"

"My father then? Would that be all right? He's very discreet."

Her mortified expression softened a bit. "All right," she said. "Mr. Hardcastle will know what to do."

I carefully folded the gown, protecting the stains and the embroidered identification. I didn't tell her that I had no intention of sharing this evidence with my father, who would only pooh-pooh it and insist that I return it to Redgraves at once.

"Thank you, Trudy. You don't know how much this means."

But I did. Now I knew that two men had been in the lily garden on the night Miss Wodehouse had died—and so had Miss Wodehouse.

∽

I pondered Father's words to Miss Judson as I prepared my next move. It was Friday, my one and only chance to get my hands on Miss Wodehouse's postmortem report before her funeral. I was therefore—naturally—spending it primping before the mirror in my bedroom.

What had Father meant when he said I had a "knack" for disrupting things? It certainly wasn't like when he said Cook had a knack with pastry crust. Didn't he want me to be clever and inquisitive? I did recognize that intelligence wasn't a highly regarded trait in the females of my species. But for pity's sake, you never heard anyone say, "What England *really* needs is more stupid girls."

Miss Judson appeared, a muslin bag draped over one arm. "Your father thought this occasion warranted a new frock," she said.

Well, that's ridiculous, I started to say, *I can wear anything*—until she unveiled the garment: navy blue silk faille, with an ankle-length skirt and a pin-tucked bodice with black frogs.* It was practically a grown-up dress, not too dissimilar to Miss Judson's own. I reached out a hand, then paused. "Do I get a corset?"

"When you need one."

"At this rate, that will be never," I grumbled. I was still wearing a babyish, button-front "waist" that only emphasized my age and small size.

"True, if your curiosity kills us both," she agreed cheerily, assisting me with the additional new layers this ensemble required (including an excess of petti-coats). "Do you intend to share any details of this plan of yours?"

I stuck my arms into the sleeves, which were almost absurdly tight. "How am I going to do anything in this?"

---

* Alas, Dear Reader, those were only knotwork clasps made of silk cord, not embellishments of an amphibious nature.

"What do you *need* to do?"

"I don't know, girl things. Play the pianoforte?"

"You don't play the pianoforte," she said. "You ridiculed too many piano teachers. Back to your plan."

I turned to face her while she adjusted the skirt. Its best feature was its pockets: masses of them, inside and out. Father was an advocate of the Rational Dress Movement, which was how he'd found out about bicycle bloomers. Giving the skirts an experimental swish, I answered Miss Judson's question, more or less. "Do you remember when we studied the medieval Mughal spies? How no individual operative ever knew all of a mission's details, so they couldn't give up sensitive information under torture?"

"Thank you for saving me from the thumbscrews," Miss Judson said. I couldn't tell if she was trying to be funny. "You realize," she continued, "this hinges on your father *believing* I know nothing of your plan. Shall I march into his office right now and say, 'Mr. Hardcastle, I am dropping Myrtle off at her next misadventure, but I have no idea what she intends, so be certain to hold me blameless when it goes cockeyed'?"

"Very good," I said. "You understand your part of the plan."

৵

Other girls were tedious. There were some in my neighborhood, middle-class girls like me, but we rarely associated if we could help it. They looked on me as some sort of contagious specimen, and were quick with "advice" about my hair or dress, which did not seem kindly meant at all. For my part, I felt they showed a dismal lack of interest in viscera. Father was constantly after me to mingle more with them, but they had declined all my invitations to join us for an afternoon of tea and dissection. Today, however, I had submitted to their clutches, and was enduring hours of boring card games (I won them all because they didn't understand probability) and discussions of sensational novels I hadn't read.

Miss LaRue Spence-Hastings, blond, fourteen, and the sort of girl who would never interrupt a murder trial, looked me over with a pitying sigh. "Caroline, don't you think Miss Hardcastle would look absolutely *fetching* in this salmon pelerine?" A pelerine, Dear Reader, was a sort of lacy half-cape, practical only insofar as it prevented a girl from using her hands or arms. LaRue's was a particularly vile shade of pink, with great pompons of fur dyed to match.

Our hostess, Miss Caroline Munjal, peeled herself off the chaise, swinging her black braid over her shoulder. "Oh, no. I have just the thing," she said. Caroline lived across the park in a four-story town house with an excellent drop from the main stairs to the marble foyer—certainly fatal—and a carriage house big enough for a private morgue. LaRue was Caroline's neighbor, and the two girls' mothers had gone off together for the afternoon on their own social calls. I was alone in hostile territory, and I knew it.

Caroline scurried off and returned a moment later, arms laden with black lace and crepe. She shook out a long black dress and a bonnet spilling over with black veils and flowers and thrust them on me. "This will let you into *all* the best funerals!" she cried, to LaRue's chants of "Morbid Myrtle, Morbid Myrtle."

The truth was, I had a most compelling reason for putting up with Caroline and LaRue's torment, and it was this: Dr. Vikram Munjal, Caroline's father, was the Swinburne Police Surgeon. Swallowing both pride and my nastiest retort, I held the dress up to myself and tried to strike a fashionable pose. LaRue was unimpressed.

"This is boring," she declared. "Let's do something fun." LaRue was the ringleader; whatever she suggested, Caroline went along with.

I stuffed my penny dreadful into my pocket. "Well," I said, trying to sound tentative, "I've always wondered what's in Dr. Munjal's office."

Caroline looked anxious. "I'm not allowed in there when he's not home."

"All the better." LaRue popped the black bonnet atop her head and tossed the lacy dress to Caroline. "Let's go."

Down the corridor, with its heavy wallpaper and shelf of commemorative pitchers from Her Majesty's

Golden Jubilee,* and all the way out to the back garden and the brick carriage house, Caroline continued to protest. "Can't we just look in the windows?" she pleaded.

LaRue scoffed. "What, are you scared?" As a rule, Young Ladies of Quality, too delicate for anything so vulgar as a morgue, did not respond to such taunts. However, etiquette experts never reckoned on the LaRue Spence-Hastingses of the world. "Afraid to see a dead body?"

"Well, there isn't any," Caroline began, which *I* ought to have reckoned on. The cadavers would have been collected and sent on to the undertaker's by now. Swinburne was too small to have a proper morgue, which is why Dr. Munjal had his laboratory at home. I'm sure the neighbors loved that arrangement.

"I'll bet it's haunted," LaRue said. "All those men your dad's cut up."

"LaRue! That's horrid." Caroline really was upset. I wanted to explain that a dead body is no different from a live body, except it can't speak to you and tell you what's wrong. You have to figure that out from other clues. All the organs, the bones and blood and muscle tissue—those were the very same bones and blood and organs inside Caroline and LaRue right now. Besides, *most* of the people examined by Dr. Munjal weren't

* EMPRESS OF INDIA, **proclaimed one.**

murdered, so there really wasn't anything to be upset about.

LaRue jiggled the door handle, obviously expecting it to be locked, but the door cracked open and she jumped back with a squeal that turned to a giggle.

"Well, go on, then," Caroline snapped. "You wanted to see it, so go see it."

"Myrtle first," LaRue said.

I stepped inside, noting the tang of disinfectant and the unmistakable—the only word is *stench*—of decomposition. The lights in the carriage house weren't lit, but the large windows provided plenty of daylight, even on an overcast day. Caroline had said there was no body here, but a form covered in white sheeting lay on the examination table, giving off an ominous buzz. I crept closer, my chest tight. It was just like the frogs in my biology textbook. Just like a chicken on Cook's dinner table.

Dear Reader, here is where I must insert a *nota bene* about honing one's Observational Skills not simply on the natural world, but on the ever-more cryptic *Human* Nature. Which is to say: I should have expected what came next. I was so pleased that my plan to enter Dr. Munjal's office had worked, I didn't notice the other girls hadn't followed me in. I heard the swish of fabric behind me, followed by a snickering laugh. I spun round to see that the mourning costume had been tossed over the threshold.

"Here you go, Morbid Myrtle," LaRue called from the doorway. "Have fun with the other ghouls." She slammed the door, which closed with a disconcerting click.

I ran back to the door and gave it a tug, but it would not budge. They'd locked me in.

Honesty compels me to remind my readers that I brought this entirely upon myself. However, let me repeat my earlier assertion that there was no reason to fear. I now had the opportunity to search the premises properly, beyond my wildest hopes for the expedition. Therefore, not in the least unsettled, I set straight to work. I sifted through the papers on Dr. Munjal's desk, my back firmly to the examination table, doing my level best not to snoop into anything that did not concern Miss Wodehouse's death. But I daresay even Caroline would have found it hard to resist a file marked ARSENIC in bold red letters, or DECAPITATED? (with question mark).

Of course, once the idea of decapitation was in my head (no pun intended!), it was not so easy to shake. The laboratory smells filled up the room, making me take shallow breaths through my mouth. Soon my breathing was the only thing I could hear. And the strange buzzing, which seemed to be growing louder. Surely the smell was worse than it ought to have been—in an *empty* room. I could not help a furtive glance over my shoulder. If those were only towels on the exam table, why would they be covered up? And wasn't that heap suspiciously *short*? Headless body short, perhaps?

"Focus, Myrtle." I was here for Miss Wodehouse's report. I reached across the desk for more files, careful not to disturb the doctor's wonderful skull-shaped (at least I think it was only shaped) paperweight, but Miss Wodehouse's report was not there, either. Dr. Munjal had left the desk drawers unlocked—really, didn't *anyone* think there was crime in Swinburne?—but they were mostly filled with blank paper and empty pen nibs.

Leaning against the desk, I tapped my finger against my lips. I had to find that report. Crikey, that smell was getting stronger. My throat burned from the antiseptic, and the light was starting to fade as more gloomy clouds moved in. I consulted my watch. It was after three p.m. The Tedious Girls knew that Miss Judson was coming to fetch me at four; surely they'd let me out by then.

I made another circuit of the morgue. Under the big back windows was a workbench full of apparatus and samples, including a glorious microscope, fancier than Mum's, with a heavy brass base and a case full of interchangeable lenses. Here was the laboratory of my dreams, and I had nearly an hour in which to explore. If only that exam table didn't keep making me turn round and stare at it. It seemed to press against my neck, taunting me.

Perhaps DECAPITATED? would prove less distracting. I flipped it open upon the bench beside the windows. Disappointingly, it was just a bunch of mundane reports, like an old letter from Schofield College and an order for microscope slides. Nobody headless, or even nearly headless. Leafing past the boring bits, I spotted the word *Ambrose* scrawled across the corner of a page. Could that mean Mr. Ambrose, the solicitor? He was a friend of Father's—and Miss Wodehouse's lawyer. I tugged the sheet from the file. It turned out to be the Police Surgeon's report for someone who had died (*not* by decapitation) in 1888, the same year as Mum. One of Mr. Ambrose's clients, perhaps? I read on.

Harold Cartwright, 67, found dead in his bed from complications of dropsy—a condition which caused excess fluid to build up in the body. There must have been an autopsy, though, for under Official Cause of Death, it read, "acute digitalis toxicity." *Poison.* I'd heard of digitalis; it was the treatment for dropsy, so the doctor should have found some of it. But evidently he'd discovered a toxic overdose. Interesting as that was, it didn't help me with Miss Wodehouse. I shoved the papers back into the file with a sigh.

A fly alit on the folder, green and bulbous and hairy. I swatted at it.

Where was Miss Judson?

Where were the Tedious Girls?

Where, for heaven's sake, was Dr. Munjal? A distant growl of thunder underscored my thoughts.

Then a horrible notion struck me.

What if Miss Judson had come back for me, and LaRue and Caroline told her that I'd got bored and left? Would she believe them? Although I did my best to circumvent Father's regulations for me, I had rarely disobeyed Miss Judson. The idea that she'd think I'd gone off without her permission made my throat ache even worse than the awful smells. I sank to the floor, trying to decide what to do. Another fly landed beside me as if sharing my indecision. I supposed they were an occupational hazard.

After a few tense moments' moping, I couldn't take it any longer. I succumbed to—yes, I'll say it—morbid curiosity. I pulled myself to my feet and crept over to the exam table. More clouds had closed in; shadows overtook the counters and medical instruments. The sample jars in the window looked like gruesome puppets poised for a show.

The table was as high as my chest, white enamel with a curved, raised rim that put me in mind of Miss Wodehouse's notorious bathtub. I wanted to know what was under the sheet, and yet I didn't. I took a deep breath through my mouth. Observations: the length of the form on the table (approximately 59 inches), the condition of the sheet (tidy), the much stronger odors present at this vicinity (take my word for it). The frightful buzzing of flies, which seemed to swarm all over. I approached the far end of the table—the feet end, hopefully—and carefully lifted the corner of the sheet.

It was *meat*. Not in a metaphorical sense. In the wildly-overspent-at-the-butcher's sense. A great ugly side of mutton, not yet cut up into shanks and chops. The stench rose up like a fog, and all over, flies buzzed and crawled and settled in the flesh. I swallowed hard, but in a flash of realization, I understood. Various insects can infest a body after death—Dr. Munjal must be studying them.

I still had the edge of the sheet in my hands when I heard someone unlock the door, and the room filled with the yellow fizzle of electric lights.

"What are you doing in here?" a voice demanded.

I spun round to confront the glowering (and gloriously moustachioed) face of Dr. Vikram Munjal.

6

ACUTE TOXICITY AND PROLONGED EXPOSURE

The study of toxins should be foremost in an Investigator's education. Many poisons can mimic common illnesses, so an Investigator must be able to distinguish symptoms that are suspicious from those that are merely unfortunate.

–H. M. Hardcastle, *Principles of Detection*

"Dr. Munjal!" I took a step backward—or tried to, bumping right into his meat-and-flies experiment. The flies spun into the room, a glittering green fog. "Quick, don't let them out!"

Apparently that wasn't what he expected me to say. He stared for a moment, then reached back and shut the door. "They'll stay with the flesh," he said. He was older than Father, with dark olive skin and very dark eyes behind his rain-spotted spectacles. "You're

Arthur Hardcastle's girl, aren't you? You were coming to lunch with Caroline."

I nodded guiltily.

"You'd better explain what happened here."

I dithered, but decided lying served no point. "It wasn't Caroline's fault," I began.

"Ah. LaRue. That girl . . ." He shook his head in understanding. "But my daughter knows better than to fool about in here. I'm very sorry they tried to scare you." His expression was full of sympathy. "Are you all right?"

"Of course," I said stoutly, partly to cover my own twinge of guilt and partly to hide how relieved I was that he'd shown up. "The flies—what kind are they?"

"*Calliphora*," he said, looking oddly at me. "Blowflies. I'm attempting to devise a more accurate method for determining time of death." I nodded. Or I grimaced. I was sure I'd be fascinated to *read* about it someday. "Well, Miss Hardcastle, shall we get you out of here?"

Oh, yes, please. But my work wasn't done, and I couldn't leave empty-handed! I seized my last chance. "Wait, Doctor—" He was halfway to the door again, so I blurted out, "Why did you say Minerva Wodehouse died of natural causes?"

He turned back, frowning. "I beg your pardon?"

"My neighbor who died—why didn't you perform a proper autopsy?" When he didn't answer right away, I refreshed the witness's memory. "An elderly woman, found in her bathtub on Wednesday." I stood very straight, professional-to-professional, not at all like a foolish child who'd got herself locked inside his morgue.

"No, no, I remember. Young lady, I do not believe we should be discussing this." He started to turn off the electricity again, and that's when he noticed all the paperwork I'd left lying about. Now, here was a lesson Miss Judson would appreciate: *clean up after yourself.* His hand came down from the switch, slowly. "What were you doing in here?"

"Trying to find your report."

He straightened up the DECAPITATED? file and sat on the edge of his desk. He didn't speak for a long time, and when he finally did, what he said surprised me. "I knew your mother, you know."

I shook my head. My eyes stung a little. "How?"

"From the teaching hospital, in medical school. Each of us outcasts in our class." Dr. Munjal gestured to himself and I understood what he meant: the female student, and the one from India. "She was wickedly clever. She'd have made a fine doctor."

"It's too bad she had to give it up, to get married and have me."

His mouth quirked. "She would not have thought so," he said. "Very well, for your mother's sake, and because anyone who has spent—how long?—locked up in here deserves something to show for it, what do you want to know?" He lifted his case onto the desk beside him and unlatched the top. "Here we are. Minerva Wodehouse. Heart failure." He handed me a sheet of paper, marked all over with beautiful official stamps and insignia, with his tight, tidy signature at the bottom. OFFICE OF THE POLICE SURGEON, it said at the top.

I devoured it carefully, not wanting to miss, or misinterpret, a single morsel. There was a brief description of where Miss Wodehouse had been found (bathtub), and the time that the police were notified (7:20 a.m., thanks to "call from concerned neighbor" [ahem]). "How do you know she didn't drown?"

"There would have been water in her lungs, and froth in her mouth and nose," Dr. Munjal said. "Heart failure was more likely, given her age and other factors."

I would come back to those "other factors" later. "But that just means she could have been dead before she went into the water. Doesn't it?" I added, trying not to seem confrontational.

"Well," he said, drawing out the word, "normally, yes. If she had been found in a pond, or something of that nature, we would wonder if she had not hit her head, or perhaps suffered a stroke and fallen in. But people do not generally fall *into* their baths."

"I think she was killed somewhere else and then dumped in her bathtub to make it look like natural causes."

He drew back. "Now, Miss Hardcastle, don't get carried away."

"I never get carried away." In my mind that was an offense akin to being fanciful, so I was quite sure I wasn't guilty. "I am *deducing*, based on rational observations of the evidence."

"Deducing," he said faintly, rubbing his temples. "I am sure I will regret saying this, but is there anything else you've deduced?"

Until then, I'd thought the conversation was going well—we were enjoying a meeting of the minds about his fascinating work. But that look of exasperation was entirely too familiar (*I'll give* you *a "knack" for disruption!*), and it made me defensive. "You can't know she wasn't murdered. Not without a proper autopsy."

"Miss Hardcastle, it wasn't warranted. When an eighty-year-old woman dies in the bath, with all the symptoms of a heart attack, in all likelihood, it's a heart attack."

"Seventy-nine," I corrected. "And don't some poisons look like a heart attack? Like digitalis," I improvised, from his file.

"Yes, but do you know what else looks like a heart attack?" He gave me a pointed look. "A heart attack."

"Did she have a history of heart problems?"

"Not that we knew of, but at her age—"

"There were bruises on her back?" I pointed to the notes, smudges sketched on an outline of a body, which lined up with the pollen stains on her night-gown. "That didn't seem suspicious?"

Dr. Munjal shook his head. "They were post-mortem, after death."

I didn't mean to stop, but this gave me pause. "Really? You can tell that? How?"

"It's the most reasonable explanation. She was injured during the heart attack–she convulsed, most likely–or when the constables removed her from the bathtub. Which was also," he added, "how the water got all over."

I nodded slowly. "What about the stains on her nightgown?"

Dr. Munjal sighed and took the report back from me. "I think we've covered everything, don't you? Again, I must apologize for your ordeal this afternoon, and I'll be certain that my daughter apologizes as well."

"That won't be necessary," I said impatiently. "I wanted to ask about–"

"Miss Hardcastle." His soft voice was heavy now. "It's five o'clock. My tea is waiting. You've had a long, upsetting afternoon–"

"I'm not upset," I said. "It was interesting."

"–and it's time for you to go home. Shall I drive you?"

I almost said yes. But then Dr. Munjal would have to explain why I was late to Father–and he'd had such high hopes for this outing, which *hadn't* included me breaking into the morgue and arguing with the Police Surgeon. It didn't take a keen deductive mind to know how he'd feel about that. So, with as much dignity as I could muster, I offered my hand to Dr. Munjal.

"No, thank you, Doctor. I can manage very well. Thank you for an enlightening conversation."

He gravely returned my handshake. "Miss Hardcastle, I'd appreciate your not mentioning what you saw in here," he said, indicating the experiment with the flies. "It's a thing many people would not understand."

I may have been frustrated by my thwarted examination of my witness—but not enough to deny a fellow Investigator such a favor. "Of course, Doctor."

And I walked out into the rain, in my dreary new silk faille gown, its fabulous pockets loaded down with the absolutely nothing useful I'd found.

∽

Father wasn't home yet, thank goodness, and Cook was too busy arguing with the hob to notice me squeezing in late, soaking wet. I tiptoed up the back stairs to the schoolroom, where Miss Judson paced, staring out the rainy windows.

"Myrtle!" Miss Judson clapped her hand to her chest. "Where on earth have you been?"

Wearily, I went over to the fireplace and stirred the embers with the poker. "LaRue and Caroline locked me in the carriage house."

Her face flamed with fury. "Those brats!" she cried. "Wait. Why were you *in* the carriage house?"

Now that I was home and safe and getting dry, I couldn't stop shivering. My teeth were chattering—which saved the need to answer her.

"Take those things off," Miss Judson commanded. "I'll fetch us some cocoa. And then you can tell me all about what you found at the Police Surgeon's house."

Said like *that*, it sounded bad.

By the time Miss Judson and the cocoa returned, I was bundled in my quilted dressing gown, and the slightly wrinkled but mostly intact new dress had been hung neatly—sort of—in my wardrobe. I had my notebook out and *Volume VIII, DEA–ELE*, of my encyclopædia, and was sprawled with them before the fire.

Miss Judson knelt on the floor beside me with the tray, knees and skirts folded smartly at her side. "What are you looking for?"

"Digitalis," I said through a mouthful of toast. "Why didn't you come fetch me?" I hadn't meant it to come out like that, so rude and peevish.

"What, planning to poison my cocoa?" she said mildly. "I *did* come. LaRue told me you'd gone home. And may I point out that had you seen fit to share your plans with me, I might have been on hand to help. Those girls are horrid. We won't go there again. Now. Tell me about your Harrowing Adventure." She made it sound that way, capitalized, like a story in a penny dreadful.

Leaving out a few details, I gave an account of my search of the files, the blowflies in their meat, and DECAPITATED?, rounding off with Dr. Munjal's defense of his findings. By that point I'd had three pieces of toast and two mugs of cocoa and was feeling quite cheered. Miss Judson was enjoying my tale immensely, laughing and exclaiming at all the right bits.

"What's this about digitalis, then?" She leaned over the encyclopædia, and I told her about Mr. Ambrose's client who'd died from an overdose of it.

"Maybe Dr. Munjal was right, and she *did* have a heart attack," I conceded. "But maybe we're right, too. What if she was poisoned with something that *gave* her a heart attack?"

Miss Judson took this in. "Digitalis comes from foxgloves," she said thoughtfully.

"Those are flowers, right?" I sat up. "Did Miss Wodehouse have any? What do they look like?" *Volume VIII* neglected to include an illustration of the plant, and I was feeling too snug and lazy to get up for *Volume X*.

Miss Judson reached for her sketchbook. "I think I have one . . . here. From that planting near the front doors." She held out a drawing of a spiky plant with rows of bell-like flowers surrounding a central stem. *Digitalis* means "finger-shaped," and it was easy to imagine foxes wearing them as mittens (though scientifically improbable).

I consulted the encyclopædia entry again. "'A treatment for heart disease, edema'—that's dropsy—'and kidney ailments,'" I read. "Did Miss Wodehouse have any of those?"

"We'd have known if she had dropsy," she said. "She was a skinny little thing, remember."

"So no swelling, then. But heart disease might not show up externally. Or kidney problems." I took a sip of my cocoa, which had grown cold. "It says it's dangerous to give digitalis to a patient who *doesn't* have a heart condition or kidney problems. Even a small amount can be fatal."

Miss Judson sat down again, rocking back on her heels. She fished a piece of toast from the tray but didn't eat it. "If she died of digitalis poisoning," she said, "which is by no means certain, then she either ate the plant or took the medicine."

"Or somebody gave it to her." Before or after shoving her into the mud.

She was silent a long moment. "I think I prefer accidental ingestion."

"Well, she definitely wouldn't eat it on purpose." I got up and paced the room. "We're forgetting Peony," I said. The cat was still missing. "This is getting hard to keep track of."

"We need a chart." Miss Judson was a great proponent of charts. The schoolroom was liberally adorned with them—Mendeleev's Periodic Table, a reproduction of the Copernican solar system, even a framed anatomy chart that had been Mum's. The only wall that wasn't covered with charts, or windows, had a full-length blackboard with an extra sliding panel. I pushed it aside, rubbed out last week's lecture on Abyssinia, and started making notes—everything I could remember from Dr. Munjal's report and my conversation with Trudy. The apparent heart attack, the bruises, the lack of water in her lungs. The messy bathroom and the pollen-stained nightgown.

"Don't forget the footprints. And the cigar cutter."

"And Mr. Hamm lying," I added. I paused, chalk in midair. They were *his* footprints I'd found, plus he lived on the grounds and had access to the plant. He was also the most likely person to encounter Miss Wodehouse in the middle of the night. "Is it easy to distill the digitalis from foxgloves?"

"I wouldn't know," Miss Judson said. "But according to this, all parts of the plant are poisonous. It doesn't take much skill to make tea out of leaves."

I turned to her. "A professional gardener would know that foxgloves are toxic. Wouldn't he?"

7
WITNESS STATEMENTS

It is common practice, when confronting a suspect, to withhold facts only the perpetrator could know, in the anticipation that he—or she—will slip up and inadvertently confess.

—H. M. Hardcastle, *Principles of Detection*

I needed to talk to Mr. Hamm. I couldn't bring myself to believe he could have killed Miss Wodehouse, no matter what our chart said about Means and Opportunity. He didn't have any *motive*. Saturday morning was the funeral, and Mr. Ambrose and Father's aunt Helena were coming over for dinner that night, but Miss Judson released me around teatime, whereupon I headed straight to Redgraves. I had the strangest feeling the gardener was avoiding me. I finally found him out near the border with the park, overturning the compost.

"Aye, lass," he said in his rich, rumbly voice. "I've not see tha' about these days."

I didn't like it when anyone else called me "lass" or "little girl," but when Mr. Hamm said it, it made me feel warm inside, as if I wasn't just the weird girl next door who was too smart for her own good, but someone worth teaching. Worth listening to. I climbed onto the lowest rail of the fence around the compost heap. "I still haven't found Peony. Trudy says she's never been gone this long."

He leaned on his rake and scratched under his rumpled hat. He still had on the black armband from the funeral, even over his work coat. "She'll turn up. Tha' munna worrit."*

"What will happen to the gardens now?"

He glanced toward the house. "Depends on the solicitors, I suppose."

"But what will happen to *you*?" I said, adding, "I don't want you to go."

Mr. Hamm gave a little grunt. "Now, don't you worrit over me, neither. A lot of gardens in England."

Holding fast to the fence, I watched the compost turn and turn. We were in a shady back corner of the grounds, far from the house, and it occurred to me that a compost heap would be an ideal place to conceal

* Mr. Hamm was from Yorkshire, where they spoke a language that was not exactly English. This translated as "You mustn't worry."

a body. There was quicklime in the greenhouse—gardeners used it to improve the soil, but murderers used it to improve decomposition.

Miss Wodehouse's body wasn't *missing*, though, and it seemed exceeding unlikely that there'd be another one just composting out here, by coincidence. Still, I'd already seen Mr. Hamm destroy evidence once—his so-called "storm debris" bonfire the morning after the murder—and it was possible he could be concealing more, where no one could see or stop him.

"Do you think Miss Wodehouse died naturally?" I asked.

The rake jerked suddenly, like it had hit a stone. Mr. Hamm didn't look up or speak for the longest time. The hush from our corner of the garden was oppressive, and I realized just how isolated we really were.

"Now, what has tha' wondering sommat like that?"

I gripped the fence and made myself ask the question. "I know you and Miss Wodehouse were in the garden that night, and someone pushed her. Was it you?"

Mr. Hamm shoved his hat back and stared at me like I'd started singing opera in Portuguese. "Push Miss Wodehouse? Tha' thinks I'd do such a thing?"

"No! But I want to know what happened. What was she doing out there that late at night? I saw your footprints—those shoes you're wearing right now. And whatever you were burning, it wasn't storm debris. It was the lilies, wasn't it? Why did you destroy them?"

"Look here, lassie," he said, his voice hot and cold at the same time. "All tha' needs to know is that I never did owt here that Miss Wodehouse didn't approve. I never were int' lily plot Tuesday night, and I never pushed Miss Wodehouse. She were an old lady! It'd be like pushing an old dog. Who could do that?"

"Well, she was mean. Maybe she snapped at you?"

Mr. Hamm scoffed at this. "She were always snappin' at everybody. I've worked here nineteen years. If I hadn't got used to Mistress's ways by now, I'd not have stayed this long. And I'd never kill her. I'd just move along. Like I said, lots of gardens in England."

I chewed on my lip and considered this. I wanted to be reassured, but he hadn't actually answered my questions. He had no alibi, and he was being evasive. I knew what Father would make of that. Mr. Hamm went back to his savage stabbing of the compost, all friendliness gone from his face.

I ventured another question. "What do you know about foxgloves?"

"Full sun. Not too much water. Anything else, lass?" His voice was hard.

There was, but he was clearly in no mood to answer me. I shook my head.

"Tha' best be along, then."

I trudged back to the main house. My Investigation was not proceeding with due haste, but I was determined not to let another frustrating interview deter me. Near the front doors, I found the flower bed where Miss Judson had sketched the foxgloves. The tall purple flowers stuck up behind a tangle of four-o'clocks and silvery lamb's ears. Mindful of the plant's overwhelming toxicity, I stepped carefully over the shorter flowers in the bed, looking for broken stems or missing leaves, but couldn't tell if anything had been disturbed.

"Hello? Can I help you?" called out a strangely accented voice. A young woman dressed in funeral black appeared on the front steps. "Little girl, what are you doing? This isn't a public garden!"

My head jerked up guiltily, and my mouth dropped open in surprise. Every Englishwoman from the lowliest charwoman to the Queen herself owned at least one mourning dress. But this lady looked like she was wearing *all* of them, all at once. Tight black skirt with black lace; black bodice studded with jet beads; a black top hat cocked far forward on her head, with a short veil of black netting; and a black handkerchief in her black-mitted fist, which she was waving at me emphatically.

"Who are you?" I said. "What are you doing in Redgraves? Where's Trudy?"

The woman had charged down the steps with more speed than you'd think her skirts would permit, but she halted before dragging me bodily from the flowers. "Wait—are you the little girl from next door? Your father was at Auntie's funeral." She clasped her hands to her breast. "You're the dear thing that notified the police, aren't you? We're ever so obliged."

Another mysterious Wodehouse relative? Where were they all coming from? The obituary had said something about an American niece. "You're Miss Wodehouse's niece? Why have we never seen you before?"

"I've just arrived in England," she said. "And I'm her *great*-niece. Well, sort of a cousin, actually. My grandfather was her cousin. It's too complicated to work that out, so I just called her Auntie."

"First cousins twice removed," I said.

"Aren't you clever!" Before I knew it, she'd hooked her arm into mine. "Since we're going to be neighbors, it's only proper that we be friends. I'm Priscilla. That little maid's set out far too much tea, and I haven't any idea what to do with it all. You will help me, won't you—oh, dear. I've forgotten your name already."

"Myrtle Hardcastle."

"How lovely!" she said, which made her exactly the first person in twelve years to admire my name.

What did she mean, neighbors? Then I spotted the ring of keys at her waist—the universal symbol of a housekeeper's authority. Was this person Miss Wodehouse's heiress?

She half dragged me into Redgraves, putting up an impressive string of chatter as we went, practically saving me the need to even look around for myself. I'd never been inside before, except to step foot in the foyer once during a garden party, when Mum was still alive. "It's a pity about the wallpaper," she was saying. "And the rugs are so worn."

Overlooking the foyer, opposite a grand staircase, loomed a fantastical, larger-than-life portrait. At first I thought it was some classical goddess, a young woman in a drapey sort of robe, leaning on a throne-like chair. In one arm, held aloft like a spear, she bore a long green stem crowned by a single snow-white lily. Looking more closely, I recognized the annoyed twist to the thin lips, the perpetually creased brow.

"It's a good likeness, wouldn't you agree?" Miss Priscilla said. "Auntie did always seem like she was just about to stab someone."

The lily was the most interesting part. It was huge, for one thing, nearly as large as Young Miss Wodehouse's head. And it wasn't just *white*. The artist had edged the blossom with a silvery halo like moonlight, with a sprinkling of palest gold down each luminous petal. The center was the brilliant golden yellow of a candle flame, the stamens weighed down with pollen, each grain picked out in perfect, glittery detail.

This was no ordinary lily.

I peered in closer. Fastened to the bottom of the frame was a brass nameplate: MINERVA & THE GILDED SLIPPER. "The Gilded Slipper?"

"Oh yes," Miss Priscilla said. "That was Auntie's great secret, didn't you know? A quest to replicate a mythical flower mentioned in an ancient book. Something that died out hundreds of years ago, if it ever even existed at all: *the Gilded Slipper lily.*" Her voice was low and dramatic; I could hear the capital letters and italics as she spoke. I felt a shiver of excitement.

"Do you think she did?" I asked, my voice hushed, like in church.

"I have no idea," she said, her words suddenly short. "I hope not. It would be worth a lot of money, after all. And where is that money now, I ask you?" She shook herself back to the moment. "Now, about that tea."

She led me down a long hallway, out to the conservatory, where a plate of limp sandwiches (leftovers from the funeral luncheon) sat on a fussy wicker table along with a vase of—what else?—lilies. "Do you think these are pretty?" Miss Priscilla said. "They seem rather bold to me."

The variety in question was an impressive shade of fiery orange with a dark brown center—*Lilium lancifolium*, the tiger lily.* Miss Priscilla poked a dainty finger at the flower's middle, flicking the pollen-coated stamen.

"Careful," I said. "That stains."

As Miss Priscilla poured out the tea—which I had no intention of drinking, mind you, at least until I was certain who at Redgraves had poisoned Miss Wodehouse—I tried to examine the lilies. But Priscilla shoved the vase aside and put her chin in her hands. She had rosy cheeks and a mouth painted like a china doll's, but I Observed that her eyes were bloodshot and her face was not as perfectly pretty as it had first appeared.

"So," she said. "You live next door, you're *very* clever, and your father is a lawyer. What about your mother?"

"She died when I was little. And Father's the Prosecuting Solicitor."

Her gaze got keen. "It's just the two of you then? That must be lonely."

And Miss Judson, I thought fiercely. "Not really." I changed the subject. "You had inconvenient timing, Miss Wodehouse," I noted, "arriving just in time for your aunt to die."

* also classified as *L. tigrinum*; Miss Wodehouse had been among the scientists who recognized these were in fact the same species.

"*Priscilla.* And don't I know it! I was hoping to get to know Dear Auntie again. I hadn't seen her in ever so long." She stirred her tea thoughtfully, but never took a sip. "Thank goodness everything has been wrapped up quickly. I couldn't have borne sitting through an inquest, could you? They're so tiresome."

I just blinked at her. "Why would there have been an inquest?" I said, all innocence.

She gave her fluttery sigh. "Well, there's always some meddlesome neighbor—I don't mean *you*, of course!"

I eyed her thoughtfully. Priscilla had all the makings of a good murder suspect, assuming she didn't have an alibi.

"You inherited Redgraves? Where were you Tuesday night?"

"What questions!" She laughed aloud. "Yes, Officer, I inherited Redgraves—or I will, once the will is read—and *when Auntie died* I was at my boarding-house in town."

I nodded, swinging my feet under the table, and the lilies bobbed, scattering a dusting of pollen onto the tablecloth. Then I was seized with inspiration. "Might I have one of these, to remember Miss Wodehouse by?"

Priscilla shrugged. "Take the whole bunch. I think they're horrid."

I finally escaped her clutches, lugging the vase of Miss Wodehouse's last lilies back home. Cook exclaimed over the flowers and wanted to put them on the dining room table for our dinner guests to admire.

"It's evidence," I mumbled through the foliage, and took the lilies upstairs, where I set to work. I plopped the vase onto the schoolroom counter, next to the microscope, and began my Investigation by inspecting the flowers with my magnifying lens and preparing microscope slides from samples taken of the plant. The deep orange petals, which looked smooth and rubbery to the naked eye, were actually studded with short, hairy spikes. Greenish liquid clung to the stigma, which protruded like a long thin tongue from the flower's center. The blossoms had opened so far that it looked like they'd turned themselves inside out, and bullet-shaped buds pointed every which way. What could this plant tell me about Miss Wodehouse's murder?

I had no idea.

When Miss Judson came to summon me downstairs for dinner, she paused reverently before the last precious remnants of Miss Wodehouse's priceless collection. I explained my latest mission at Redgraves, including my unproductive conversation with Mr. Hamm. "The niece gave me these," I concluded. "Priscilla. She thought they were ugly."

"Mmm. I disagree, but I accept that they might be an acquired taste." She curled a petal around one finger. "Did you learn anything else?"

I scrunched up my face. "Not really. She's rather weird."

Miss Judson waited. "Many people are 'weird' by your estimation."

"Oh, she'd fit yours as well. She was worried there'd be an inquest because they're *tiresome*."

"Well, how many has she been to?"

I looked up at Miss Judson. "That's what I was wondering!"

8

AGGRAVATING
FACTORS

A skilled Investigator is impartial, never allowing his
emotions to distract him from the task at hand.

          –H. M. Hardcastle, *Principles of Detection*

Downstairs, our guests were just arriving. I was
playing hostess tonight, despite Father and me *both*
begging Miss Judson to save us. But her notions of propriety were absolute, and that included "the help" not
mingling in family dinners. I watched her retreat with
some envy. And unless I was very much mistaken, so
did Father.

    Mr. Ambrose arrived first, and I ushered him
grandly into the foyer. I was bubbling over with questions about the case, but first we had a ritual.

"Well, Myrtle, my girl, what can you tell me about this?" He handed over his hat and coat for my inspection, and I set about examining them for clues to his recent activities. The coat was new—gone was the familiar garment with its frayed cuffs and threadbare lining, its scent of tobacco smoke and moustache wax. This one sported a velvet collar and polished silver buttons. The pockets were empty, save for a single wrapped sweet I knew was meant for me. The hat was new, too, a black silk top hat with a label from a men's haberdashery in London—not the sort of indulgence I'd expect from Mr. Ambrose! Perhaps he was on his way to the theater or something after dinner.

"You've recently come into money," I posited. "Did you win a big case?"

He smiled at me, blue eyes glinting in the lamplight. "Clever girl. Can't hide a thing from you." He was stooped slightly, rubbing at his knee.

"What's wrong with your leg?"

"It's as old as I am," he said. "What else can you tell, you cheeky child?"

I started to say, *You've been to London*, but changed my mind. "You've been to a funeral. For a client you've had for many years."

"Not fair," he said. "You didn't deduce that. You know very well I was Miss Wodehouse's lawyer, and I've heard you know quite a bit about her death as well."

"I did so deduce," I said. "Look, see the indentations from the armband in the wool of your sleeve? If you rub the pinholes, they'll come out, you know." I shook my head sadly. "Criminals never hide their tracks."

"Well, not from you!" He gave his crinkly grin, then produced a smallish wrapped parcel. "I've got a present for you, *if* you can tell me what's in there."

"Let me see!" I held it before me. "It's lightweight for its size, and the shape is awkward, so it's not a book." Mr. Ambrose was expressionless. I shook it. No sound. "The wrapping isn't from Swinburne; no shops here use that type of brown paper." This was wild speculation. I had no way of knowing what *every* shop in town wrapped their parcels in. I'd mainly been hoping for some reaction from Mr. Ambrose, but he was just as good at this game as I was.

He watched me skeptically, whiskered mouth downturned. "Disappointing, my girl, disappointing. And it was so *elementary*." He reached to take back the present.

"Wait! I know what it is." I didn't. And then I did. "You gave it away!" I wailed. "I'd have worked it out. It's a deerstalker cap!" Triumphantly, I ripped off the paper to reveal my prize: the signature hat of Mr. Sherlock Holmes, Consulting Detective. "Oh, it's wonderful. How does it look?" I popped it on my head and stood on tiptoe to examine my reflection in the secretary mirror—at which point, our second guest of the evening arrived.

"Take that ridiculous thing off, Helena Myrtle, it doesn't go with your frock." And there was Aunt Helena, my unfortunate namesake. "Good evening, Whitney. I see you're still a bad influence on the girl."

"Happy to oblige, Helena." Mr. Ambrose got out of the way. Aunt Helena was Father's aunt, my great-aunt, and had to be at least nine hundred years old, but she strode through the world like someone much younger. Without preamble, she dropped her fur wrap onto me, stepping out in a glittering silver gown. Did everyone think that dinner at the Hardcastle house was now a formal event? I hated to admit it, but I suddenly felt rather shabby. I wrestled free of the creature and tossed it haphazardly onto the hall tree. Defiantly, I kept my new hat on, turned, and followed everyone to the dining room.

One thing I could say about Aunt Helena's visits, they weren't boring. Poor Father looked exhausted already, and dinner hadn't even started.

"Dear Arthur, you look weary." She glared at him through a lorgnette. "Taking on too much work again, no doubt. Ambrose, you should take him back."

"I didn't let him go!" Mr. Ambrose took a drink of his wine. "Arthur has a mind of his own, you know."

Peering around the vase of lilies, I Observed that Aunt Helena managed to take generous helpings of all the most expensive dishes Cook had served, but Mr. Ambrose wasn't eating much at all, just rearranging the food on his plate. He was looking rather peaked, actually, pale and rubbing occasionally at his eyes. Probably from the strain of being seated next to Helena Hardcastle.

Father ignored their quibbling. "Aunt Helena, how was Paris?" This ought to have been a safe topic.

"Filthy. And absolutely riddled with crime. Do you know, someone was murdered in my hotel?"

I started. "While you were there? Did you get to talk to the police?"

Now she glared at me. "Don't be pert. Of course not. It happened years ago. But honestly, it's the sort of thing they should warn people about!"

"Quite right," Mr. Ambrose said. "Decent people can't go anywhere these days without tripping over a body." He winked at me.

Father gave him a look. "Whit, please don't encourage her."

"What's this?" Aunt Helena trained her lorgnette on me like an artillery sight. "Oh, yes. I heard about your antics this week, Helena Myrtle."

"Which ones?" I grumbled.

"Well," she declared, "I don't believe that nonsense about a heart attack for a moment. Minerva Wodehouse was far too eccentric for such a mundane death."

For a moment, we were all silent. I stared at my great-aunt, scarcely believing that of all people, *she* was the one who agreed with me. Mr. Ambrose gulped his wine, and Father fairly flung the platter of fish down the table. "Anyone for more flounder? Flounder, Whitney? Helena?"

In a small voice, I said, "How do *you* think she died, Aunt?"

She wheeled on me and in a clipped voice said, "Impertinence, no doubt. I can't see how you put up with her all this time, Whitney." It sounded like she'd meant *me*. I wasn't convinced she hadn't. "What will happen to her estate now? Carved up to creditors, I suppose." Aunt Helena reminded me of a hyena circling the carcass of a wildebeest.

"Well, now, I'm not sure this is really the time—" Father began, but I pounced.

"She didn't die intestate, did she? And even if she did, she has heirs—that niece and nephew, Priscilla and Giles. Everything would be divided between them, unless the estate was entailed. Otherwise it escheats to the Crown. Right?"

Mr. Ambrose gave a tug on his collar. "My word, Myrtle, you have been studying."

I nodded happily. "I've been brushing up on inheritance law." I didn't say it was because I was researching what would happen if Father married again.

"This is exactly why I don't approve of this trend of overeducating girls," Aunt Helena said. "It encourages just this sort of behavior. When girls get ideas that are too modern, they get in trouble."

"How can an idea be *too* modern?" I demanded. "That's the stupidest thing I've ever heard." In retrospect, I might have chosen my words with more discrimination.

Aunt Helena's gaze was hard and icy. "Case in point," she said. "It's downright disgraceful how forward some children are these days, and it's a *most* unbecoming trait in a young lady. Girls need to learn modesty and civility, not mathematics. If you ask me"—no one had—"that foreign governess of yours has been deplorably lax in her duties."

"Well, now," Father began, "I wouldn't go that far—"

"You can't talk about Miss Judson like that!" I burst to my feet, jostling the table. I meant to make some scathing and final comment that would put Aunt Helena in her place once and for all. But something much, much better happened instead.

I knocked over the lily vase.

Right into her lap.

Her plate toppled, too. All onto Dear Aunt Helena's silver Parisian silk gown careened a cascade of gravy, wine sauce, sticky silverware, gaudy orange flowers, indelibly staining pollen, and vile vase water that had started to turn. Aunt Helena was a woman of exceptional composure, so instead of letting out a satisfying wail of horror, she merely froze, still as a statue, as all the color drained from her face.

For a moment I was terrified. Then I wanted to laugh. Then I was terrified again. Father leaped to his feet, and even Mr. Ambrose hopped up to help. Unfortunately, this only made matters worse, for now the vase tumbled all the way to the floor and shattered.

"I'll get the broom," I said meekly. We kept a silent butler at hand—everybody did—and I grabbed the little silver dustpan from the sideboard.

"Let me help." Mr. Ambrose knelt with me at Aunt Helena's feet, collecting the greater shards of broken vase as I swept up the rest. Some pollen had got on his pants, a pale smear near the hem. I glanced up to see Mr. Ambrose wink at me. I was still too mortified to even smile back, but the camaraderie warmed me.

I reached my brush under the table as far as I dared, between Aunt Helena's legs. Beneath a curve of orange petal, I spotted something that was neither silverware, plate, broken vase, nor flower—a sparkle of brass against the dark floor. A key. Thinking swiftly, I palmed it around the brush handle and kept sweeping. Where had that come from? Unless Aunt Helena had dropped it, it must have been inside the vase.

A very odd place, indeed, to store one's keys.

Aunt Helena had recovered enough to begin bellowing at us again. "Get off me, you stupid girl!" she howled, and shoved her chair back almost onto my hands. Mr. Ambrose pulled me backward, like a comrade in arms saving a fellow soldier from a bullet. "Somebody, get my coat. And *you*," she snarled at me, "will learn to behave yourself before I set foot in this house again!"

"Well, Aunt Helena," said Father mildly, "if you think that will help."

9
PLEA BARGAINING

Although every defendant is entitled to a fair trial, the courts will sometimes grant the accused a lesser sentence in exchange for a guilty plea.

—H. M. Hardcastle, *Principles of Detection*

After Aunt Helena swept out of our house like a storm blowing away, it was obvious that I was, yet again, in disgrace. Father stared down at me gravely, passing judgment long before speaking.

"The incident with the vase was an unfortunate accident, and Aunt Helena handled it poorly," he conceded. "And I'm very sorry you've lost your keepsake from Miss Wodehouse. But what *preceded* that incident has me deeply concerned, Myrtle. It's not seemly for you to have so many opinions, and on so many inappropriate subjects."

I frowned, trying to remember. "But *you* were all talking about the murder."

"For the last time, Myrtle, there was no murder! I don't want to hear that word in this house again, do you understand me?"

Well, *that* was an impossible demand, given his own profession, but I was finally wise enough to keep my mouth shut.

I was sent to bed immediately. Miss Judson was spared a trial, at least: Father sent her with me. She bustled soberly about my room, turning down the lamps and gathering my things. Her hair, loosed from its prim daytime twists, was a soft dark cloud around her face. It was hard to imagine there was a time when she hadn't been part of my life.

But before Miss Judson, there had been Aunt Helena. When Mum was ill, and for the entire next year, Father's aunt had lived with us, and (according to her) taken care of me. Those were the days without Stansberry pie, of barked orders and tense silences, and I'd spent many long hours in Father's study, where it would never occur to Aunt Helena to look for me. It was beneficial for my Latin, at least. Father and I hadn't spoken much during that time, but he'd never shooed me away or pried his beloved books from my hands. What had changed?

Finally, having Done Her Duty, Aunt Helena made one last decision for us, and advertised for a governess. Out went Aunt Helena and her Morally Beneficial storybooks, and in came Miss Judson with her sketchbooks, her practical plaid cape, and her Socratic Method. And Father's smile returned. Miss Judson had indulged my curiosity and *encouraged* my questions—beginning with her own heritage: French and Maroon* on her mother's side; Scottish and English on her father's. She'd described French Guiana in such fascinating detail† that I'd longed to run away there with her. But I'd grown up enough now to understand that there were probably Aunt Helenas and LaRue Spence-Hastingses everywhere, and you had to hang on tight to the Miss Judsons when you found them.

Miss Judson brought me my nightgown. I had doffed the dress I'd worn at dinner and was perched on the bed in my underthings, studying the key I'd rescued from the broken vase. It looked like an ordinary key, except that the handle was shaped like a fleur-de-lis—a sort of stylized lily. I showed it to her.

"That was in the flowers?" Miss Judson turned it over, examining the intricate design. "How curious!"

* Miss Judson's French word was *Marron* (*not* to be confused with the word for chestnut!). The name comes from Arawak roots, and means the descendants of enslaved Africans who took back their freedom and settled with indigenous peoples.

† frightful conditions of the prison colony notwithstanding

"I wonder what it opens. I've never seen a key with a handle like that. It must be important." Perhaps it even had something to do with the mythical Gilded Slipper lily!

Miss Judson set the key on my nightstand. "That, my dear, is a mystery for tomorrow. Time for bed." She handed me instead my encyclopædia, but paused before turning away. "Do you want to talk about what happened tonight?"

I scowled so hard my face hurt. "No."

"Your father loves you," she said, homing in on the subject I least wished to discuss. "You know that."

"But I don't understand!" I cried. "He always says he wants me to be clever and curious and study hard. But whenever I show him how smart I am, he's embarrassed by me. He thinks I'm morbid." I hadn't meant to let that slip, but it hardly mattered now. "What's wrong with me?"

"Oh, Myrtle." She bundled me to her, her tight embrace just as crisp and reassuring as the rest of her. "There is *nothing* wrong with you. Nothing. And your father loves you. He adores you. He just—" She hesitated, and I tried to read all the unspoken words fleeting past as she worked out what to say. "He wants the best for you and doesn't always know what that is or how to go about it."

"*You're* what's best for me! And for him." I hadn't meant to let that slip, either.

"Yes, well." She chose to ignore that. "Don't worry. This will blow over, and you and I will be absolutely fine." She bent over and kissed the top of my head. "Don't stay up too late."

ↄ∽

I snuggled under the covers with *Volume X*, rereading my favorite passages about the Galapagos Islands. But the giant tortoises and unique volcanic soil could not soothe me tonight. Finally, I put the book aside and turned to peer out the window, lowering the flame on the lamp in order to see out. The telescope was in the other room; I'd have to content myself with what I could Observe with the naked eye.

Gravesend Close had one gas streetlight, right near our house, and under the yellow halo of the lamp lurked two figures. I hunched closer to the window. One was easy to identify: the narrow bell-shaped skirts, the black top hat, and the overall height pegged her as Priscilla Wodehouse. The other I didn't recognize at all. It wasn't Mr. Hamm or Nephew Giles, whom I hadn't seen since the morning Miss Wodehouse died. I unlatched the glass and cracked the window. It was a clear night, and the wind was in my favor—and they were arguing loudly enough to overhear.

"This is the last time. Do you understand me?" said Priscilla. "If you come here again, I'll call my solicitor."

"Ain't for me to say," said the other figure, a burly man in a bowler hat. "Now hand it over."

Priscilla looked about anxiously, then withdrew something from her bodice. I was too far away to see what. It was smallish, about the size of a pack of playing cards, but it could have been anything—an envelope, a book, a bundle of banknotes. The burly man stuffed it into his jacket pocket, tipped his hat, and hiked off into the night. Priscilla stood under the light, watching him disappear into the thicket of dark cottages. Finally, she turned back toward Redgraves—but not before swinging her gaze straight up to my bedroom window.

I darted back, my elbow cracking against the encyclopædia and knocking it off the table. Had she seen me? I froze, not nodding or blinking or anything, until I was sure she had left.

My thoughts rattled, I fished around in my night-stand for my notebook, found my pages on Priscilla, and started making more notes by moonlight. My first thought, naturally, was blackmail. That happened all the time in Billy Garrett, and it had happened once in one of Father's cases.

Who would be blackmailing Priscilla? I chewed on the end of my pencil. Perhaps a better question was, what secret did Priscilla have worth blackmailing her for?

Monday morning, when we were barely out of bed, there was an urgent knock at our door. I was half afraid Aunt Helena was back, despite her vow, but I was astonished to discover Priscilla waiting on our doorstep. What could she want?

She gave me her gay, faintly hysterical smile and bent as if she were going to pat me on the head. "Look, it's you!"

"Who else would it be?" I said, before thinking better of it. She just laughed.

"I need to speak with your father. Is he in?"

It was unseemly early for a social call; we hadn't even had our breakfast yet. "I'll see if he's dressed. Won't you come in." Instead of ushering her to the parlor, I unceremoniously left her where she stood and went to fetch Father. He was up in his room, still getting dressed. He'd already trimmed his whiskers and was buttoning his collar stand into place, and I saw with dismay that he'd laid out his burgundy foulard waistcoat. I scurried over and swapped it for the gold check one that made him look cross and sallow.

He turned to me, bemused. "That doesn't match my tie," he said.

"All the better. Miss Wodehouse is here."

"Here? In our home? Why?" Instantly his brow came down. "What did you do?"

"I answered the door!" I said, indignant. "I swear. I am inculpable of any malfeasance."

He actually smiled. "I rue the day I ever let you read my law dictionary."

"*Ex post facto*," I said cheerfully. We hadn't entirely forgiven each other for our quarrel, but this was more how things were supposed to be.

He shrugged into the nearest jacket at hand—the oldest one with the threadbare elbows, which he only wore at home, and *only* Miss Judson and I could find appealing—and hurried for the door. He was almost out when I spotted something amiss.

"Ring," I said softly, and he froze in the doorway. He patted down his pockets and, finding nothing, spun back to the dresser and retrieved his wedding ring and pocket watch from their leather-lined tray. He passed me on his way out and squeezed my shoulder as he went. I trotted down with him; there was no way he was going to meet Priscilla unchaperoned anywhere in my house!

"Miss Wodehouse." Father stumbled into the foyer as though his shoes, or the act of walking, were unfamiliar to him. I noted his appearance with approval. He couldn't help being charming and intelligent and a widower. Those were stipulated facts in evidence. But I could emphasize the precocious daughter who lurked about everywhere being impertinent and morbid. I could thrust the attractive, smart, and infinitely more appropriate governess before The Rival—since it was hard to rely on a flummoxed man automatically identifying the better choice.

"Oh, Mr. Hardcastle." Priscilla curtsied like it was her profession. Her dress was buttoned up tight, all the way to her sharp little chin, which was cupped in a tiny ruffle of black lace. "I need to speak with you. I know you're not in private practice, but I really don't have anywhere else to turn."

"Um, certainly, Miss Har—Wodehouse. Please, let's step into my study." He led the way, one arm held out as if to shield her skirts from harm (from what, the chair rail?). He frowned as I followed, giving me a nearly imperceptible shake of his head. I shook back and went right on following.

"Myrtle, I believe Miss Wodehouse wishes to see me in private. It's business."

"It's inappropriate." I was certain this argument would work; adults used it constantly. "I'm chaperoning."

Miss Wodehouse turned that smile on me again. "I promise you nothing untoward will happen, Myrtle. Or don't you trust your father?" This with an altogether too-pert wink that I did not trust at all.

Unfortunately, she'd won and she knew it. I gave Father the fiercest scowl I could muster, and said, "Miss Judson and I will be waiting for you at breakfast."

"Oh, don't bother," he said absently. "I don't know how long this will take."

My scowl got fiercer still. *"We'll be waiting."*

I realized my own error the moment the study door closed in my face. My pledge to sit at vigil at the breakfast table would preclude me from stationing myself in the water closet to listen in on their meeting. With a growl of frustration, I stomped to breakfast.

Miss Judson was typically imperturbable. She went on stirring her tea and buttering her toast with the same unflappable precision as every morning, each pleat, pin tuck, and twist of dark hair perfectly in place. Normally I found that serenity and exactitude soothing, but today they exasperated me.

"Don't you know what's going on in there?" I leaned far over the table, trying to get her attention, and upset the honey pot in my urgency.

She scooped it up without even looking, before a single drop had a chance to spill. "No, and nor do you. Your father has a client."

"My father has a *caller*. A *woman*! At his house. At eight o'clock in the morning. And he's the Prosecutor, not a common solicitor. He doesn't have clients anymore."

"Mmm." Toast, butter, tea, calm. "Don't jump to conclusions. One breakfast meeting does not a stepmother make."

"Miss! You said it!"

"So I did. You realize that your father has an entire life that happens away from this house, about which we—you—know almost nothing. Anything at all could be going on, all day long, when he's at work. You need far more evidence before drawing a conclusion."

I stirred my porridge and swung my feet. It would be nice if I'd ever grow enough to put them on the floor like a sensible person. "I suppose you're right." I glared at her, although that glare was really meant for someone else. Two someones. "But I'll be watching for more evidence, and I'm not responsible for what happens if I find some!"

Finally, after *forty-nine minutes*, three pots of tea, and an entire loaf of toast, Father and Priscilla emerged from the study—and *both* of them came into the dining room. I looked urgently to Miss Judson, who smoothly stepped into the exact role I wanted for her, like a heroine.

"Good morning, Miss Wodehouse. Have you eaten? There's plenty left. Won't you sit down?"

I could have kissed her. Governesses generally did not invite the neighbors to dine with the family, like the lady of the house. Father didn't notice, of course. But I was sure Priscilla did.

"I—no, thank you. Judson, is it?"

"*Miss* Judson," I corrected, because I knew she wouldn't bother. "Ada."

"I can't stay," said Priscilla. "Myrtle–Arthur, shall I tell her the news? Or do you want to?"

I stared between them. It was far too early for this sort of development! "What news?"

Her fluttery smile grew. "Your father is lending you to me."

"Miss Wodehouse needs some assistance sorting through her aunt's records," he said. "I thought you might like to help her." In this light, Father's gold waistcoat did not look quite as unflattering as I had intended.

"Mr. Ambrose was telling me you're quite the little legal clerk!"

I was torn. On the one hand, I had no desire to assist in any enterprise that could strengthen ties between Priscilla and our family. On the other hand, here at last was my chance for a really proper Investigation of Redgraves.

Father crouched beside me. "I know you're still concerned about Miss Wodehouse, and I thought this might help you come to terms with what happened."

Well, that wasn't exactly what I planned. But I nodded, touched by his understanding, incomplete though it was. "Can Miss Judson come?"

"Oh, I don't think that's necessary," Miss Judson put in, too swiftly. In one elegant movement, she poured

Father a cup and set it at his place. I twisted my fingers together, not sure I approved—Father was *entirely* capable of pouring his own tea—although I think Miss Judson's maneuver worked. Father sank down into his seat, looking faintly dazed. The last thing I saw, before Priscilla led me away, was Miss Judson watching me, mirth in her eyes.

10

GAINFUL EMPLOYMENT

Although common belief tells us that the poor and unfortunate commit most crimes, do not overlook those offenses perpetrated by the well-to-do. They can be the most egregious, and the hardest to comprehend.

–H. M. Hardcastle, *Principles of Detection*

Priscilla explained the project on the walk to Redgraves. "Mr. Ambrose can't read the will because the version he has was never signed. We need to find my aunt's copy, to prove that it really reflects her wishes." Her mouth was a thin line. "I can't afford a proper clerk to help me, but I'll pay you ten shillings."

Ten shillings! That would certainly be a nice cushion in my Laboratory Fund.* Of course, financial gain

---

* I was saving to buy more professional chemistry equipment. The Boy's Own Chemistry Set I'd bought from Leighton's Mercantile Shop had proved a disappointment.

was hardly my main motivation. Questions simmered in my brain like in an overheated beaker: Who killed Miss Wodehouse? How, and what for? Why had Mr. Hamm destroyed the lilies? Where was Peony? I was determined not to leave Redgraves that afternoon without answers.

As we passed through Redgraves's gloomy foyer, Miss Wodehouse scowled down on us from her giant portrait, like she was daring somebody to find her secret lily. Or her will—or her murderer. *I'm trying*, I thought back at her, flinching away from that intimidating glare. I noticed a curious mark in the worn carpet, a sort of furrow veering toward the stairs, and there was a great raw gash in the newel post where something had crashed into it. An over-exuberant Trudy with a tea cart? Unlikely. I made a mental note to Investigate that as soon as I had the chance.

Priscilla led me to a room on the main floor that might have been a parlor, once. Now it was a maze of shelves, cartons, clay pots, and piles of papers. Amid the clutter I caught glimpses of furniture—a red velvet sofa that was probably nice before someone left a pair of wet boots on it—and the biggest photographs I'd ever seen, nearly life-sized pictures of the Redgraves gardens, covering the walls. If anything in this room opened with the fleur-de-lis key, it was well hidden.

"At least she was organized?" I said hopefully. Priscilla didn't laugh this time. She just lifted a box from the top shelf and plunked it into my arms.

Dear Reader, I shall spare you the details of that morning's toil, save to note that surely Billy Garrett had never endured anything so dull as Miss Wodehouse's dusty files. Unintelligible order forms and random newspaper clippings piled up alongside flattened sweet wrappers and forty-year-old brochures from the Great Exhibition. The towering shelves blocked the windows, making the room even gloomier. Fifteen minutes into the work, I knew it was hopeless. It would take *weeks* to find the will—if it was even here—and longer still to find anything that pointed to Miss Wodehouse's murderer.

I tossed aside a dog-eared advert for Thompkin's Guaranteed Beard Generator and glowered back at Miss Wodehouse's portrait. Her gigantic pearly gold lily shone from the canvas, so realistic you could almost smell its mysterious fragrance. Had she really grown it?

"Maybe there's something about the Gilded Slipper lily in these files," I suggested. "You don't remember ever seeing it when you were little? It would be worth a lot of money, you said. Do you think it could have made her any enemies?" Perhaps someone driven mad by the tedium of searching through all these ancient papers?

Priscilla gave a nervous laugh. "Well, aren't those just the funniest questions! Your father warned me about you!" But she didn't answer me.

"Who was that man you were talking to the other night?" I said, hoping to catch her off guard.

Her face was blank. "What do you mean?"

"I saw you. Outside under the streetlamp, meeting some man."

"I don't think so," she said, neatening and re-neatening the edges of her papers.

"You were arguing," I insisted. "And then you gave him something to make him go away."

Now she was frowning. "You really have *quite* the imagination, Myrtle."

I had seen Father do this a hundred times. He could force the truth out of anyone. "What was it?" I pressed. "Is he blackmailing you?"

She let out a strangled laugh. "Oh, yes. For the heaps and piles of money I have lying about!" She tossed her handful of papers in the air, scattering them hopelessly.

Glaring at her, I got up to fetch another demoralizing file. Even on tiptoe, I couldn't reach the top shelf, but my craning fingers found the corner of a loose folder and coaxed it into my grasp. PRISCILLA, it read, in spidery red handwriting. Without thinking, I said, "Oh, Miss Priscilla—this one's about you." And then I could have kicked myself.

"What? Hand that over." She sprang up and snatched the file from my hands, not noticing a photograph slip to the floor. As Priscilla flipped through the contents, her face grew even more pinched and disagreeable. "This is nothing. Just some old letters I wrote her." She shook off the cross expression. "Goodness, who'd have thought dead people could be so *boring*?"

I'd retrieved the photograph, a cabinet card of a young family outside Redgraves, dressed for an old-fashioned lawn party in boater hats and flouncy white dresses. In the middle were two blurry figures: a thin woman in a severe dark dress with upswept white hair was swinging a little girl by the arms and laughing. I glanced over. Was that Miss Wodehouse and a very small Priscilla?

What in the world had happened to estrange Miss Wodehouse from all those happy family members?

And which one of them had finally decided to kill her?

A jostle at the front door made us both glance up, and a moment later, someone's shadow filled the doorway to the drawing room.

"Well, hullo there, girls." It was that nephew fellow, the one who'd been here the morning Miss Wodehouse died.

"Giles!" Priscilla cried. "Tell me you've come to save me from this drudgery!"

"I thought that's what *she* was for." He peered over my shoulder at the photograph. "Finding anything interesting? Auntie was such a pack rat." He noticed me staring. "Pris forgot to introduce me. Giles Northcutt. I'm Priscilla's cousin."

Priscilla stuck her tongue out at him. "*Second* cousin. And ever so jealous because I'm the heir."

For a moment, I thought I saw a flicker of darkness cross Mr. Northcutt's clean-shaven face. Then it was gone again in a laugh. "Rather. Who'd want this old rubbish heap? You ought to sell it, Pris. Good riddance."

"You *would* think that," Priscilla said. "You have no respect at all for the family name."

"Maybe if I had the family name," he said cheerfully. "Giles *Wodehouse* Northcutt," he elaborated. "I'm a matrilineal cousin. That means I'm related through my mother."

"I know what it means," I said indignantly.

"Clever, are you?" He glanced around the room. "What's she roped you into here, anyway?"

I saw no reason to keep it a secret, and thought his reaction might be interesting. "We're looking for your aunt's will."

He just looked bored. "Ambrose is still on about that? Why he can't keep up with his own files is beyond me. That's the whole reason I stopped working there, you know."

"Really," Priscilla said. "I can't imagine any other reasons."

"You're a solicitor?" I couldn't quite keep the disbelief from my voice.

"Alas, no. Too dull. Now I'm in shipping. International commerce." He made it sound very grand, but Priscilla gave an exaggerated yawn.

"You must know my father, then," I said. "Arthur Hardcastle, the Prosecutor?"

"Well, I'd better stay on your good side!"

Priscilla looked cross with both of us. "I'm not sure she has one, Giles," she said. "She asks some very probing questions. Myrtle, dearest, I think Giles here can take over for you for the afternoon. No, don't you *dare* run away, cousin. There may be something for you in that will, too, you know."

"Quite," he said. "A ceramic elephant or her antique spoon collection. No, thank you."

I wasn't sure what I'd learned from that exchange, but I'd had more than my fill of Miss Wodehouse's files—not to mention her disagreeable niece and nephew—for one day. Happy to make my escape, I grabbed my bag and headed for the front door. I passed Cousin Giles, who was just now lighting a cigarillo, its sour smoke twisting through the grand foyer. My hand on the doorknob, I turned back.

"Do you smoke cigars, Mr. Northcutt?"

He looked surprised. "Me? No. Can't stand the things. Don't you know they're bad for your health?"

⟳

I expected the next day to go much the same, but when I got to Redgraves, no one was about. Mr. Hamm was nowhere to be seen, and even the gardens felt desolate. It was eerily similar to that terrible quiet morning last week when I'd arrived to find a silent house and nobody working. My heart fluttered anxiously—had something else happened? When nobody answered my first, second, or third knocks on the big front doors, I headed around back to let myself in through the conservatory.

The conservatory door was open (well, in the name of accuracy, I should say it was *unlocked*), and inside, Redgraves was just as quiet. I called for Trudy and Priscilla with no answer. "Peony?" I tried, without much hope. With a tentative step into the hallway, I saw that the curious furrow in the carpet I'd noticed yesterday led all the way down here. I followed it back to the stairs.

"Morning, Miss Wodehouse," I said to the painting. My voice sounded overloud in the cavernous space. The clock on the sideboard had wound down, so I gave it a few firm twists and set the hands in the right place, whereupon it set about an orderly ticking that instantly made the house feel less empty. Beside the clock was a small book, encircled by a rime of dust. It was a novel, *The Green Widow* by Edgar Corey, author of the Billy Garrett serials and other mysteries in the penny dreadfuls. Not the sort of reading I'd expect from Miss Wodehouse! Cracking the book to the middle–beginnings were often boring–I discovered a pressed flower petal, a long, narrow slip of pale creamy brown, like old parchment. I felt a spike of excitement–was this from the Gilded Slipper?

"Oh, hello there! You're back." Priscilla stood above me on the stairs, looking like she'd just fallen out of bed. She was in a threadbare pink dressing gown and bare feet, her blond hair a frizzy halo.

I stood up straighter, feeling unaccountably caught out at something. "I didn't mean to come in uninvited."

"Oh, you're fine. I was just up very late and told Trudy not to disturb me." She rubbed sleepily at her face. Her sleeves were smudged with grey smears of ink, the sort you might get if you rested your arms on freshly printed pages.

"Do you have a typewriter?" I asked eagerly. There was a typewriter at Father's office, and I'd been advocating for one for our house. But for some reason, Miss Judson would not support me on this. (She kept saying things about refined penmanship being a hallmark of a lady's education.)

"What?" Priscilla shook her sleeve down and looked at it. "You *are* observant, aren't you? Well, I'm impressed." She gave me a broad smile. "What's that book you have there?"

"Just a novel," I said. "It was on the shelf here." I handed it to her—along with the lily petal caught between the pages.

Instantly, her expression changed. Her fluttery fingers froze on the edges of the pages as she stared at the cover. She forced a laugh. "Who would have guessed Auntie was the lurid novel type! Goodness. I should get dressed." She looked around, still flustered. "Keep going through those boxes from yesterday. I might be a while. If you finish up in here, or get bored, then . . . I don't know, look around the rest of the house."

Well, keen as I was to dive back into Miss Wodehouse's riveting collection of faded receipt books and decades-old planting almanacs, I waited a full twenty seconds for Priscilla to disappear before deciding it was *not* too early to plead boredom. I commenced my proper examination of the crime scene at last.

I studied the giant swirl of a staircase, Observing that the track in the carpet, the one that had left such a gash in the woodwork, continued up the stairs. Something heavy had been dragged up. Or down? No, the dent in the newel post had definitely been made by something banging into it on the way up; the damage was on the underside of the wood. I crouched down and saw that the track was caked with dirt. Some vehicle had come in from outside, then. Was

Miss Wodehouse riding a bicycle in here? But I dismissed that charming thought. Bicycles left *two* tire tracks, and this had just one (a unicycle seemed even more unlikely, alas). Or none: the wheel that had left this track had no tire at all, or at most had a metal band, like a cart wheel.

Or a wheelbarrow.

My breath caught. We'd seen wheelbarrow tracks in the lily garden, too—the lily garden where someone had killed Miss Wodehouse then somehow transported her body inside, then up the stairs, and dumped her in the bathtub. The skin on my neck prickled—not *entirely* with excitement—as I crept along the track, down the hallway to a set of double doors. Miss Wodehouse's bedroom? I peered through the keyhole, but everything looked ordinary enough. A spare brass bed with a plain green coverlet, a washstand holding an old pitcher and basin, curtains drawn over the French doors with their broken pane (presumably). And curled up in the very center of the bed like a black-and-white Chelsea bun, Peony the cat.

I gave a squeak of surprise, and the knob turned in my hand, spilling me into the room. Peony startled off the bed with a mew of indignation and darted into a corner, disappearing once more. Ignoring propriety, I dashed in after her.

"Peony?" Where had she gone? I poked my head around the corner she'd run to and found myself in the

Famous Modern Bathroom. I pushed the bathroom door wider and stepped reverently across the threshold, but there was nothing to see here (cats included). If the wheelbarrow had made it this far, Trudy had long since mopped up the evidence. Morning sunlight filtered in through an etched glass window, making the glossy white room seem anything but sinister.

I turned to leave again, when a thought struck me. Two doorways accessed the bedroom, the one from the hallway that I'd used, and the French doors to the balcony. Both were shut when I'd arrived.

So where had Peony gone?

More to the point, how had she got *in*?

I prowled slowly round the bedroom, calling her name, peering under, above, behind, and inside all the improbable places—curtains, desk drawers, the wardrobe with its catless array of depressing black dresses—but Peony had concealed herself in none of them. Nor was there any evidence of what she'd been using as a water closet, let alone where she'd been eating or drinking. Cats had a reputation for being tidy animals, but it seemed impossible that she would not have experienced some biological functions recently. She just didn't seem to have experienced them *here*.

Back out in the hallway, I found someone waiting for me. "Hello," I said, somewhat foolishly.

"Meow," Peony replied politely. Whereupon having spoken once, she released the floodgates and a torrent of feline monologue poured forth. It would be scientifically irresponsible to anthropomorphize the creature, but she began with small sharp meows that sounded cross, followed with a series of petulant yowls, and concluded with a sort of relieved chirrup— this last as she trotted forward to greet me personally.

"Where have you been?" I said. Before you scold me, Dear Reader, she started it.

Peony halted a few steps away and lowered her eyes in a slow half blink. Her black fur was matted sleek against her head and back by some sticky substance, like she'd squeezed under something. Fearful of some ghastly cat emission, I reached tentative fingers for her head, but the substance had a fresh, surprisingly *pleasant* scent. "What's all over you?" I asked.

Peony butted her head into my leg, which I defy even the most unbiased Observer to call meaningless. Her wide green eyes staring up at me, she really did seem to be asking a question, deep and solemn. I only wished I had the answer for her.

In a sudden moment of insanity, I scooped the sticky, complaining cat up in my arms and stuffed her into my bag (an act that took far longer to accomplish than explain), then hurried out of Redgraves before anyone could ask why my bag was squirming.

11
RES IPSA LOQUITUR

Occasionally there is that piece of evidence whose meaning is so obvious as to be indisputable: it speaks for itself.

–H. M. Hardcastle, *Principles of Detection*

I collided with Miss Judson, who was balancing an
armload of books, as we both tried to enter the schoolroom at once. After a moment of squeezing and jostling, we made it inside together.

"Library books!" Miss Judson said with triumph.
"While you were working at Redgraves, I went . . . to . . .
the . . ." Her voice wound down as she saw *my* armload.
"Peony! My lord, Myrtle, where did you find her?"

"She found me. I'm still not sure where she came
from."

Miss Judson visibly discarded several questions
before settling on one. "What's that—goo on her?" I

put the mildly protesting cat on the workbench, whereupon she instantly set about bathing herself, and Miss Judson peered in closer. "Why is it shiny?"

I reached across the desk to retrieve a spatula, vial, and microscope slides. Miss Judson endeavored to hold the cat still, chanting nonsense in a voice I did not recognize at all—*"Who's a soft kitty? Who's a pretty Peony kitty?"*—as I collected samples of the "goo," which would not discharge without a generous bounty of black fur adhered to it. It was viscous, mostly clear, and faintly sparkly.

I held a sample to the light. "Paint?"

"I don't think so," said Miss Judson. "Where in the world have you been?" She held the cat aloft, and Peony regarded her with wide, suspicious eyes the color of jade. "Was oo hiding in awful sparkwy sticky paint?"

"What is that language you're speaking?"

"It's *Cat*." Miss Judson spoke directly into Peony's face. "I speak Cat." She gazed into those green eyes, slowly half-blinking. Peony solemnly blinked back.

I whistled. "You *do* speak Cat. Quick, ask her who killed Miss Wodehouse."

Miss Judson covered Peony's ears and looked at me with shock. "Hush," she said severely. "She can hear you."

"She's a cat."

Miss Judson nuzzled the cat's sticky head, murmuring, "Ignore that nasty girl. She doesn't mean it."

"I can't talk to you like this," I said. "I can't take you seriously."

With a sigh, Miss Judson released the cat. She went to the basin and dampened a handkerchief, and then tried to wipe Peony's head. The black ears sank flat against the skull and Peony stiffened, but she let Miss Judson dab at, rub at, then scrub at her fur.

Meanwhile, I prepared a microscope slide. Under the lowest magnification, there was something familiar about the substance, a smear of clear liquid and faceted particles in soft pearly gold. It had a faint but striking odor, fresh and sweet, but it was obscured by the warm furry scent of the cat herself, and the same old musty odor I'd smelled everywhere at Redgraves. Whatever Peony had climbed through, she'd done it somewhere inside the house.

As Miss Judson deftly wrestled Peony, I had a sudden image of her wrangling a squirming toddler in much the same way—a little brother or sister for me, perhaps. In the hands of an average governess, no doubt, that cat would have rocketed away in an instant, but Peony had snuggled into Miss Judson's chest and now issued the most pitiful meow any creature has ever uttered. The whole of feline misery seemed to be caught up in it, and only now, in Miss Judson's arms, was she safe to express how unhappy she'd been.

I knew how that felt.

An average governess would *also* have scolded me for going into a dead woman's bedchamber uninvited, not to mention kidnapping her cat. I kept my mouth shut and reached for the books Miss Judson had brought home.

"Christison's *On Poisons*!* I've been trying to convince you to get this for months. It took a murder to talk you into it?"

"Mmm. There's also one on medicinal plants."

I wrinkled my nose at that one; it was clearly written for the layman. Or the lay *lady*—its green cloth cover was adorned with a silhouette of a female gardener, bent over a flower bed with a watering can. Miss Judson snatched it back. "I like the illustrations. You go study your toxic chemistry. Peony and I will look at the pretty pictures."

"You'll traumatize her," I said vaguely, but I was already lost in Dr. Christison's introduction to forensic toxicology. "I need a Marsh apparatus, some arsenic, and something to dissolve a stomach."

"Yes, I'm sure your father will be eager to approve that expense," she said. After a suspicious pause she wrapped her arms around the cat. "What *exactly* were you planning to test? You didn't happen to find a

---

* Sir Robert Christison's 1845 volume *A Treatise on Poisons in Relation to Medical Jurisprudence, Physiology, and the Practice of Physic*. We had none of his books in the house, as he'd been a strident opponent of women studying medicine. I felt a twinge of disloyalty to Mum cracking into this, but it could not be helped.

vial labeled DIGITALIS in Miss Wodehouse's bedroom, did you?"

"No such luck," I said.

But Miss Judson was distracted from our murder. "Don't you worry, Peony," she was saying, "I won't let that nasty girl do *any* experiments on you."

"She's an eyewitness," I pointed out. "Or a fur witness, in any case. Perhaps she got some of the poison on her fur."

"That would be convenient," she said, not really listening. Peony had finally squirmed away from her and was exploring the schoolroom, with rather strong opinions about everything. Miss Judson translated:

Peony: *Meow.*

Miss Judson: "I do not approve this cupboard."

Peony: *Meow-rowr.*

Miss Judson: "I do not approve this flooring."

Peony, rubbing her face against my chair: *Mrrrrow.*

Miss Judson: "This is my stool. And this is my counter. And this bookcase is mine."

After a few minutes of this, I couldn't help giggling. Peony, who had endured Miss Judson's silliness, narrowed her green eyes at me and said sharply, "*No.*"

Miss Judson collapsed in helpless laughter and scooped the cat onto her lap. "Oh, kitty," she said. "I think you'll fit in nicely here."

I looked at her with alarm. "We're not *keeping* her!"

Miss Judson looked back seriously, Peony's face next to her own. "And whyever not?"

"She's not ours, for one. She belongs to Priscilla now, probably."

"Priscilla doesn't want her," she said; and before I could ask how she'd possibly arrived at *that* conclusion, she added, "Peony told me."

I rolled my eyes. "What will Father say?"

"Possession is nine-tenths of the law?"

༄

The Matter of Peony remained unresolved for the time being. Father was late again that night, coming home looking strained, but brimming with distracted energy. He patted me and Peony on the head before telling us to go to bed. I'm not sure he even really noticed the cat.

"What are you working on?" I asked, scurrying at his heels. Peony scurried down the corridor before us, as though she knew where we were headed. "Is it interesting?"

He turned back and gave me a tired smile. "You might think so. We'll talk about it in the morning," he said.

"I'm still working with Priscilla," I reminded him.

He paused before answering, regarding me solemnly. "I'd like you to stay away from Redgraves for a few days, Myrtle."

"Why? Is something wrong?"

The tired smile again, no mirth in it at all this time. "Just—stick close to home, would you?"

My lungs felt too small, and I tugged on his sleeve. "Father, you're scaring me. What's going on?"

He frowned now, and gestured me into his office. I followed silently, though it was an effort. He lifted his case onto the desk, unlatched it, and handed me a piece of paper. It was a search warrant for Redgraves. For a shocked moment I couldn't breathe. "What, really? What's happened?"

He rubbed at his beard. "The Police Surgeon revised his report, for some reason. I've just come from an emergency inquest. You were right, Myrtle. Miss Wodehouse was murdered."

∽

I could hardly sleep that night, I was so excited. Miss Judson kept poking her head in with admonishments (*Put out the light. Put away the toxicology textbook. The cat is not plotting your murder. Let her sleep.*). Dr. Munjal had revised his report! It could only have been because of our conversation. What a triumph! Now that this was *officially* a murder investigation, I ought to hand over all the evidence. The nightgown, obviously. But what about the cigar cutter? Or the key from the vase? I wanted to share my discoveries, but once I gave anything to the police, it would be lost to me forever, and I'd be shut out of the case. In the end, I decided I would just wait and see what happened. . . .

. . . which was easier said than done. I listened to the minutes tick away on my clock, one span more interminable than the last. I tossed this way and made an alphabetical list of African mammals. I tossed that way, mentally reciting *The Iliad.* In Greek. But thoughts of tomorrow's search kept invading, pushing aside any efforts of sleep to do me in. Finally, Peony crept over and descended upon my chest.* I reached a hand to scratch her chin, but she gave her sharp dissenting *no* and proceeded to perform an exotic dance, feline hindquarters raised in my face, forepaws kneading the coverlet. Mesmerized by this alien behavior, I eventually dozed off. I awoke one time, and found Peony sound asleep on my lap. This time she made no objection to the stroke of my fingers across her neck, and we were both asleep again in moments.

* I may have discovered the origin of the folk superstition that cats will "steal your breath" as you sleep.

12

INCRIMINATING
EVIDENCE

> With careful observation by an Investigator, a victim or
> crime scene has much to tell us.
>
> —H. M. Hardcastle, *Principles of Detection*

The next morning, Redgraves was a flurry of activity,
like a grim, businesslike carnival. Father was allowed
to attend as a professional courtesy, and before heading over, he had rushed through breakfast, refusing
to answer even the simplest of questions (*What happened at the inquest? Who is your suspect? What took you so
long?*). Now Miss Judson and I were confined at home,
permitted to monitor the proceedings only via telescope. I was glued to the eyepiece, and had shoved the
window all the way open—dreadful weather notwithstanding—the better to Observe the goings-on. Peony

occupied the windowsill, folded into an impossibly small space and somehow managing not to get rained on. I was convinced she was defying natural laws of physics. I spied Priscilla among the onlookers, clutching Father's arm and whispering anxiously to him.

"You can't possibly tell she's whispering from here," Miss Judson said, pausing in her telegraph-tap pacing.

"What are they doing over there? What are they looking for?" I sounded peevish, even to my ears. I trained the scope on a constable toting a box from the house, but could not make out the contents. I was dying to know what, exactly, they were seeking. Search warrants had to be very precise, specifying the exact offense and evidence expected to be found during the search. "I can't hear anything."

Miss Judson turned to cross the room again, for approximately the forty-seventh time that morning. "You don't need to hear—oh, this is just silly." She pointed toward the door. "We're going for a walk."

Since it was a rainy, cold, ugly morning, we could hardly be heading out to enjoy the fresh air. We took a moment to wrap up well, left Peony in Cook's care, and set off across the park for an improved vantage point. But first I made sure my bag was packed with all the essentials. I might be called upon to contribute to the Investigation, and I would be prepared.

Uniformed constables swarmed over the house and grounds, like the flies on Dr. Munjal's morgue meat. I spotted Inspector Hardy talking to Father, and nudged Miss Judson closer. Trudy and Mr. Hamm huddled together outside the carriage house. Even Cousin Giles had turned up, strolling about like the mayor at a village fair.

"But I don't understand," Priscilla was saying. "Arthur, surely they don't suspect *me*?" Her flutters had become quivers, and she held on to Father's arm for dear life. She had chosen an awkward moment to come out of mourning.* Her pink plaid pelerine flapped in the gusty rain, completely inappropriate to the proceedings, not to mention the weather.

"Miss Wodehouse, there's nothing to worry about. The constables are very discreet, and I'm sure they won't disturb anything private. But in a house as big as Redgraves, you understand they have to go through everything."

"But that could take days! I'd better go inside."

Inspector Hardy blocked her path. "Not permitted, miss."

"Oh, Arthur, this is *really* too much!" She yanked Father closer, and he turned a peculiar shade of red I'd never seen before.

"Look here," Inspector Hardy said. "I'd hate to think there was some kind of conflict of interest."

---

* not to mention premature—custom dictated at least four weeks of black attire for a cousin's death. Even a twice-removed one.

"No, no, of course not," Father said hastily, pulling his arm away. Not fast enough, if you ask me.

Priscilla gave a sudden cry of outrage and set off for the house. "You, there, put down that typewriter! You're not going *anywhere* with that!"

Father had finally noticed me. "I suppose this shouldn't surprise me," he said. "Although I feel I should make some remark about telling you to stay home."

"I thought it would be educational," Miss Judson said. "Besides, if she didn't see it for herself, you know she'd never stop peppering you with questions about it. This is far more efficient."

"Efficient," Father murmured. "That's what we're going for."

"I'll make certain Myrtle doesn't interfere."

Which I found rather insulting, although she may have had a point.

I stepped forward, clutching my bag before me. "Father, I must show you something. It's important." With a surreptitious nod toward the police, I withdrew the folded bundle from my bag. I'd wrapped it carefully, given the rain, although water hadn't damaged this evidence so far.

He frowned. "What on earth's that?"

"It's Miss Wodehouse's nightgown. The one she was wearing when she died."

Father stared, mouth frozen open for lack of words.

"Trudy gave it to me. There are stains all over it. I knew it was important, so I've kept it safe."

"What sort of stains?"

I described the pollen all over the hem and the "handprints" on the back that coincided with the bruises on Miss Wodehouse's body. "What did the Police Surgeon say at the inquest? Was it digitalis?"

"What? Digitalis?" Father shook himself from a stunned stupor. "Look, we'll talk about it later. This isn't the right place."

"I understand," I said. I sounded very solemn and mature, but inside I was crushed with disappointment—again. Father put a hand on my shoulder; the other held Miss Wodehouse's nightgown. There were a dozen things he could have said, and I braced myself for all of them.

"This was good work," he said. "Well done, Myrtle." And he squeezed my shoulder, leaving me absolutely speechless after that.

～

The morning rolled on smoothly, as entertaining as a show. Even the rain couldn't dampen my good spirits. Miss Judson had an umbrella propped impressively against her shoulder to protect her sketching, and her charcoal raced across the page. I watched with satisfaction as constables carted away the wheelbarrow, loading it into one of their wagons, and wondered if they'd also rip up the marked carpeting or pull out the notorious bathtub. It was as I'd always imagined, like going to court with Father, but even better. I wanted to absorb every detail, memorize the exacting procedures, Observe the reactions of the suspects.

"Well, my girl, isn't this exciting? You ought to be very proud of yourself." I spun round to find Mr. Ambrose right behind me, wearing his black overcoat and carrying a black umbrella as glossy as a crow's wing.

"What do you mean, I ought to be proud?" I tried to make that sound demure, but my chest gave a little squeeze of pleasure.

"I don't know what you did, but you talked your father into this, my girl."

"All he said was the Police Surgeon revised his report." I'd have loved to share my involvement in that development with someone, especially Mr. Ambrose, but I had a feeling he'd boast about it to Father.

"Still, you were the one that pointed it all out. Be careful, lads," he called out. "This girl will put you lot out of a job."

I stifled my grin—it seemed impolite—but Mr. Ambrose gave a hearty laugh. He was rubbing his leg again, and this morning his eyes were puffy, like he hadn't slept well. I *knew* that was an impolite Observation, so I refrained from remarking upon it.

"But why are you hiding over here in a corner, girls?" Mr. Ambrose thoughtfully included Miss Judson in this. "Come on out to where the action is."

I glanced at Miss Judson, who I was sure only *appeared* to be absorbed in her sketching. "I promised Father I'd keep out of the way."

"That's nonsense, I say. Why, you've got front-row seats to one of the most educational things you could possibly see, and you're missing half of it. Come on, then. I know these men; I'll introduce you to some of them."

Down across the grounds we went, into the gardens, the pristine paths now ground to muck by all the tromping constables' feet. Mr. Ambrose really did know everybody, and paused to introduce me to each policeman we passed. They tipped their helmets to him, and to me, and I gravely curtsied back. One day I might be working among them, so it was vital I make a good impression. Or, really, no impression might be better.

As we passed the walled lily plot, I drew him over. "I want you to look at this, sir. I'm not sure anyone else has realized what's happened." There were two men searching the area—what was left to search, that is.

Mr. Ambrose let out a whistle of surprise at the bare plots, scarcely a leaf or stem remaining. "Well, well," he said. "What's this, then?"

"Mr. Hamm destroyed the lilies," I said, voice low so no one else could overhear. "Why would he do that?"

"Why indeed?" After a moment of distraction, he glanced down at me once more. "What else did you find out here, my girl?"

Eagerly, I walked Mr. Ambrose through my Theory of the Crime. I began with the footprints, and Miss Judson's Deduction about the wheelbarrow, and where we'd found the cigar cutter. As I described the scene I'd pieced together, Mr. Ambrose's expression grew darker and darker. "I think she must have encountered someone in the gardens that night—surprised him, maybe—and they . . . quarreled." I was strangely reluctant to say *he attacked her.*

"Someone?" Mr. Ambrose said.

I hesitated only a moment. The truth was more important now. "I saw Mr. Hamm's boot prints."

"Ah," he said. "Have you told anyone else this, Myrtle?" He turned to me, and his normally merry blue eyes looked cold and grim.

"I've *tried* to," I said. "But no one listens."

Mr. Ambrose regarded me with a slow, sober nod. The drizzle was slowing, leaving behind a puddle-strewn, mud-filled plot of depressing grey and brown, where once it had sparkled with glorious color and life. I hoped Miss Wodehouse would appreciate what we were doing on her behalf, even if she'd no doubt find the methods distasteful, if not downright intolerable.

"Well," Mr. Ambrose said, "we'll see about that, my girl. Let's go."

Heedless of his sore leg, he set off back toward the house, on the shortest route to Inspector Hardy. When we got there, the detective was talking to Priscilla again, with Cousin Giles in tow this time. Priscilla was clutching her typewriter as desperately as she'd held on to Father's arm, even though the thing must have weighed over two stone. There were black inky streaks up her arms, like she'd had to wrestle it away from someone.

"Do you know of anyone your aunt might have had problems with?" the Inspector said.

"Only everyone," Cousin Giles said. "She was a cantankerous old bat, and the whole world knew it." He nodded our way. "Ambrose may have been her only friend in the world." With a last drag on his cigarillo, he dropped it to the wet ground, where it instantly snuffed out.

"Since I can't interview the whole world," said Inspector Hardy, "how about we narrow down our suspect pool to people she's had problems with *recently*."

"Well, I hadn't seen her in months," said Giles. "Pris?"

Priscilla shook her head. "It's probably nothing."

"Priscilla, dear, if you have something to say, it's important you tell the Inspector," Mr. Ambrose said.

"I did see Auntie quarreling with someone last time I was here—last Monday. I couldn't hear everything they were saying, but it sounded like she was accusing him of something."

"Of what?" I asked, breathless with the suspense. Everyone forgot to glare at me.

"I'm not sure. Stealing from her? But that doesn't make any sense, because . . ." She trailed off, frowning across the lawn. I followed her gaze, deep into the gardens.

"Because what, Miss?" Inspector Hardy prodded. "Who was she arguing with?"

She looked regretful. "Her groundskeeper. Mr. Hamm."

Mr. Ambrose and I turned to each other. I didn't know what to think, but Mr. Ambrose nodded grimly. "I think you'd better tell him everything, Myrtle. Just what you said to me."

I did, starting with the footprints (again), Mr. Hamm's boots, the stained nightgown, the destruction of the lilies, the bonfire, the wheelbarrow tracks leading to Miss Wodehouse's bedroom. I stayed focused on Mr. Ambrose and Inspector Hardy, who asked careful questions and recorded everything I said. I was dimly aware of Miss Judson slipping away to fetch Father, but I kept up my declamation. By the end of it, more and more people had clustered round me. Out here in the chilly gloom, I was finally starting to feel the weight of the evidence, the *preponderance* of what I'd discovered, and what I was saying. Mr. Hamm had killed someone. *My* Mr. Hamm, with the strong weathered hands and the crinkly eyes and his warm *lasses*.

I felt my voice slow down, though my heart pounded faster than ever, and I was shivering. Mr. Ambrose held me close, but it didn't warm me up. My teeth were chattering by the time Inspector Hardy thanked me and turned back to the men.

"Find that gardener," he said. "Get me those boots. And *you*, Miss Hardcastle—don't go anywhere."

13

REASONABLE DOUBT

An Investigator must piece together the facts of a crime, step by step and bit by bit, until the assembled evidence reveals the truth.

–H. M. Hardcastle, *Principles of Detection*

The story should have been over–or my role in it, at any rate. That evening at dinner, I did my best to keep silent and not bombard Father with questions. Miss Judson had joined us, which was indication itself of how strange a day it had been. My thoughts were as thick and murky as Cook's gravy. How could Mr. Hamm have done something so awful? *Push an old lady into the mud? Tha' thinks I'd do such a thing?* I hadn't, but now it was *all* I could think of.

Father kept stealing heavy looks at me, and I

couldn't make out what I saw in his blue eyes. But Miss Judson must have understood it.*

"I'm sure he never meant Myrtle any harm." Her voice was soft. "We didn't know about his criminal record." That detail had come out during the arrest, supplied by Mr. Ambrose, who knew all the Redgraves affairs. Nobody would tell me what the record was for, though.

"Is that an apology?" Father said sharply, then pulled himself up with a little shake. "I'm sorry. That was uncalled for." He put a hand atop the table, fingers very close to Miss Judson's. His pale, ginger hand looked like a slab of cold fish next to hers, but I liked the way they fit together. "Myrtle, will you give us a moment?"

I looked between them, torn. On the one hand, it seemed they were about to share an intimate conversation, discussing their nightly concerns over coffee, and I applauded that.

On the other hand, it seemed they were about to share an intimate conversation about *me*, and I certainly felt I ought to be present for it. I wasn't even sure what they were both so unhappy about. I was upset that Mr. Hamm had killed Miss Wodehouse—but they seemed upset that he might have hurt me, which

---

* I was beginning to entertain the scientific possibility of telepathy, watching those two together. Certainly on Miss Judson's part; she also seemed capable of reading Peony's mind. It went without saying that the cat was telepathic.

didn't make any sense. Of course, I supposed proper girls like LaRue Spence-Hastings would never have been allowed to spend time alone with the neighbors' gardener who turned out to kill helpless old ladies.

"I want to stay," I said, though I rose and scooted back from the table, "but I'm not very hungry. I ought to check on Peony, anyway. Cook said she didn't eat any dinner."

Upstairs, I sat in the schoolroom with only a single lamp lit. It was too dark for the microscope, and I felt like I'd already learned everything useful about digitalis from Sir Robert. Peony was curled in the corner, facing the wall. She hadn't even let out a *no* of protest when I came into the room. Was she missing her old home? Did cats have such thoughts? Science told us no, but I wasn't sure how I felt about Science tonight. It had never let me down before, and I couldn't tell if I was worried that it *had* let me down and Mr. Hamm was innocent, or that it *hadn't* and he'd killed Miss Wodehouse.

I drew open the curtains, letting the shadow of Redgraves loom over us. It was quiet there now, the only light coming from a single second-story window, the library where Priscilla must be working at her precious typewriter. What was so important about that thing that she'd had to practically wrench it from the police?

"Stop, Myrtle," I said aloud. "The mystery is *solved*. There is nothing more at Redgraves to wonder about."

If only that were true. The trouble was, Mr. Hamm's arrest raised more questions than it put to rest. The police thought they had a motive and means and all the rest—but that still didn't entirely explain it. My hands on the windowsill, I stared hard out the glass, trying to picture the horrible scene in the lily garden a week ago. But try as I might, I could not bring up a mental image of Mr. Hamm striking Miss Wodehouse to the ground and killing her. Instead, all I could see was his head bowed under the floppy felt hat, shoulders slumped as the police led him away to jail.

∽

The next morning was Miss Judson's half day, and she had risen early and bicycled off on some undisclosed errand. Father had left much the same way, off to work before even taking breakfast. I sulked around the empty house, feeling dull and sluggish. As much as the *idea* of Father's renewed request to stay away from Redgraves galled me, I didn't really feel like going over there, either. It was thus in a disgruntled frame of mind that I answered Cook's summons that we had a caller. To my astonishment, Caroline Munjal stood in the foyer, twisting her gloves in her hands as she stared around her, as if our pictures or bric-a-brac might lunge off the walls and attack her.

"What do you want?" That wasn't half as rude as I'd hoped.

Caroline whirled round, perfect black ringlets bouncing. "Myrtle." Then she was silent. After a tense moment, she reached into her reticule* and pulled out a crumpled magazine. "You left this at my house." It was the penny dreadful I'd had that afternoon. "I read it," she offered. "*Billy Garrett and the Rajah's Jewels*? It was quite thrilling. Do you have any others?"

I came down a few steps. "All of them," I said. "But that one has just started. There aren't any more numbers in that series yet." In fact, we'd been expecting one for more than a week now, but the newsagent said they were delayed.

"Oh." Caroline just stood there. I knew I should invite her upstairs, or into the parlor at least, but I didn't quite manage it. "Look, Myrtle, I'm sorry about what happened with LaRue and the carriage house. I wanted to let you out, but . . ." She trailed off, looking at her feet.

I shrugged. "I wasn't scared," I said.

"I know!" Her words came out in a rush. "You were sensational, the way you solved that genuine murder! Just like Billy Garrett! Wasn't it horrible?" She said *horrible* the same way she'd said *thrilling*, and I wasn't sure what to make of it. "I wanted to come earlier, but Father was working on the case and asked me to

* a dainty little bag, wholly impractical for collecting specimens of anything

138 }

wait until–" She broke off. "What's wrong with your kitty?" Without waiting for a reply, she sprang up the steps two at a time, to where Peony huddled on the landing. "Is she sick?"

Peony, who just yesterday had been busy exploring, as opinionated as ever, *had* seemed poorly that morning. She'd eschewed her fish heads from Cook, had indeed suffered some gastrointestinal distress (politely and conveniently on the schoolroom lino), then listlessly retreated to a corner of the stairs, where now she crouched unhappily. Caroline crouched beside her, offering her fingers for a sniff. Peony couldn't even muster the smallest of her mews.

"Myrtle, I think she's been poisoned!"

"What?" I rushed up beside her. "What do you mean?"

"Look," Caroline said. "She's drooling and lethargic." To demonstrate, she tugged on poor Peony's paws, but the cat just ignored her. "Could she have been into anything? Rat killer or the like?"

"I don't know," I said helplessly. I admitted I knew very little about what Peony had been up to the last few days, and told Caroline about the sticky substance the cat had been covered with, which she'd almost certainly ingested during her efforts to clean herself.

Caroline scooped Peony up. Peony made barely a protest. "Let's take her to my father. He'll know what to do."

"She's still alive!" I cried.

"He has a regular practice, too," she said, impatient. "The police department post doesn't pay anything."

"A practice treating animals?" I asked.

"No, of course not. He's a human doctor, not a veterinarian. But he's done a lot of—erm—tests on cats."

She didn't need to elaborate on the sort of tests she meant. Not all toxins had modern methods of detection. That wasn't Dr. Munjal's fault. I gave a shudder, but I had no choice but to trust her.

After a short carriage ride across the park, we pulled up in front of the Munjal home. Caroline clambered down and sped toward the back of the house, and I scrambled after her. Her arms were full of sick kitty, so I opened the door and once again surprised the Police Surgeon by appearing unexpectedly in his laboratory.

"Dear me," he said. He hastened over and tenderly accepted Peony from Caroline's arms. My opinion ratcheted up a notch or two. "What's this?" He peered intently at Peony's eyes and mouth as Caroline explained the situation.

"Can you help her?" I asked.

"If anyone can, it's Father," Caroline assured me, but the look on Dr. Munjal's face was not quite so hopeful.

"The biggest concern is dehydration," he said. "Followed by kidney damage. And that's assuming we can even neutralize the toxin. Do we have any idea what she was exposed to?"

I shook my head. "We've only had her a couple of days. And Cook is very careful with her supplies."

The doctor had set Peony gently down upon the laboratory bench and had fetched a container–two, actually. One apothecary jar, and one that looked suspiciously like a chamber pot. "I'll administer charcoal to absorb the toxin, then treat the dehydration. After that, we'll just have to wait and see."

He gave the treatment, which Peony endured more or less willingly. Caroline served as a surprisingly able laboratory technician (she *had* used the word *lethargic*, after all), restraining Peony and fetching supplies with deftness and familiarity. I stood back, chewed on my fingers, and fretted. When the treatment (which turned out to be most unpleasant, for all of us) was accomplished, and they had managed to convince Peony to take some water, Caroline wrapped her in a towel and cuddled her on her lap, in the same corner where I'd waited for Miss Judson that rainy afternoon just a few days ago.

The doctor washed his hands and turned back into an Investigator. "Now, back to what's happened to her. Has she been exposed to any poisonous plants?"

"She's Miss Wodehouse's cat," I said flatly.

He sucked in his breath. "I see." He stood silent for a moment, looking at Peony.

"That's two suspicious poisonings at Redgraves," I said. He had to be thinking the same.

"One poisoning," he said. "One *exposure*. And we have no evidence that it's intentional, let alone 'suspicious.'" But I heard doubt in his voice.

"Who in the world would want to poison a poor little kitty?" said Caroline. (Present company excepted, of course.) "That's horrid." She gave Peony a protective little squeeze, and Peony managed a tiny *no*.

I paced the office, nervous energy burning through me. I wanted Peony to be well, but simply wanting didn't make it so. "She stands the best chance of recovery if we identify the toxin?"

"There may be an additional treatment," he said, evidently relieved to turn his attention back to the medical details. "But I don't want to treat her for one toxin if it's something else altogether. We don't want to make her worse."

"Oh, I'm so *stupid*!" I cried. "I have samples, but I left them back at the house."

He stared at me. "Samples of what?"

I explained about the substance that had covered Peony when I found her.

"Keep talking." Dr. Munjal got up and went to his bookcase and withdrew a heavy volume. I could not see what the book was, so I scurried over. "Can you describe it? It was clear and viscous? Sticky—like sap?"

That was it. "Yes, exactly. Like sap. No—like *nectar*."

He looked up sharply. "Nectar. Excellent." He strode to the door and called for the carriage driver. "Hobbes, return to the Hardcastle home and collect the—"

"I should go, too," I said, though I was loath to leave Peony. There was no way Cook would be able to find the samples I'd collected.

"She'll be fine for now," he assured me. "You'll be back in no time."

The errand home and back was less than ten minutes, and I handed over my entire collection—snips of fur, smears on paper, and microscope slides. Caroline still held Peony, who had dozed in her arms, and watched her father and me with wide, attentive eyes. I was grateful she was there, both for Peony's sake and for mine. Her father was taking me seriously now, and it wasn't just because Caroline was there, too.

"You're right," he was saying, peering through his microscope at one of my slides. "It's definitely nectar. Take a look. The question is what it came from."

He slid aside for me to look through his microscope. It felt like a huge honor, even though I had to stand on tiptoe to even come close to reaching. Once I had finally arranged myself so I could see, I let out a gasp. Why hadn't I noticed this before? I like to think it was the superior quality of Dr. Munjal's equipment—and *not* the inferior quality of my intellect. I recognized this substance after all.

"It's from a lily," I breathed.

"What's that?" Dr. Munjal returned. "Did you say lily? Well, that makes sense," he said. "Lilies are definitely toxic to cats. But we've given her the appropriate treatment, and if she's just consumed the nectar, and not the plant itself—its leaves or petals—she should make a full recovery."

"But that's impossible," I said. I gazed down at Peony in awe.

"No, I assure you, she should be fine."

"Not that," I said. "I mean, thank you, Doctor. Really." I tapped the microscope. "But this means there are still lilies somewhere at Redgraves."

14
LILIUM FEBRICULA

A wise Investigator never underestimates the contribution of the human factor in an Investigation, cultivating a network of informers from all walks of society.

–H. M. Hardcastle, *Principles of Detection*

After a long nap in Caroline's arms, Peony had improved enough that Dr. Munjal felt she could be removed to the house proper.

"Can I take her home?" I asked, but he shook his head.

"I'm sure she'll be fine now, but I'd like to keep an eye on her overnight."

Caroline hopped up–goodness, that girl had energy (perhaps she, too, was *irrepressible*). "Mother's flower show is tomorrow. You could come with us, if Peony is all right by then."

Dear Reader, there is no word to describe the sensation engendered in me by the notion of accompanying the Munjals on a family outing. That was probably something regular girls did, go with . . . friends, to Events. But Caroline couldn't *really* want Morbid Myrtle tagging along with her, where someone might see us together. Could she? It was on the tip of my (suddenly alarmingly dry) tongue to decline, but somehow what I said instead was, "Is that Miss Wodehouse's flower show?"

Caroline was nodding. "She was president of the committee. Mother was in *such* a state last week because Miss Wodehouse missed the meeting, and it was the last one before the show."

"Caroline." There was a note of mild warning in Dr. Munjal's voice. Both of us gave him Significant Looks, and he relented. "Very well, yes. Mrs. Munjal related that to me as well."

"Those ladies take their flowers *seriously*."

I glanced from Caroline to Dr. Munjal and dared voice my next thought. "Seriously enough to kill for?"

"Now, really," the doctor said.

But Caroline gaped at me, a hand to her throat. "Oh, hardly. No. Do you think?"

"What time does it start?"

⁓

At breakfast the next morning, Father could scarcely contain his delight at the prospect of my spending more time with Caroline Munjal. He set aside his papers and *looked* at me—and not with a frown, either. "Flower show, eh, Myrtle?" he said. "That should be fun. Very, er, botanical."

"Botanical?" Miss Judson hid her smile behind her teacup.

"And fragrant," he affirmed. "Perhaps even leafy."

"Don't make it sound so exciting," I grumbled.

"I'm sure it will be marvelous," Miss Judson said, and I could not tell whether she meant it or was just humoring us.

"Won't you come?" I asked again. She'd demurred earlier, but had offered no explanation for her refusal. Asking her directly, here in front of Father, seemed more likely to elicit a credible response.

"No, indeed," she said. "I have plans of my own."

"Is that so?" Father said. "Do you care to share?"

Miss Judson set down her teacup. "I've decided to attend a luncheon at the church."

Father set down his own tea—physical telepathy, perhaps? "Really? That's wonderful. You haven't gone in years."

Miss Judson looked a bit uncomfortable. "Yes, well, it seemed like a good time to return."

"What does that mean?" I said, but Father looked satisfied.

"It will do you good," he said—but I was still very much *un*satisfied.

"It's not even Sunday. What could you possibly have to do at a church?"

Miss Judson continued stirring her tea, while Father tapped his fingers against his cup.

"What?" I demanded. "Is it some kind of secret?"

"Of course not," Miss Judson said swiftly.

Father tried to laugh. "Nothing like that. A church luncheon is the sort of place young ladies, like Miss Judson, can go to mingle with and meet other young . . . people."

And suddenly I understood. "You mean young *men*," I said. "She doesn't need that! Why would she need that?" I was perilously close to upsetting my own breakfast plate, so I shoved it to the center of the table. Some eggs spilled off anyway. Everything I did lately just ended in a mess.

"Myrtle—" both of them said, together.

Miss Judson touched Father's sleeve. "You know I would never lie to you, Myrtle." She put up a hand to forestall citations to the contrary.* "Yes, there will be some young men there." I noted she did not come out and admit that those young men were her *reason* for going.

I jumped up. "You're leaving us?" There was no other reason she would need to cultivate acquaintances with gentlemen besides Father.

---

* There was a notable incident involving Wee Willie Winkie and the physiology of sleep that I still maintain could have been explained with more accuracy.

"That's not it at all. Don't jump to conclusions." But she had no defense, and she knew it. "If it truly upsets you, I can come to the flower show."

"Oh, go ahead," I said savagely. "Enjoy your luncheon. I'll expect *your* report on it this afternoon!" Which, all things considered, was not a particularly scathing exit line, since I really did not wish to hear anything about it.

I slammed out of the house and planted myself on the stoop to await the Munjals.

∾

I was still in a Mood when they arrived. Caroline was wearing a sailor suit with a wide collar, her thick black hair long and loose all the way to her backside. She was thirteen and taller than I by about six inches, and the outfit made her look like an overgrown eight-year-old. In her arms, and looking much improved this morning, was a chatty and purring Peony. Caroline released her, and the cat sprang down and dashed up our front steps, whereupon she demanded entry as if she'd lived here all her life.

"I'm glad you're coming today," Caroline said as I climbed aboard the gig beside her. "These things are so frightfully boring."

I did not ask what, exactly, she expected *me* to do to alleviate the tedium. I wasn't sure I wanted to know.

The flower show was downtown at the Social Hall, a place for ladies' groups to hold salons and suffrage rallies. We followed a grand staircase to an upper story set off with an iron railing painted invisible green.* Striped bunting hung from the balcony, along with a banner emblazoned SWINBURNE LADIES' GARDEN CLUB INVITATIONAL FLOWER SHOW 1893. Dear Reader, I am not sure I can do justice to the Swinburne Ladies' Auxiliary Social Hall ballroom that August morning. The marble floors were almost totally obscured by makeshift garden plots, which did not in any way appear *makeshift*. It looked as though their builders had been at work for months, installing the beds and plantings and—"Is that a pond?"

"The Belvedere twins always have to outdo everyone, Mother says. There aren't supposed to be water features at indoor shows, but some people simply can't follow the rules. Come on. Mother's expecting me to pose in her display. It's a vivid tableau."

"*Tableau vivant?*" I said. Evidently French was not a priority in Caroline's schoolroom.

"Whatever. We pose like a living painting. *All day.*"

The floral club members had turned the ballroom into a virtual paradise, with varied *tableaux* vying for attention—and, indeed, ribbons. Stern-looking gentlemen strolled the aisles, inspecting each display, their

* The nearly black paint used on railings and lampposts is not truly invisible, of course. That would be dreadfully inconvenient when trying to chain up your bicycle, not to mention keeping people off park grass.

stony faces giving away no sense of awe or appreciation. It was impossible to tell if they even *liked* flowers. For my part, I could not decide where to look. A Japanese garden with a bed of combed sand and a blossoming cherry tree? A medieval knot of herbs surrounding a stone bench, upon which posed a little boy dressed as Cupid, brandishing a golden bow?

"Your wings are crooked, Simon," Caroline remarked as she dragged me past, dispelling the illusion. Someone had released a colony of butterflies, which flitted about in confusion. "That'll be a mess later." Caroline sighed. "Here we go. Hello, Mother, Nanette."

We'd reached a display where a commanding Indian woman dressed as a sea captain—complete with an Admiral Nelson hat with gold braid and bejeweled cockade—was pointing authoritatively at her booth with a spyglass. "Caroline, *where* have you been? We need crewmembers! Get in place. Oh, who's this?"

"Myrtle Hardcastle, ma'am." I curtsied.

Mrs. Munjal gave me a closer look. "Oh, dear. You're the one—" She clammed up, looking uncomfortable.

"Oh," I said. "Miss Wodehouse. Right."

"Don't worry, dear. It's not your fault. But you'll find it's quite the topic of conversation today—Minerva managing to get herself murdered, and at such an inconvenient time. And by her *gardener*." She shuddered, as if afraid the notion might be catching and her own gardener would take it upon himself to bean her with some garden shears.

"Caroline said she missed the last meeting," I said.

"I should have known something was wrong—that wasn't like her at all. Imagine my surprise to step out of the hall after the meeting and find her out in the alley, arguing with someone! A terrible row, it looked like."

"Another club member?"

"No, of course not. This was a man."

"Mr. Hamm?" I put in swiftly.

"What? Heavens no. Some *young* man, in a ghastly yellow tartan jacket. I scared him away."

I felt my pulse quicken, despite the fact that I told myself, *It's over.* "Could you hear what they were arguing about?"

"Minerva said it was nothing, but I could tell she was upset. Nanette, stop *moving*! I'm sorry, dear, this ship's about to run aground. Can you amuse yourself for a bit? The judges are coming this way, and we need all hands on deck." She gave a chuckle, to which Caroline, mounting a platform that really did resemble the deck of a ship, rolled her eyes.

The Munjals' *tableau* was impressive. Climbing vines and pots upon pots of flowers all contributed to the illusion of a vessel on the high seas. A bed of silvery ferns made the white-capped waves; the ship's sails were a trellis of tropical plants with wide white leaves. Caroline's older sister Nanette perched on the bow as the figurehead, a role for which her stout figure suited her perfectly, while a row of golden pansies spelled out the ship's name.

"HMS *Victory* has three gun decks," I said helpfully, and Mrs. Munjal's brow furrowed.

"I could only get six dozen poinsettias to whiten properly. They are *incredibly* fussy, you know. I do hope the judges will overlook that! Oh, here they come. *Places, everybody!*" This last was bellowed with enthusiasm that would have done Admiral Nelson himself proud.

"England expects that every man will do his duty," I said—and she saluted me.

⁓

The second half of the ballroom was more like Miss Wodehouse's lily gardens: starkly simple by comparison. Gardeners stood along rows of plain tables, stationed protectively behind their exhibits. At one long table stood six men, each with a single cabbage before him. This is where Miss Wodehouse would have been, too—not out among the foolish frippery of the artistic displays, but here with the pure scientific perfection of perfectly grown specimens.

I approached one of the cabbage men. "What's first prize?"

He regarded me like I was some vile insect that had crawled out from beneath his prized vegetable.

"Ten pounds, a feature in *Cottage Garden Weekly*, and the Cup," he said archly. I looked closer at his clothes—Sunday best, but old and worn. Most of the people on this side of the show were working class, and that prize money was no small sum.

He was a little intimidating, but I forged ahead. "Would anyone kill to win this show?"

If possible, his look grew even colder. "We know who you are. You got Hamm in trouble. No one here will talk to you. *Miss*," he added, a threatening hiss of an afterthought.

I stood my ground, a flutter of misgiving in my chest. "You think he didn't do it?"

Mr. Cabbage would say no more, but the look he gave me made me grateful I *wasn't* an insect, since he'd clearly like to stamp me out with his own steel-plated boot.

The rest of the contestants were just as forthcoming. He was right: nobody wanted to talk to the little girl who'd had Mr. Hamm arrested. How in the world did they *all* know who I was? Did the *Tribune* publish my picture alongside the murder suspect's?

I was beginning to think coming today might have been a mistake when I caught a glimpse of something familiar across the sea of cold, unwelcoming faces: a flash of pink, blond hair, and frantic energy. Priscilla. Oddly relieved, I made my way toward her table. Trudy was with her, and they stood amid a bewildering heap of sweetpeas, colorful blossoms and tendrils spilling everywhere. Priscilla had on a giant, old-fashioned pink bustle, and her hair was pulled into a tight knot on the very top center of her head, like a sort of knob. Trudy was desperately trying to rein in the unruly sweetpeas, and they were both looking completely out of their element.

"How was I to know you were only supposed to bring *one* flower?" Priscilla wailed. "That doesn't even make sense. Myrtle! How lovely! Have you gotten separated from your nanny? She must be worried." She reached an arm over the escaping flowers and reeled me toward her.

"My—Miss Judson? She's not here. I came with . . . friends."

"But I just saw her," she said. "There she is!" She gave an enthusiastic wave.

There indeed, strolling our way, was Miss Judson in her crispest twill walking suit.

And strolling along with her, arm in arm, was Mr. Northcutt. The obnoxious Cousin Giles, wearing a ghastly yellow tartan jacket.

15

ACCESSORY
AFTER THE FACT

Efforts to conceal a crime, or any involvement therein,
may go on long after the event itself.

—H. M. Hardcastle, *Principles of Detection*

I told myself I did not care one whit where, when, or
under what circumstances Miss Judson had encountered Mr. Northcutt and his ghastly yellow tartan
jacket, much less how she'd come to arrive at the
flower show in his company. And I'd have enjoyed
reasonable success, too, if it hadn't been for Priscilla.

"What's she doing with him?" she said, voice
sour.

"Aren't you fond of your cousin, Miss Wodehouse?"
I asked, scarcely sweeter.

"Him? Oh, he's well enough, I suppose." It wasn't exactly a rousing endorsement—but neither was it outright defamation.

I decided to Focus on the Case. "What about your aunt?"

"How would I know?" Trying to laugh, she said, "Oh, don't mind me, darling. I'm just out of sorts today. How *could* Mr. Hamm get himself arrested right now? I really don't know how I'm supposed to manage."

I bit my lip to keep from rather rudely reminding her that he hadn't been arrested on his own. She and I might have had something to do with that. "Can you remember what Mr. Hamm and your aunt were arguing about?" I asked instead. "That time, the one you told the police about? What do you think he stole from her?"

Priscilla didn't have a chance to answer, because Miss Judson and Cousin Giles were upon us.

"Miss Wodehouse, these are lovely." Miss Judson lifted her fingers through the fluttery sweetpeas. "I think your aunt would be pleased to see Redgraves exhibiting after all. Do you mind if I record the scene?"

"You mean to draw us, Miss?" Trudy piped up.

"Well, I'll get in on that." Jabbing a stem of sweetpea in his teeth, Giles struck a jaunty pose between Trudy and Priscilla.

"I don't think she does wanted posters," Priscilla snapped. Miss Judson only laughed as her charcoal flew across the paper. Minutes later, she blew on the page, then tore it neatly from the sketchbook.

"Here you go, Trudy," she said, passing her the sketch.

Trudy's watery blue eyes grew large. "For me, Miss? I've never had a picture of meself. Thank you!" She clutched it to her breast, but we all caught a glimpse of it—a sweet little drawing of a wide-eyed girl with wild curly hair and an armload of equally wild blossoms.

"I think we've disturbed you Wodehouses long enough," said Miss Judson. "Myrtle, will you show me around the exhibitions?"

Just then, I wasn't sure whom I wished to be with less, but since I could not come up with a compelling reason to stay with Priscilla and Giles, I set off across the ballroom at a pace even Miss Judson was hard-pressed to keep up with.

"Myrtle, wait." Miss Judson pursued me through the aisles, past funeral displays and a life-sized statue of Her Majesty made entirely of carnations. "I didn't go to that luncheon to hurt you, you must know that. But it has upset you, and so I do apologize." She caught up to me, and turned me to face her. "Now. Are you going to tell me what you've learned? Because I don't believe for a minute you came here solely out of your newfound affection for Caroline Munjal, the girl who *locked you in a morgue.*"

"I like her. She's smart," I said.

"Your father will be glad to hear that."

With a deep breath, I stood my ground before my heretofore beloved governess. "I *do* like her. She saved Peony, for one thing. She reads penny dreadfuls, and she wants to be a physician. Or a veterinarian." I made this sound as enviable as I knew how, but even as the words left my lips, I knew I'd fallen short. "I'll be wanted at their booth. Come along if you like."

I whirled on my heel and stalked off, down a corridor lined with—of all things—lilies, their ivory and scarlet and orange heads bobbing into the aisles like a tropical, pollen-laden death trap. The colors and fragrances were overwhelming, and I felt for a moment that I'd stepped into Miss Wodehouse's world. I could not help searching among the flowers for a mysterious moon-white blossom, petals smeared with glittery gold nectar.

Miss Judson caught my hand—not to restrain me, I realized, but to share the moment. "I feel like we should whisper," she whispered. I nodded back, and together we made our way through the lilies. Miss Wodehouse seemed to be everywhere: her name on the tags of flowers named for her, framed photographs of her from flower shows past.

"This is extraordinary." Miss Judson paused before a specimen of *Lilium wodehouseia* prominently displayed at the front of a booth. She touched the pink, frilled petal of a flower as utterly unlike Miss Wodehouse as I could imagine.

"That's not for sale!" The exhibitor rose up from behind her booth to snatch the pot back—revealing five-feet-two-inches of haughty expression, golden curls, and salmon pelerine. My heart sank. It was LaRue Spence-Hastings. Her mother, an older copy of LaRue, materialized beside her daughter, and Miss Judson gave them her sunniest, most dangerous smile.

"Good afternoon," she said, as I tried desperately to be anywhere else. "The Munjals never mentioned that you'd be here."

LaRue's eyes narrowed. "*You're* here with Caroline?"

I gave a shrug. "I know her father."

Miss Judson made a show of admiring the lilies, and Mrs. Spence-Hastings beamed at her. "The rhizomes for those were given to me *personally* by Minerva Wodehouse, from her own stock."

With a tragic cluck of her tongue, Miss Judson said, "It's such a shame what happened to her gardens. You might have the only original *L. wodehouseia* left in England."

LaRue looked at me smugly. I Resisted the Urge to stick my tongue out at her.

"Well . . ." Mrs. Spence-Hastings said, "they say the flowers are still out there, *if* you know the right people."

"Surely that's impossible." Miss Judson's voice was hushed. "Her gardener destroyed them all."

Mrs. Spence-Hastings looked down the aisle to see who else might be listening. When it was apparent we were alone, she went on anyway. "I don't know anything about it *myself*, of course, but I've heard that Hamm fellow wasn't the most *reliable* of servants, if you know what I mean." It was obvious she meant his criminal record, which had been reported in the papers. "He might have had something going on the side."

"Selling the flowers?" Miss Judson sounded aghast.

"He wouldn't do that!" I hadn't meant to burst out like that, and LaRue seized on it.

"You don't know everything, do you, Myrtle?"

I glared at her. "I know what you can do with your pelerine."

Miss Judson gave a little cough. "Well, he's been arrested, so even if the flowers were still out there, they're gone for good now."

Here Mrs. Spence-Hastings's smile grew even more secretive. "Minerva wasn't the only Wodehouse, was she?"

"Priscilla and Giles?" I said. "I mean, Miss Priscilla and Mr. Northcutt?"

Mrs. Spence-Hastings and LaRue gave us identical knowing looks, but would admit no more. Miss Judson looked gravely at LaRue. "Myrtle had a wonderful time last week," she said, voice cool. "She *can't* *wait* to return the favor sometime."

"That would be lovely," Mrs. Spence-Hastings said, but LaRue made a strangled sound. "Mother!"

With a final wave that only the Exceptionally Perceptive would find foreboding, Miss Judson deftly steered us along.

Once out of earshot, I said, "Was she telling the truth? Mr. Hamm was selling Redgraves lilies?"

Miss Judson grimaced. "That woman is an inveterate gossip, and I shouldn't have encouraged her. It's probably no more than rumor."

Considering the reception I'd had from the groundskeepers here, I added, "And nobody else is going to tell us, either."

"Hmm," she agreed. "Come along. We should check in with the Munjals. And I can tell you all about Mr. Northcutt on the way."

"Wait." I stopped in the aisle beside a pot of small red blossoms that smelled vaguely like roast beef. "Aren't you going to tell me that the case is over and it's time to mind my own business?"

Miss Judson answered carefully. "I think there are still a lot of unanswered questions." Still holding her sketchbook, she flipped back a page and handed it to me. "Here."

"That's Mr. Northcutt!" And he was decidedly *not* at the New Reform Ecumenical Chapel, where Miss Judson's luncheon had been. She had sketched Cousin Giles outside a shop with a round awning. "That looks like that shipping agent's by the courthouse. But who's this other fellow?"

"That's the place," Miss Judson confirmed. "I stopped by the courthouse to let your father know I was coming to meet you and spotted Mr. Northcutt when I came out. That jacket was too extraordinary to pass up. I don't know who he was meeting, but they were having rather an animated discussion." If she'd caught the scene accurately, "animated" was an understatement. Mr. Northcutt was leaning forward, jabbing the other fellow in the chest.

"I know this man." The squat form and bowler hat were unmistakable. "I saw him with Priscilla. The night Aunt Helena came over, she met him out in the street. She gave him something, and I thought he might be blackmailing her." Our conversation with the Spence-Hastingses had just put that encounter into a new light. "When I asked her about it the next day, she lied to me. Maybe it was seeds!"

Miss Judson sighed. "We mustn't jump to any conclusions. We have no idea what anyone said to anyone else. It's just as possible that Priscilla and this gentleman have a relationship, and her cousin doesn't approve."

I frowned. "It didn't seem like *that* kind of a meeting. Not like a church luncheon or anything."

Miss Judson let out a bark of laughter. *"Touché, ma râleuse."**

---

* Miss Judson claimed this was a pet name, but you be the judge, Dear Reader. It means "my complainer."

Now that I knew Miss Judson was still firmly on my side, it was time to share the other evidence I'd collected. I glanced around to see who might be lurking about, eavesdropping on our conversation. But the middle-class ladies in their visiting dress, reticules dangling from gloved hands, swept along in pairs, utterly indifferent to mysteries brewing below their very noses. "Mrs. Munjal saw Miss Wodehouse arguing with someone during the last flower club meeting. It was serious enough that Mrs. Munjal felt the need to scare him away."

"Mr. Northcutt? Or Bowler Hat?"

"'Ghastly yellow tartan jacket,'" I said.

Her eyes grew wide. "Giles told the police he hadn't seen his aunt for months before she died."

I nodded. "It hardly seems likely he'd forget an argument in public that had been interrupted by a stranger."

Miss Judson glanced past my shoulder. We could scarcely see through the forest of lilies, let alone all the way across the venue to Priscilla's table of desperate sweetpeas, where we'd left Cousin Giles, but I knew that's where she was looking. "No," she said. "No, it does not."

16

UNDUE INFLUENCE

After an arrest, every effort is made to convince the suspect to admit his guilt. Fortunately, the police no longer employ primitive methods such as torture to elicit a confession. But even today, there is no more compelling evidence than the suspect's own words.

—H. M. Hardcastle, *Principles of Detection*

Monday morning I dashed into the dining room, still pulling on one of my boots. Breathlessly (and half shoelessly), I dropped into my seat and heaped my plate with eggs. I caught Miss Judson's eye from across the table and poured myself a more ladylike cup of tea. She was wearing one of my favorite suits today, a soft tawny brown a shade deeper than her own skin, and her hair was twisted neatly away from her face. I wondered if Father had noticed.

"Has my copy of the *Police Gazette* come?" I asked.

Father drummed his fingers on the tablecloth. "I thought we were going to encourage her to find more appropriate reading material."

Miss Judson calmly stirred her tea. "She canceled her subscription to the *Girl's Own Paper.*"

That had been a gift from Aunt Helena. It was full of articles on Improving Yourself and how girls could embrace the heavenly pleasures of domestic toil. "It was preposterous. And *juvenile.*"

"*You* are a juvenile, Myrtle." I do not know what Father was going to say next, thank goodness, for Cook appeared just then with the post. "Your newspapers, Mr. Hardcastle, Miss Hardcastle," she intoned. Her spanner peeked out from her apron pocket, ready for the week's battle with the hob.

As always, I skimmed the more sensational front page (another article rehashing Miss Borden's trial in America, even though she'd been acquitted months ago), and opened it directly to the summary of the Coroner's inquests and Police Surgeon's reports. Most newspapers took liberties with the truth, but the *Police Gazette* was the official newspaper of the Metropolitan Police and was generally reliable. After the crime logs came the confessions. I knew from Father that an accused criminal's confession was the single most important piece of evidence the Prosecution could have: proof of guilt, from the suspect's own lips.

Confessions trumped any other evidence, which was why the police were so keen to elicit them. I was not supposed to relish these, but I could not help myself. The details of the crimes were often so delightfully gruesome.

Today, huge black letters bawled out:

CONFESSION IN DASTARDLY REDGRAVES MURDER!!!

With a little cry of surprise, I read the headline aloud.

Father looked up. "That's a new development," he said. "Very good. It will make our jobs easier, certainly. What does it say?"

Scarcely believing my eyes, I read for everyone to hear:

"The true & lawful Admission of Mr. Llewellyn Hamm, lately arrested in Swinburne for the murder of Minerva Wodehouse, his employer. What follows are his words, in his own hand, recorded under presence of counsel:

"I, Llewellyn Jones Hamm, do freely confess to being the sole person responsible for the death of Miss Minerva Wodehouse. On the night of 1 August 1893,

*I did procure a quantity of arsenic in the
form of rat poison from the garden shed
in my workplace at Redgraves, after
which I stole upstairs and under cover of
night did enter Miss Wodehouse's private
chambers for the purpose of administering the same. There I discovered a carafe
of water, which her maid Trudy did set
out for her nightly. I placed the poison in
the carafe, and likewise put some powder
in the glass for good measure. I thereafter
hid in the shadows until she had imbibed,
after which I returned to my quarters
until summoned the next morning by
the maid."*

I sat in stunned silence for a moment after this. At
last I managed, "What rot!"

"Myrtle! Language!"

"But this is completely wrong! It doesn't match any
of the facts of the case." It said nothing of confronting
her in the lily garden, destroying the flowers, or covering up evidence afterward with a bonfire—let alone
offering any kind of motive. "And *arsenic*? Why would
he say that when it was clearly digitalis poisoning?"
Arsenic produced ugly and violent symptoms, which
might be mistaken for death by illness—but not a heart
attack.

Father's eyes narrowed. "Where did *you* hear about the digitalis?"

"Dr. Munjal, of course," I said. "How could they accept this? Why would Mr. Hamm say it was arsenic?" The natural conclusion dawned on me too late, and I stared at Father and Miss Judson, stricken. "Unless he didn't do it."

Father let out an audible groan. "Oh, come now, not this again! Miss Judson, this is *exactly* what we were talking about–"

"Mr. Hardcastle, I think you should let her finish." Her words were soft, calm–and cutting. Father fell silent, but now that I had the floor, I wasn't sure what I wanted to say. I looked at them both, feeling unaccountably panicky. No, not unaccountably. And not just panicky.

Guilty.

"This is wrong," I managed again. "Can't we do something? Tell somebody?"

"Myrtle, he's confessed." Father's voice was gentle. A bad sign. "Why would he lie?"

"I don't know." The crime described in the criminal's own words* was the strongest evidence against any suspect. Father had told me that often enough. It didn't even matter if the confession didn't match any

* *These* words didn't sound anything like Mr. Hamm's broad Yorkshire speech, but sometimes the police "translated" their dictations to make them easier for the public to read.

of the other findings. A mind-set of guilt was the same as guilt, and an admission of guilt was better still. An open-and-shut case, as they said. "But that's not what happened."

"We don't know that," he said. "Now, wait. We might *think* we have other evidence, but so far it's all circumstantial. A confession is *proof.*"

"This is my fault," I said.

Miss Judson jumped in. "Oh, Myrtle, of course it's not."

"Don't try to comfort me! There wasn't even a murder before I got involved. And *I* got Mr. Hamm arrested. He's told them some ridiculous story, and now he's going to hang!" I was shouting, my voice shrill and close to breaking.

Father stood up and collected all the newspapers— mine included. "Miss Judson," he said, voice dark, "my daughter is distraught. Will you see her to her room, please, to calm down?" He stood there, glowering over the table, the way he did over the suspects who *didn't* confess. I wanted to sit there and glower back, but I felt shaky and brittle. I could not stand up under Arthur Hardcastle, Prosecutor, this morning. Trembling with fury, I let Miss Judson gather me up and take me back upstairs.

☙

The knock on my door that night at quarter past ten wasn't half as unexpected as the identity of the knocker.

"Father!" I could not recall the last time Father had visited me here; I think I was nine and had scarlet fever. I was so surprised I froze, guilty for no logical reason, my book gripped in my fingers until they hurt.

"May–" He coughed and tried again. "May we talk?" He sat beside me, taking a closer look at the book. "I remember your mum reading this in bed, too."

"Even after you were married?" She'd given up her medical studies by then, I'd thought.

"She didn't want to get rusty." His finger joined mine inside the book, and we pried it open together. "Thinking of another career path?"

The truth was, I *was* starting to doubt myself. I had been so certain I'd interpreted the evidence correctly, until Mr. Hamm's confession. I had to admit that it wasn't terribly likely that a twelve-year-old girl was going to be better at solving a crime than professional detectives, lawyers, and police surgeons. Still, it was hard to give up on the conviction that I was right, and Mr. Hamm's confession was false. I just couldn't figure out why he was lying.

Father's gaze traveled round the room until his eyes fell on the little pot of chrysanthemums I'd brought home from the Munjals' *tableau*. He picked it up. "Did you have a nice time at the flower show?"

Was that what he'd come in to talk about? That was three days ago. "Caroline's nice," I said, because it seemed like he was waiting for me to say something. Something an ordinary girl would say. "She's asked me back for tea." And to look at Dr. Munjal's textbooks—but Father didn't need to know that.

He was nodding absently. "And Miss Judson? How was her luncheon?"

Now I stared at him. He was looking everywhere but at me. "What do you mean?" I said warily.

"Oh, nothing. I just wondered how it was. Naturally."

"You mean, did she *meet* anyone."

His long fingers fidgeted on the quilt. "Well, Myrtle, you know I'm very fond of Miss Judson, of course, but you're getting to be a young lady now, and you won't need a governess forever. It's only natural for her to make plans for when that time comes."

That was his Courtroom Voice. Who was he trying to convince?

"Why can't she always stay here? Why should we encourage her to leave us? Isn't she part of our family?"

If possible, Father looked more distant and uncomfortable than usual. "And what would she do here, without you to teach?"

Now we were both in danger of blushing, but I plunged onward. "Maybe you would have other children."

"Well, er, that would require a wife, Myrtle."

"Exactly!" I cried, with triumph.

"And how would you feel if I got remarried?"

I could have secured a happy future for everyone in our house, and yet somehow I failed. I prevaricated. I lost my nerve. "I suppose it would depend on who you married," I mumbled. "But you should be happy."

After a long moment, he said, "I'm glad to hear you say that. I've worried that you wouldn't want someone here, in your mother's place."

Neither of us said anything for a long time then, both of us thinking about Mum, about that time years ago when everything changed. Awful, at first, and then gradually turned into something I wouldn't give up for all the world. *Miss Judson* had done that. She hadn't taken Mum's place—not for me, anyway—but she'd filled the hole left behind, like a key somehow refitting its keyhole around itself.

But something else had changed back then, too. "Why did you leave your practice to join the Prosecutor's Office?" I asked.

Father looked surprised. "It was time for a change, I suppose. With your mum dying, and Whitney and me not always seeing eye to eye, it seemed like a good time to move on."

"You could have made more money in private practice," I said. I'd been to Mr. Ambrose's house; he had a butler and three different housemaids, and it was full of velvet furniture and medieval antiques.

Father's head cocked quizzically. "It wasn't about the money. We're comfortable, aren't we?" he said. "It was about the law, the reasons I had for practicing it. I didn't want to draw up wills for rich old families, or negotiate contracts between railroad barons and actual barons anymore. I wanted to do something that mattered."

I understood this. I saw it every day when he went off to work or stayed up late in his office, poring through casebooks. "Like Mum did," I ventured.

The nostalgic smile faded. "Something like that. But after she got sick—it sounds strange, but I felt like medicine had betrayed her. Us. She'd loved it, but in the end it was no help to her. And I looked around, and I just felt like those railroad contracts didn't mean anything. Good people were dying, and I was quibbling over land easements. I needed to do something different."

"Mum wasn't murdered," I said, not entirely understanding, logically. But I *felt* the meaning settle somewhere in the middle of my chest.

"No," he confirmed.

"But murders make sense. Like Miss Wodehouse."

Father gave me an odd look. "What happened to Miss Wodehouse makes sense to you?"

"Not yet," I admitted. "But it will. We'll—*you'll* put the pieces together, figure out the motives and the reasons, and then the culprit will be punished. I like that. Every day, you make sure that when someone is killed, the person responsible is punished."

"I try, anyway," Father said. "But when someone like Mum dies . . ."

"There's nothing you can do," I said. "She got sick, and she died, and even if we know the science of why it happened, you can't put cancer in jail or send germs to the gallows."

He smiled at this. "Don't we wish." He reached out and almost took my hand—laid his palm against my book, our fingers nearly touching. "You are an insightful young woman, Myrtle Hardcastle. I'm sorry I don't tell you that more."

I pressed my lips together so that I wouldn't beam like a ninny, but I nodded a solemn thanks. "Then you'll help Mr. Hamm?"

"What?" He pulled his hand back.

"We have to do something. This is all my fault."

Father rubbed at his beard. "I'm glad to see you appreciate the severity of the situation, but you didn't make Mr. Hamm confess. He did that all on his own, under the advice of counsel."

"He has a lawyer? Is he any good?"

"I hope so. It's Mr. Ambrose."

I felt the first glimmer of hope since I'd opened the newspaper. Mr. Ambrose could stop this before it went all the way to the high court. "But why would he let Mr. Hamm lie?"

"Why are you so convinced he's lying?"

"You read the post-mortem report—you know there was nothing in there that even suggested arsenic poisoning. It doesn't look anything like heart failure, for one thing." Too late, I realized my blunder. I hadn't meant to reveal my source about the medical details of Miss Wodehouse's death.

His face was hard. "Yes, I did read the post-mortem report. And I've seen the materials collected from the search of Redgraves. And I've gone over the witness statements. And none of it explains what happened or who killed her. But now someone has confessed. That is the strongest evidence we can get."

"Even if it's wrong?"

"Who's to say it's wrong?" he asked.

"We are! Science! Forensics! The Police Surgeon, for one. Doesn't *his* word carry any weight?"

But even as I said it, I remembered Father saying, just a moment ago, that medicine had betrayed us when Mum died. Perhaps he didn't trust it anymore. The statement of an accused man carried more weight for him, too.

17
CONFLICT OF INTEREST

A good Investigator is impartial. He is not motivated by personal gain, nor does he let his own interests corrupt his search for the truth.

—H. M. Hardcastle, *Principles of Detection*

The next morning, Father summoned us to his office. It wasn't even breakfast yet, and there we stood, Miss Judson and myself, before the grand mahogany desk, like parties to a plea negotiation. Father was pin-neat in a black suit and the foulard waistcoat, his whiskers combed and moustache freshly waxed. Indeed, he looked as though he'd just been turned out of the mold and given a polish before being set upon the shelf for display. I turned a questioning face to Miss Judson.

Her eyes were wide with curiosity, but she betrayed no other emotion.

"Good morning," Father said formally. "Thank you both for joining me." This was obviously a prepared speech, after which he was apparently at a loss for words.

"You wanted to see us, Father?" I prompted.

"Yes! I have been thinking about what we discussed last night, Myrtle. And I believe you're right. To that end, I've decided to invite Miss Wodehouse— Miss Priscilla Wodehouse, that is—to dinner tomorrow night."

I was baffled. "How will that help Mr. Hamm?"

"What? No, I meant the *other* matter we discussed."

Horrified, I stared at him, willing him to be the one to say it out loud, because I certainly wasn't going to. The "other matter," of course, was the notion of Father marrying again. But marrying *Priscilla*? Where on earth had that idea come from? Was she the only single female remotely of marrying age he'd encountered recently, and nobody else came to mind? What about the one, the *perfect* one, standing right under his nose at this very moment?

The one, indeed, who first managed to find her tongue. "Very good, sir. Shall I have Cook prepare a particular menu?"

That was a peculiar thing for Miss Judson to say; it wasn't the governess's duty to plan menus for the master of the house and his dinner guests.

"Yes, thank you, Ada—Miss Judson. Whatever

you think best. Do—do you suppose Miss Wodehouse would like trifle?"

Miss Judson's serene smile did not falter, but I felt cold from my knees to my throat. Trifle was her favorite. "Oh, I don't think so, sir," she said coolly. "Being American, she's surely used to more exotic fare. Was there something else, sir?"

Father gave a self-conscious fidget of his tie. "No, no. That will be all, I think."

"I see." Miss Judson made no move to leave, which was just as well, because my feet were rooted to the rug. "Mr. Hardcastle, I believe Myrtle expected to discuss quite another matter this morning. If you'll recall, she was rather preoccupied with it yesterday." Her voice was as calm as ever, but there was an edge to it.

Father flushed. "Of course. I was just coming to that." But he fell silent, and for a troubling moment I doubted him.

"You *will* help Mr. Hamm, won't you?" I said. "There must be something you can do."

He regarded the two of us, seeming to grasp for the first time that something might be amiss in this room. "This is not an easy matter," he said.

"Can't you talk to Mr. Ambrose? Or the Magistrates? They can decline to bring charges, can't they?"

"The man has confessed to murder, Myrtle. There's not much that can be done at this point."

"What if we uncover other evidence?"

"Now, wait a moment," he said. "I don't want you involved in this any more than you already are."

"But that's the point!" I cried. "I *am* involved."

Miss Judson laid a hand on my arm. "Mr. Hardcastle, please. Don't say there's nothing to be done. Nothing *you* can do. I know you'd never send an innocent man to the gallows."

Father's red face drained of color, and he gave a heavy sigh. "No. No, I would not. Not if I could help it. But listen to me, both of you. The situation is more complicated than you imagine." He came round the desk and looked me straight in the eye. "And I must tell you, Myrtle, as Prosecutor, I'm not altogether convinced Mr. Hamm *is* innocent. There are facts here that point firmly in his direction."

"What facts?" I demanded.

"I'm not going to go into this with you."

That voice was final. He'd said all he meant to. "Father, please," I begged. "We must do something. We have to be sure. *I* have to be sure."

Father held my shoulders. "I know," he said. "We will be."

But the look he gave Miss Judson was full of uncertainty.

ೞ

After Father dismissed us, Miss Judson charged into the schoolroom like it was on fire. I scurried after, nearly tripping over Peony, who was trying to get out of her way. Miss Judson went directly to the black-board and commenced vigorously rubbing out yester-day's lesson on Latin declension.

"Don't I need those?" I asked tentatively.

"Then you should have memorized them." Her voice came out in little snips. "Is this your doing?"

Perplexed, I looked around the room for evidence of malfeasance. "What do you mean?"

"Did you encourage your father to court Priscilla Wodehouse?"

"Of course I did," I snapped. "And then I said Aunt Helena should move in with us. It's my dastardly plan."

The chalk squeaked, and I was rewarded with a microscopic quirk of Miss Judson's lip.

"What are *you* so upset about, anyway?" I said. "You went to your church luncheon."

"Oh, this is *not* the same."

"How?"

She whirled on me. "Well, because it's not."

This conversation was bordering on ridiculous, but I felt as twisted and knotty as Miss Judson seemed to be. She was so rarely overset that her mood was a sci-entific curiosity in and of itself—and worse, she was right. This, too, was all my fault.

Briskly—as she would—I took charge. "There's only one thing to do." I slid aside the blackboard panel to reveal our chart. "If Father won't listen to reason, then we must find another culprit and make him confess."

"I thought we were talking about dinner." She still sounded cross.

"It's all the same thing."

She was silent for a moment, then said, "Very well, I look forward to your defense of that position. Proceed. And I remind you, time is of some urgency. Mr. Hamm will go before the judge soon, and dinner is in thirty-four hours."

I was pacing now, trying to perfect the efficient telegraph patter of Miss Judson's stride. "We start at the beginning. Who had motive to kill Miss Wodehouse? What was it? Money? Hatred? Revenge?"

"Romance?" suggested Miss Judson, acid in her normally pleasant voice.

I ignored that. "Insurance money is a good motive for murder."

"Kindly clarify your use of the word *good* in that sentence."

I wrote INSURANCE on the blackboard, followed by INHERITANCE.

"I think I see where this is going." She had taken a seat on the other stool, like an attentive schoolgirl. "Fairness compels me to note that we have no evidence against Priscilla."

I raised a finger. "Ah. But you'll recall *she* was the person who accused Mr. Hamm of arguing with her aunt. She might be lying. Furthermore, there's the matter of the will. Why would Mr. Ambrose delay the reading if *he* weren't suspicious of Priscilla's claim on the estate?" The more I thought about it, the more I liked this theory of the crime.

"All right," she said. "How did she do it? I'm struggling to imagine Priscilla attacking an old woman, then dragging her body into the house by herself."

"There was the wheelbarrow. And the second set of footprints. She had an accomplice."

"The cigar-smoking man?" Miss Judson studied the chart, chin cradled in her fists. "It's an intriguing possibility, I'll grant you. However, none of it explains why Mr. Hamm would confess."

No, it didn't. I only had one idea that did—and I didn't like it one bit. "Maybe they were working together, and now he's covering up for her."

Miss Judson's face twisted with disbelief. "To what end? It's not a terribly profitable thing to do, after all, confess to murder. If Priscilla paid him to help her, it's not like he can spend the money after they hang him."

I turned back to my list. After a thoughtful moment, I wrote down the motive she'd suggested earlier: ROMANCE.

"Oh, surely not. Mr. Hamm sweet on Priscilla?"

"Why not?" I said. "Priscilla's convinced Mr. Hamm to kill her aunt—or take the blame for it. She's convinced the police that Mr. Hamm is guilty. And she's about to convince my father to–" I couldn't say it.

Miss Judson let out all her breath. "Now, wait a moment, Myrtle. Don't you think you're getting carried away?"

I looked hard at her. "No, I do not. Priscilla Wodehouse must be stopped."

❦

The next afternoon I sat on Miss Judson's bed, watching her paint. We had not succeeded in solidifying our plan to prove Priscilla guilty of murder, let alone get her to confess. The only other idea I'd come up with involved arsenic, but I supposed it would look awfully suspicious if *two* members of the Wodehouse family were felled by poison within days of each other, not to mention reflect poorly on Cook. Unfortunately.

I surveyed the room, where Miss Judson's few keepsakes were on display: a well-loved Bible in French on the nightstand; a tiny plaid turbanlike hat, its tied ends sticking out in jaunty tufts; and a portrait in progress of her parents for their upcoming anniversary. Reverend Judson was still a sketched outline, but she'd begun to fill in the rich colors of Maman's image: the blue silk of her formal gown, the deep reddish umber of her broad, thoughtful face. I had one drawing Miss Judson had done of the two of us, our heads bent together over a book, but it was just a charcoal sketch. When I'd asked why she hadn't finished it—why she'd never colored it in—she'd looked at me a little sadly but gave no answer. Now, watching her parents' faces take shape, I was beginning to grasp the matter. If only we lived in the West Indies, too, instead of stodgy little Swinburne, maybe things would be different for her and Father.

As if she'd picked up my thoughts, Miss Judson gave me a flicker of a smile. "It will be fine," she said. "In a few hours, it will be out of his system. After all, you know Aunt Hardcastle is coming."

"Aunt Helena?" The vague anxiety in my stomach solidified into genuine pain. "How is that going to help anything?"

She eyed me over the easel. "It would take a soul of extraordinary forbearance to marry into a family with an Aunt Helena."

When the offending parties at last arrived, Miss Judson and I were summoned to the foyer to present ourselves like evidence before a judge. Priscilla was enduring the scrutiny of Aunt Helena, who was clad in a gown that made her look like a glittery green dustbin. Given the circumstances of her last appearance, I was surprised she hadn't gone with an apron.

"It's so hard to find a good lady's maid these days, isn't it?" Aunt Helena was saying.

"There's just Trudy," Priscilla said, hands smoothing her pink skirts. "I gave her the night off."

"I can see that," said Aunt Helena. "Well, this house isn't what you're used to at Redgraves, I'm sure, but it's cozy enough."

Priscilla glanced about as if taking in the decoration—but I thought she was really seeking an avenue of escape. "It's lovely," she said. "Arthur, how touching that you haven't changed anything since your wife died. It proves what a devoted husband you must be."

"Er," said Father.

Aunt Helena regarded them with satisfaction—and then she saw me and her expression shriveled up. "Of course, you know Arthur's daughter, my namesake. And her governess," she added, as an afterthought.

"Myrtle! I brought you something." Priscilla shuffled over to the stairs and handed me a book. It was *The Green Widow*, the novel I'd found on the sideboard at Redgraves. "Your father told me you like mysteries."

I gave her a questioning look. "Thank you?"

"I figured out the killer by chapter ten. Let's see if you can do better." This was accompanied by a conspiratorial wink.

"Are you fond of children, Miss Wodehouse?" Father put in awkwardly.

Priscilla smiled eagerly. "Ever so," she said—and I had a sudden moment of horror (induced, no doubt, by tales inflicted upon me by Aunt Helena) of being usurped by little blond stepsiblings who would gobble up Father's funds and affection. I scurried back to the protection of Miss Judson.

Aunt Helena was nodding her approval. "You'll find Helena Myrtle an *exceptionally* well-behaved child, Miss Wodehouse," she lied.

Miss Judson held me firmly in place.

"Oh, Myrtle and I are great friends already, aren't we?" Priscilla said. "She's so terribly clever."

Aunt Helena's face fell. "Yes, *terribly*. Arthur, you're not planning on leaving your guests standing in a draft all evening, are you?"

Priscilla clutched her hands together as she trailed my aunt into the dining room, and I couldn't help myself.

I felt a little sorry for her.

18
MOTIVE, MEANS, AND OPPORTUNITY

A suspect must have the *motive*, the *means*, and the *opportunity* to commit the offense. Did he have a reason to kill? Did he have access to the murder weapon and the skill to use it? And was he in the right place at the right time?

–H. M. Hardcastle, *Principles of Detection*

The morbid curiosity about what was happening in that dining room, among Father, Aunt Helena, and Priscilla, felt like ants crawling under my petticoats. I'd stationed myself at the top of the stairs, straining to hear, but could make out nothing useful. Peony perched beside me, serenading the dinner party with an undulating song of woe and betrayal. I thought she was spectacular.

Until Cook stepped into the foyer (dressed tonight

as a butler). "The master requests that the cat be removed," she intoned.

"*No*," said Peony.

I gave a sigh and untwined my legs from the balusters. "Yes, ma'am." I scooped up Peony, who responded with one parting utterance shrill enough to break wineglasses, and carried her into the dark schoolroom. The curtains were still open, and I noticed lights on across the way at Redgraves. Some lights were normal, even with Priscilla over here; no one wanted to come home to an absolutely dark house. But these lights were upstairs, in empty bedrooms, not down in the main areas of the house.

And the lights shouldn't *move*. As I watched, one set of windows went dark. A moment later, the adjacent room brightened as someone turned up the gas. I chewed on my thumbnail, trying to decide what to do.

I had three options, two of which were sensible.

One: Notify Miss Judson.

Two: Alert the diners downstairs, one of whom would certainly be concerned by nefarious goings-on at Redgraves. But to whom I owed no duty of care.

Three: Investigate on my own.

Dear Reader, I will allow you to Deduce what choice I made.

Before I could talk myself out of it, I tightened my bootlaces, checked that my skirt hems weren't likely to be stepped upon, and loaded up my bag. Onto my head went my deerstalker cap. Last, I opened the cabinet and retrieved the key with the fleur-de-lis handle. Peony, watching my preparations, almost gave me away. She twined about my ankles, complaining, and ignored all my admonitions to shush.

"Do you want to come?"

"*Yes*," she replied, and trotted out of the schoolroom, down the back stairs, to the scullery door. Thus we prepared to commit the most egregious transgression of which a Young Lady of Quality is capable. I was about to Go Outside Alone After Dark.

Dear Reader, surely I need not enumerate the dangers posed by my present course of action; they are drilled into every girl from the cradle, by every possible means. I knew all about Spring-Heel'd Jack, the fiend who stalked the pages of the penny dreadfuls. Not to mention Jack the Ripper, the fiend who'd stalked the real-life streets of London only a few years ago. There were body snatchers and burkers;* press-gangs waiting to drug the unsuspecting and ship them off to sea; and all manner of Deviants, ready to Defile the Innocent. I was not certain what this last meant, precisely, except that it was practically *guaranteed* to occur the instant the Young Lady of Quality touched her bootheel to the moonlit earth.

In the kitchen behind me, Cook bustled about, getting the next course ready. I could turn back now, no one the wiser. But Priscilla was in my home, eating at

* **named for Mr. Burke and Mr. Hare, the notorious Scottish grave-robbers-turned-murderers**

my table, beguiling my father. And she'd practically *dared* me to prove her guilt, giving me that book. *I figured out the murderer by chapter ten. Let's see if you can do better.* This was my best chance.

I put my damp hand on the knob, took a deep breath, and opened the door.

Beyond our yard, it really was like walking into the wilderness. The rustle of crickets and trilling of frogs sounded terrifyingly large; the evening breeze might have been a typhoon. The hedge loomed monstrously, a perfect hiding place for any number of fiends.

It's just darkness, Myrtle—the same frogs and hedge that were there in the daytime. I crept onward. All my dithering had cost me, however, for the suspicious lights in the main house had disappeared, and Redgraves stood dark and quiet once more. Now what? Scowling, I looked about. Straight ahead was the carriage house, where Mr. Hamm had lived. And where a light now burned in an upstairs window.

Clearly, in the interest of public safety, I ought to Investigate and extinguish the lamp or candle, before it burned down the house—and, by extension, the entire neighborhood.* Gripping the key for reassurance, I made my way, as stealthily as Peony, toward the carriage house.

---

* I direct your attention to the fire that ravaged Chicago in 1871, or the one that took out London in 1666. I did not wish to be Swinburne's Mrs. O'Leary. Or her cow.

I was holding my breath by the time I crept up the stoop. The door stood open a crack, and I hesitated—but Peony pushed her small black head against the door and nudged her way through. "Peony!" I whispered.

"*No*," she snapped, and disappeared into the dark.

Thereupon I may have uttered a few words that are not suitable for a Young Lady of Quality, no matter how wide her vocabulary, and went after her.

This always seemed easier in Billy Garrett and Sherlock Holmes. They would stride purposefully to a window and throw open the drapes (revealing a critical clue in the process) to admit generous moonlight. I could hardly see through the murk to *find* said windows. Gradually, though, my eyes adjusted to the gloom, and I made out the vague shapes of overturned furniture and the white silhouettes of papers strewn everywhere.

It must have been the Fiend with the Lamp, searching for something.

But what? What secrets lay concealed in Mr. Hamm's apartments? Money? Stolen flowers? An incriminating vial of digitalis? Had the intruder found anything? I picked up a folder and some of the dropped papers, though it was too dark to read them.

"Meow," said Peony, in accusing tones, from upstairs.

"Well, hullo there, puss," replied a man's voice.

I clapped a hand over my mouth to suppress a gasp. He was still here!

"You miss your friend, eh? Nice kitty."

"*No.*"

I heard their voices as clearly as if they were in the room with me. Which meant I would be equally audible to them as well. Who was it? Perhaps not a fiend of Spring-Heel'd Jack's mettle—but absolutely, expressly the very danger I had been warned about.

A lifetime of warnings all clanged in my head at once, and—over the protest of my rational mind—my body heeded them. I fled, tiptoeing hastily past an overturned chair, across the uneven stone floor, and out into the chittering, croaking, shadowy safety of the night.

By the time I was back outside in fresh air, I had recovered my senses. I positioned myself to Observe the intruder as he left the carriage house. Evidently his own search was over as well, for it took but a moment for Peony, tail raised like a white-tipped signal flare, to lead him out the door.

I recognized him at once by his haughty, jaunty stance, not to mention his jacket, which was scarcely tamed by the darkness. Cousin Giles.

He sauntered deeper into the gardens, proceeded to light a cigarillo, then lingered in the summer night, smoking lazily away. He looked like he was waiting for somebody, an accomplice, perhaps, or an Illicit Rendezvous. I crouched by the hedge long enough for my legs to cramp, but nobody else appeared. Indeed, it seemed for all the world as though *Peony* were the liaison he was expecting. She twisted about Giles's legs like a shameless hussy. I wasn't supposed to know what that meant, either—but tail up, ears pitched forward, and head bumping into his ankles, there was no mistaking her mens rea at all.

I couldn't wait here all night; eventually he'd see me, too. But between Giles and home was the long, wide-open pathway, where a twelve-year-old girl in a deerstalker cap sneaking away would be clearly visible. I unclenched my fingers, still gripping the papers I'd collected from the carriage house. Behind me, however, only steps away, was the greenhouse. I could hide in there until Giles went on his way.

I crawled through a bed of lavender, waking the pungent scent. The greenhouse rose before me like it was made of the faint moonlight, glass panes misty grey. The door was unlocked, and I slipped inside.

How long did it take to smoke a cigarillo and flirt with a cat, anyway? I peered back out the door and nearly swallowed my heart. The path where Giles had been standing was empty. There was no sign of him or Peony. I jerked back against one of the plant racks, hitting a stack of trays that all came crashing to the floor. I froze, scarcely breathing, afraid to even move my eyes to the doorway. But after a count of thirty, nobody appeared, and I carefully let out my breath.

Now what? I pushed my cap away from my eyes and considered my situation.

Had Giles well and truly left? Or was he still lurking outside somewhere? My best course of action, while I was stuck here, was to make up for any Observational shortcomings from my prior visits—which is to say, Investigate the greenhouse for clues. It was mostly empty now, at the height of summer, with only some tropical plants and a few spindly orchids, the sorts of things that didn't grow well in our climate. Normally I was quite interested in greenhouse science: the capture of the sun's warmth within the glass walls and the complex irrigation system were technological marvels. But night left the deserted building cool and dark, and the pipes were ominously silent.

I passed down the aisles but found nothing of note until coming face to face with a rack of smocks and aprons guarding the back room. It looked like they hadn't been disturbed in weeks. Was it possible the police had missed this room during their search? Heart racing, I pushed my way in, fleur-de-lis key at the ready.

And was instantly disappointed.

It was only the boiler room, a tiny closet of a space taken up by the cast iron boiler and its snaking network of pipes and valves, which heated the greenhouse and pumped water for the sprinklers. A single gas mantle lamp, always burning, cast just enough light to see by.

And *be* seen, unfortunately, by anyone happening past outside. I felt like I was inside a vivarium.*

I was about to squeeze back out when I spotted something. The cover of the coal chute wasn't quite closed, a scrap of white caught in its latch. Peering closer, I saw that it was a bit of lace, torn off—like from the sleeve of a nightgown. With a thrill, I swung the hatch open and reached my bare hand inside and found a file folder, hopelessly streaked with black. I flipped it open to reveal a single page, one brief hand-written paragraph, barely legible in the dim light. An unusual word leaped from the page: *Llewellyn*. That was an eye-grabber in any scenario. I held my find closer to the lamp.

> *In respect for his loyal service and his devotion to the gardens, and in recognition of his contribution to the efforts of development, my signature herein denotes my full and complete intent to transfer rights and ownership of all lily species, and all associated ancestors and hybrids, along with the research thereto and moneys therein associated, to my partner and groundskeeper, Mr. Llewellyn Jones Hamm, upon my death.*

* a glass enclosure for observing live biological specimens. There would be a card posted: SMALL HUMAN FEMALE (JUVENILE). PAY CLOSE ATTENTION TO THE WAY SHE SNOOPS THROUGH OTHER PEOPLE'S BELONGINGS.

This was from the missing will! Miss Wodehouse had left her lilies to Mr. Hamm! She must have hidden it in here, for some reason, the night she'd died, ripping her nightgown in her haste. But why? And where was the rest of the will? I started to reach into the chute for more, but something flashed past outside. I froze. I could see nothing but black mirrors shining the room's image back at me, but from outside I'd be as visible as a goldfish in a bowl. My lungs constricted. It might have been a bat flitting past. Or a hare, startled by a stalking feline.

Or it might have been Cousin Giles.

I shoved the paper into my bag, pushed the coal chute door closed, then squeezed back into the greenhouse proper and tried to look like I belonged there.

19

Appearance of Impropriety

There is no substitute for conducting on-the-ground Investigations yourself.

—H. M. Hardcastle, *Principles of Detection*

When the greenhouse door opened and a waft of tobacco smoke swirled in, I was sweaty and disheveled and probably looked like a criminal myself. I tried to remember that I ought to be excited. I had caught a subject in the act and was about to Interrogate him! But it was hard to shake the feeling that *he* had caught *me*.

"Well, well." Cousin Giles strode in like he owned the place. "And what brings the little girl from next door to the greenhouse on a Wednesday night?"

"Homework," I croaked, trying to look busy at one of the potting benches, although it was too dark to be doing any work in here. I made myself face him. "Were you in Mr. Hamm's rooms? I saw lights on in the carriage house."

"Your friend Ambrose sent me over to get some of Hamm's things." He came closer, and only the workbench kept me from shrinking back. "Conditions at the jailhouse being what they are."

"That's nice of you," I said, nodding slowly. "Where are they?" And why had he needed to tear the place up to find a spare shirt and shaving tackle?

He took a drag on his cigarillo. "You do ask a lot of questions."

"Yes. I'm known for it."

If he was here tonight under entirely innocent circumstances, then why not mention the ransacked state of Mr. Hamm's quarters? Something like, *Say, quite a mess in there, do you think we ought to alert the authorities?*

"Does Priscilla know you're here?" I asked.

He dropped the cigarillo and stubbed it out with a toe. "What about you?" His voice was amiable, like we were friends. "Does my cousin know you're over here, playing in her greenhouse?"

Playing! "Of course," I said stoutly. "I'm authorized." Because a *really* responsible Young Lady of Quality certainly wouldn't be Outside Alone After Dark without letting somebody know. *Well done, Myrtle.*

I noted that Giles hadn't really answered any of my questions. I started to ask what he'd been doing in the main house, but at that moment, Peony stuck her head through the open greenhouse door and scolded the both of us. Giles laughed and scooped her up in his arms. She struggled, but he held on to her and strolled deeper into the greenhouse. "Not much to see here, is there?"

"Everything is *outside*," I said, mentally pushing him in that direction. But he wouldn't budge.

"You probably know the name of every flower in this place," he said. "What's this thing?" He flicked a plant with one tobacco-stained finger.

"Orchid," I said warily. "*Phalaenopsis*."

"Is it valuable?"

"Not really. Everyone has one."

He let the stem drop in disappointment. "Have you had any luck with that will?"

My eyes flew to his, and it took all my willpower not to grab my bag, where I'd stuffed the papers I'd found. "What?"

"The old lady's will. Did you ever find it?"

I shook my head, a little too vigorously. "No, we never did." One page was not a will, I told myself. "We found her cat, though."

Giles regarded Peony, pinned against his chest by his bulky arm. "Maybe *you* know where it is," he said. "Probably knew all the old lady's secrets. Where she hid that will, where those flowers are . . ."

In reply, Peony wriggled free of his grip and darted out the greenhouse door.

Giles gave an oily laugh. "No love from the Redgraves girls," he said, sounding not in the least disappointed. "Shall I walk you home, Miss Hardcastle? Your pretty nanny must be missing you."

"*Governess!*" I snapped. I ought to refuse—it violated several elementary precepts of propriety *and* common sense—but Giles hadn't told me anything useful, and I couldn't think of another way to get away from him.

When we reached the border between Redgraves and my house, Giles gave me an exaggerated bow.

"Thanks for the botany lesson. *Phalaenopsis.* I'll remember that." He tipped his nonexistent hat to me and Peony, then sauntered back into the night, whistling. I closed my eyes and let out all my breath.

A shadow had appeared in the window of the scullery door, which cracked open slowly, the light from the hallway slicing out like a yellow blade. Cook was waiting for me, with a look like murder I could see even from across the yard. The instant it was evident I was safe and unharmed, she reached out and pinched me by the ear, yanking me into the kitchen.

"And just what do you think you're about, Young Miss?" she demanded, plopping me down in a chair at the table.

"Peony—" I began tentatively, but she cut me off.

"And don't give me any of that nonsense. That cat is an innocent." Indeed, the "innocent" bystander was now rubbing plaintively against Cook's ankles, face pressed into a gravy stain on her apron. "Explain yourself, and it had better be good."

Cook piled a plate with steaming buns and a thick slab of leftover chicken—and I saw a Stansberry pie heating over the stove—so I was inclined to obey her. Tucking my feet under my backside, I pulled out the documents I'd found: the folder from Mr. Hamm's ransacked rooms and the page from the greenhouse coal chute.

"What's this, then, all over my table?" Cook frowned at the sooty papers. "This one says *Priscilla*." Her voice was thick with suspicion.

I swallowed my mouthful of bread. "Let me see that." It was the file I'd scooped up from the floor at Mr. Hamm's—the very one Priscilla had so swiftly appropriated from me that day at Redgraves. But why would Mr. Hamm have it? "It's just a bunch of newspaper articles."

Most were from American newspapers—not particularly respectable ones, if the headlines were any indication. **REAL FALL RIVER KILLER CONFESSES!**, a reference to Miss Borden's case again. And if the *Daily Questioner* were to be believed, Jack the Ripper had emigrated to Chicago, where he was enjoying renewed notoriety at the fabulous Exposition. What did these have to do with anything?

Then I flipped one over and saw Priscilla's face staring up at me, accompanied by a headline that made me sit bolt upright.

BLACK WIDOW POISONER
STRIKES AGAIN!

BOSTON, JUNE 22, 1893: Police have confirmed that the recent demise of Mr. Branford Babbidge, 45, Corey Gardens, was due to a DELIBERATELY ADMINISTERED toxin. Mr. Babbidge was discovered early Thursday morning in bed, by his daughter Camille, just 14. When questioned by police, Camille was swift to point the finger: "My new mamma did it." The Babbidges appear to have fallen prey to the wicked schemes of a mysterious woman (see SKETCH). She had called herself Mrs. Scharpe, a widow—and which she most certainly was. The *Examiner* has linked Mrs. Scharpe to incidents in Boston, Philadelphia, and Providence—all involving well-to-do gentlemen who died under *suspicious circumstances* soon after making Mrs. Scharpe's acquaintance. Mrs. Scharpe's preferred poison appears to be the perennial favorite "inheritance powder," arsenic. The diabolical witch has thus far eluded capture and may have fled overseas.

Gentlemen, beware! Guard yourselves against the Wicked Machinations of this Wanton Killer!

I stared at the article for the longest time, my food forgotten. There were two pictures, both unmistakably of Priscilla. One was a dramatic pen-and-ink sketch showing Priscilla's fair curls and pointy little chin graced by a diaphanous black veil. That was obviously a fabrication; she held a mortar and pestle in her hands, as if she were posing for *Who's Who Among Society Poisoners.* The other picture was a wedding photograph, a fuzzy image of a white-clad Priscilla gripping the arm of a moustachioed gentleman in an army uniform. The caption read, *Captain Overland, Mrs. Scharpe's Third Victim.*

I jumped to my feet. She was upstairs! She wasn't even really Priscilla Wodehouse! And she had designs on my father! Well, Arthur Hardcastle wasn't about to become Mrs. Scharpe's *fifth* victim, not if I had anything to say about it!

"Well. I *never*," said Cook. "That's that Miss Priscilla!" She picked up the paper and turned it to the backside, perhaps for evidence of a trick ending. "And Himself's not seen this yet?" I found her slow-simmering suspicion oddly calming, and I sat back down.

I shook my head. "Nor Miss Judson. I just found those, in Mr. Hamm's house."

There was a moment in which Cook's expression made it plain she was showing Exceptional Forbearance by not inquiring after the reason I had been inside Mr. Hamm's residence to begin with. "I never did like the look of that one," she finally said. "Not a patch on your dear mum, rest her soul, not to mention Miss Ada."

"Do you think I should show Father?" Even as I asked that, I knew the answer. He'd find some reason to dismiss the article or turn it into something *I'd* done wrong (although it might be interesting to see how he would make Priscilla being a murderess my fault). I wasn't foolish enough to confront Swinburne's Prosecutor with anything less than ironclad evidence. This article, he would tell the jury, was hearsay—sensational rumor designed to drum up scandal and divert attention from the real culprit.

Cook was pondering the same. "Best not tell Himself yet," she said. "You'll need more proof."

"I could Investigate these other poisonings," I suggested.

"And how long will that take? Nay, you'd best go straight to the source."

"Priscilla? She's not going to tell me anything."

"Not that one," she said scornfully. "I mean it's time for a word with Mr. Hamm."

I sighed. "How? They won't let me in to see him. Only his lawyer is allowed."

"And family members," Cook pointed out. "I've just remembered my dear long-lost nephew, locked up cruelly for a wicked crime of which he is so obviously innocent."

The words made sense—sort of—but coming from Cook's mouth they were too surprising to be understood. "You're going to visit Mr. Hamm?"

"Harrumph," she harrumphed. "There's a noon tram into town tomorrow. You can drop off a nice meat pie for me while I do some shopping. That young tart wants a lemon cake to match her sour looks."

"Do you think that will work?"

Cook just gave a dismissive wave of her hand. "I'll put in an extra for the desk sergeant." She tromped across the kitchen and began pulling out ingredients for pastry. I noticed for the first time that she was wearing a pair of oversized men's Wellies over her butler's trousers, like she did when she mopped the stoop.

"Why do you have boots on?" I asked. Something was niggling at me.

"I was coming out to the garden to fetch you," she said. "And I didn't want to get mud in my kitchen." Cook eyed me warily. "Why?"

I stood up. "I'm not sure," I said. "You put the boots on because you were going outside."

"I just said that."

She put the boots on because she was going outside. And then I almost had it. "Cook," I said urgently, "can you come outside again for a minute? I want to test something."

Upstairs, the bell rang to summon the next course. "That'll be coffee," Cook said doubtfully.

"Please?" I pleaded. "It'll only take a second."

She whipped off her apron. "They can wait," she said, and there was an alarmingly gleeful spark in her eye. "Test away, Young Miss."

Outside, I directed Cook into position, as close to the light from the open door as possible. "I want to see your footprints," I said. "Step here." She did as I asked, and I peered closer. "I can't really tell . . . Again, please, only harder this time—like you're stamping out a roach."

"Harrumph." The very *notion* of roaches was insulting to Cook, and she stomped robustly in the soft earth, pulling her foot back with satisfaction. For good measure, she stomped again with the other foot. "So?"

"We should have brought a lamp." I crouched down to get as close a look as I could. "Why do you have men's boots anyway?" I asked, tracing around her footprints with my finger.

"They were Mr. Stansberry's.* Always thought they were useful, so I kept them."

Studying the impressions, I nodded absently. Cook's footprints, in the oversized boots, were sloppy and indistinct, very different from the crisp, clear outline of my own prints in my properly fitting shoes. I had seen footprints just like this before—and now I knew what had been so strange about them.

* No one was *entirely* certain what had become of Cook's husband, although we all presumed she was a widow.

"It wasn't Mr. Hamm in the garden that night with Miss Wodehouse!" I breathed. It was someone lighter, with much smaller feet. Someone like Priscilla.

∽

At half past midnight I was summoned back to the foyer to bid Aunt Helena and Priscilla good night. Both of them were smiling. As was Father, I noted with a sense of dread. I mentally clutched tight to "Black Widow Poisoner" and felt my spine stiffen with resolve. I managed to descend the staircase to deliver my farewells with dignity.

"And what have you been up to this evening?" asked Father, with a fond (and humiliating) tousle of my hair. It was already tousled beyond hope by my deerstalker cap, but still. I wasn't a puppy.

I looked evenly at Priscilla when I answered. "Reading."

She brightened and stepped my way. "Oh, good. Did you figure out the murderer yet?"

I gave her a slow Peony blink. "I think so. It wasn't too hard."

"Well. You be sure to let me know if you're right." Her smile, overbright and overwide, reminded me of a shark.

"Oh, I will," I said. "You can count on it."

20

EVIDENCE OF
BAD CHARACTER

Every crime scene tells a story. From the tiny details
to the whole picture, the truth will emerge and point to
the guilty.

–H. M. Hardcastle, *Principles of Detection*

I worried about explaining my forthcoming errand with
Cook to Miss Judson, but the next morning's excitement overshadowed any alibi I might concoct. Father
and Miss Judson ate in stony silence, while I swung my
feet with nervous energy, willing the clock to tick faster
(despite all scientific evidence against the telepathic
manipulation of time). Then Cook burst into the room.

"Sir, I tried to stop her, but she insisted–" Cook
squeezed against the doorframe to avoid being mown
down by a pink cyclone.

Priscilla was back.

"Arthur! Oh, Arthur, thank goodness. It's just too awful!" She was wide-eyed, barely dressed in her pink wrapper, blond curls loose and chaotic.

Father leaped up, toppling his chair, as Miss Judson slid out of the way and rescued the tea service. I stayed put, not believing her hysterics for a moment.

"Miss Wodehouse, whatever's the matter?" Father barely had the words out before Priscilla flattened him in a desperate embrace, sobbing into his shoulder.

"It seems there's been some to-do at Redgraves," Cook said in a deep, expressionless voice.

Miss Judson stepped in. "Cook, dear, could you freshen the tea? Miss Wodehouse, please have a seat and explain what's happened."

Priscilla gave no signs of releasing Father, although he gamely attempted to disentangle himself from her octopus-like grip. She seemed to sprout another arm as soon as he got part of himself free, reeling him back in. By the time Cook returned with another tray of tea and our most scanty biscuits, Priscilla was at least coherent. Somehow Father managed to wheedle the story from her, and amid tears and sighs and flutters, it finally emerged.

"I've been *robbed*!"

I sat very still in my seat and stared hard at my tea.

"Someone broke into my house last night," Priscilla said. "They upset poor Trudy—I had to put her to bed with a hot-water bottle, but now she says she won't stay in a house where people are being murdered and robbed and I don't know *how* I shall get on without her and Mr. Hamm—"

"Did you call the police?" asked Father. I chewed my lip and made a focused study of the tablecloth.

Priscilla faltered. "I didn't want to make any trouble. I can't bear having those dreadful men back again." I noticed that she didn't mind making trouble for *us*.

"But I knew you would help me, Arthur." She put a hand on his arm, and I suddenly understood why Cousin Giles had been so calm about everything last night. They had *staged* this—together! To gain Father's sympathy, and—probably some other reasons I hadn't quite worked out yet.

I got up from the table and paced behind my chair, ignoring Miss Judson's quelling look. "Miss Wodehouse," I began, fingers laced behind my back, "when did you first notice something amiss?"

Priscilla spun in her seat to stare at me. "Right after I got home—no, before that. There was a light on in the carriage house. The planter on the front step was knocked over, and my door was open."

"Was anything taken?"

"Myrtle?" Miss Judson's voice was soft, but Father put up a forestalling hand. I was, after all, getting her to talk. And while she was talking, she was not strangling my father.

Priscilla's forehead creased daintily, as if it pained her to think this hard. "I can't be sure, of course. But I didn't notice anything. I don't have any valuables, so they can't have been after anything of mine."

"Maybe you have some *secret* in your past someone is trying to uncover."

"Myrtle, that will do, thank you," said Father gently, and Miss Judson really did tug me back down to my seat again. I seethed.

"Won't you come over and make sure everything is all right?" Priscilla pleaded. "You'll come, too, won't you, Myrtle? You're so clever—you'll figure out what they were after." She said this with a teasing smile, and I glared back at her, eyes narrowed. What was this, some sort of challenge? A sick game to ensnare my father and dare me to stop her? Well, I would. This Black Widow wouldn't cast her web around *my* family!

❧

Scowling all the way, I followed Father and Priscilla to Redgraves. Peony joined us, and we could not shake her off.

"Do let her come," Priscilla said. "Maybe she'll be able to tell if anything's missing."

Father frowned. "And how would the creature then communicate that to us?"

Priscilla laughed and hit him lightly in the chest with her fan. "Oh, Arthur."

Priscilla and Father would have barged right inside, heedless of any evidence on the exterior of the premises. With only a *slight* pang of dishonesty, I stopped them. "Shouldn't we check out here first?"

Father and Priscilla made a show of wandering about and peering under bushes while I made notes. Peony offered her opinion by planting herself on the steps and having a bath.

"Do you see anything?" I called. "Footprints? Cigarillo stubs?"

Father unearthed himself from the holly. "No," he said. "Are you sure they broke in? There's no damage to the doors or windows. Could you have left it unlocked, Miss Wodehouse?"

"I hope I wouldn't be so careless, but . . . I suppose I *was* a bit nervous last night. Perhaps I did."

Father gave her hand a comforting pat, and I looked intently at the brim of my hat, as Miss Judson would do.

Inside, in the foyer, the "break-in" was more obvious—the coatrack and an ornamental pedestal had been toppled over, some of the pictures torn from the walls. I stooped to retrieve one, another framed photograph of the lawn party. The glass had broken and the picture slipped in the frame.

Priscilla cooed, "Those are my parents! Wasn't Mother lovely?"

Father peered over our shoulders. "And that downy little chick must be you, Miss Wodehouse!" He gave a fond chuckle. "But who's the young lad there in the back?"

I felt Priscilla's scowl and peered closer myself. "Is that Giles? I mean, Mr. Northcutt?" A sour-faced little boy sulked beside a disapproving lady in black.

"I suppose it must be," Priscilla said, kneeling to pick up pieces of broken glass.

Father was down beside her in an instant. "Careful, you'll cut yourself. Myrtle, can you find a broom?"

I rolled my eyes but took that as leave to explore further.

Priscilla certainly was playing the Damsel in Distress. Plainly she'd kept up *her* subscription to the *Girl's Own Paper* and learned all the tricks for how to snag a widower. How could Miss Judson, with her calm, unflappable poise, possibly compete with a sobbing, fluttery, *desperate* Priscilla that Father could rescue?

I gripped my magnifier tighter and stalked up the steps, Peony bounding ahead of me. Giles had stormed through here as well, knocking off paintings, dumping ferns on their sides, tossing chairs about. The ceramic elephant guarding the staircase was now a pile of rubble, recognizable solely from its genuine ivory tusks, the only bits still intact. There were books and furnishings and oddments scattered all over, but nothing except the elephant and the picture frame seemed to be out-and-out broken.

In short, it was a grand mess that could be tidied right up again.

Miss Wodehouse's doors stood open. Her room, too, had been ransacked.

"Mrrow?" Peony gave me a questioning look.

"I know. It's all a mess," I said. "But we can't fix it before the police have a chance to see it."

"No." Peony nudged past me to Investigate the Famous Modern Bathroom, giving me a detailed report of her findings as she went.

It looked like Giles had gone after the bedroom with especial vengeance. The covers and mattress were half off the bed. The great heavy wardrobe was shoved aside, its drawers emptied out and Miss Wodehouse's unmentionables spilled onto the floor. After a minute or so, I no longer heard Peony complaining from the bathroom. Scrunching my nose over the thought of a seventy-nine-year-old lady's corset covers, I edged my way inside. It was drafty and spotlessly clean; I heard the thin teakettle-whistle of air in the boiler's pipes. But there was no sign of Peony. She hadn't slipped back past me through the doorway, but she wasn't under the shiny white pedestal sink, in the enormous clawfoot tub, beneath the cold copper boiler, or under the commode.

"Peony?" I said, expecting an answering meow. But there was nothing.

I froze. She'd done this before—disappeared from the room then reappeared later in the hallway. Somewhere in the bathroom, Peony had a secret entrance and exit from the master suite.

Magnifier in hand, I gave the bathroom walls and floor a serious inspection. A painted-shut window opened (or rather, didn't) onto the balcony. I closed the bathroom door, but there was no crack to squeeze under or transom to climb over. And no secret gap behind it, either—no linen chute or chimney access or dumbwaiter. No loose tiles, backless cabinets, or false walls. There was no way at all for Peony to have escaped this room unnoticed. And yet she had.

And I'd stake money that her escape route led straight to the secret cache of lilies only Peony knew about.

Peony and whoever had killed Miss Wodehouse, that is.

It was seeming more and more likely that those lilies *must* have been the motive. Priscilla had arrived from America, eager to claim Redgraves and her Wodehouse legacy, including the priceless, mythical flowers. Impatient with the Wodehouse who was currently in possession of it, Priscilla had dispatched Dear Aunt Minerva, but she'd been unable to find the lilies on her own. Recruiting me had failed as well, so she'd hired Cousin Giles to give the place a more frantic search, thereby also providing an excellent excuse for sympathy from the charming widower next door.

I headed straight for the one room at Redgraves I hadn't yet searched: the library, which Priscilla was using as an office. She'd halfheartedly scattered a few books around the room, but the key evidence was exactly where I expected it to be. Her beloved typewriter sat upon the desk, untouched. A real burglar might have upset it in his furor, but Priscilla would never have let anything happen to it.

Triumphant, I approached the machine for a closer look. A half-typed page poked out of the roller, and I leaned in to read it.

Dearest Branford,

By now you'll have heard the terrible things the police and the press are saying about me. Whatever you may read, I have done none of the wicked things of which I am accused. I am the Victim of a spiteful campaign of Rumor and Innuendo. I am sorry to leave you in such a way, but I knew you could never look at me the same way again. You may not believe me, but I had to tell you the truth. If you can find it in your heart, please give my love to Camille.

Yours, ever loving,

Mrs. Evalina Scharpe

Mrs. Scharpe—the Black Widow from the newspapers! Here was the proof I needed. I was dying* to snatch that page right out of the typewriter, but Priscilla would instantly notice it missing and just as swiftly realize what had become of it. Instead, I dug through the wicker wastepaper basket. It did not take me long to find another copy—a rough draft, perhaps (she'd added *wicked*, *spiteful*, and *Innuendo*). Grimly satisfied, I stuffed it into my bag.

I stole back into the foyer, where Father and Priscilla were still straightening the pictures and bric-a-brac, their fingers almost brushing as they reached for the same overturned vase.

"Shouldn't you wait for the police?" I said loudly.

They started and whirled around, two naughty schoolchildren caught out by their schoolmarm. I felt a swell of pride and power, and imagined myself as Miss Judson at her strictest. I glared. "We don't want to disturb anything before they have a chance to investigate."

"Oh, Arthur, it's not necessary, is it?" Priscilla clutched his arm for support.

Father looked very serious. "If you're quite sure nothing was taken . . ."

"I've looked upstairs." I turned pointedly to Father and said, directly to him, "It doesn't look like they

* fanciful hyperbole

broke anything, or did any damage that can't be cleaned up easily."

Father's frown deepened, and I thought I had him.

"At most," I continued, "they were trying to scare her, not do her any actual harm."

Father was nodding. I had the jury on my side, eating up my every word. "Or maybe there wasn't any intruder. Maybe this was just meant to *look* like a break-in. Wouldn't real intruders have done more damage?"

Father seemed taken aback—indeed, he stepped away from Priscilla and looked around the space again, more thoughtfully this time.

"But—" Priscilla gave me a curious look. "Do you think she could be right?"

And then I overplayed my hand. "It would explain why she doesn't want to notify the police, and why she came to *you* instead."

They turned to me, wordless, one deadly frown shared between them.

"You think *I* did this?" Priscilla's voice was shrill. "Arthur?"

"Myrtle." Just that. Just that single word, and a finger pointing dangerously toward the front door. "I will speak with you tonight. In the meantime you will consider how you might best apologize to Miss Wodehouse for such an outrageous accusation."

Heat crawled up under my collar. How could he talk to me that way? Side with Priscilla, against me?

Against *logic*? Against the evidence laid out plainly before him? I gritted my teeth and started to turn away—but I couldn't hold my tongue any longer.

"You'll see I'm right about her," I said darkly. "I'm going to prove it to you."

21
NIHIL DICIT

A good Investigator will always seek evidence to corroborate–
or refute–a witness's testimony.

–H. M. Hardcastle, *Principles of Detection*

All the way downtown, I crackled with indignation over how Father had treated me. It was so unfair! How in the world could he listen to somebody so fluffy-headed and eyelash-batting and ignore the clear, logical evidence before him? It probably wouldn't even matter if I showed him the article about Mrs. Scharpe now; he'd just see the pretty pictures of Priscilla and swoon all over her, all over again.

Well, if I couldn't save Father from Priscilla, at least I could try to save Mr. Hamm from the gallows. That disaster was my responsibility, and I would get *someone* to listen to me, if it killed me!

Swinburne's police station, Est. 1892,* sat a few blocks away from the courthouse. Modeled on New Scotland Yard in London, its stately redbrick walls, tall windows, and electric lighting gave the place an exceptionally modern air I found efficient and reassuring. Here was a place where reason and justice would prevail.

Inside the station, I approached the sergeant's desk, a high counter like a judge's bench. I had to stand on tiptoe to reach the visitors register, but saw that Mr. Hamm, the jail's only current resident, had been visited no fewer than three times by Mr. Ambrose, the latest yesterday morning. I plopped my basket onto the desk and announced myself, surreptitiously sliding the extra pie toward the desk sergeant, as instructed by Cook. "I'm here to visit Mr. Hamm. His, erm—aunt—sent him a hamper."

"Wot's this?" He eyed the pie with suspicion. "Are you trying to bribe a duly sworn member of the constabulary?"

I felt my face flame, but held my ground. "Pork and egg. Just the thing on a hot summer morning."

He shoved it back at me. "You can't be wasting police time like this. We're very busy."

---

* Renovations had been necessitated when a careless guard at the old jailhouse allowed an inmate to smoke, who then subsequently burned down the building, releasing all three prisoners. It took almost forty minutes to round them up again.

"I can see that," I said. Several constables chatted near a tea cart, while another was reading the newspaper, feet propped upon his desk. A lady about Miss Judson's age typed away efficiently at a desk in the back. "Very busy arresting the wrong people for crimes *someone else* had to point out to you even happened!"

"Is there a problem, Sergeant?" I heard a familiar voice and saw Inspector Hardy coming down the hall.

The desk sergeant looked relieved to see him. "Inspector, this . . . person is asking to see the prisoner."

"Oh, is she, now?" The detective's voice boomed through the station, echoing off all the marble. "He'll be right pleased to see a friendly face. Is that Mrs. Stansberry's pork pie?" Inspector Hardy plucked the pie from the desk and slipped it into his uniform pocket. He offered me his arm. "You've been busy, then, Miss Myrtle. Right clever police work, if you ask me."

I swallowed my treacherous pride. "Thank you, sir. But you've got the wrong man."

"What's that?" He looked taken aback. "We followed the evidence *you* gave us. And it led us straight to the man."

"But he gave a false confession. Miss Wodehouse didn't die the way he claimed. You have to let him go."

"That's a very serious charge, Miss Myrtle. Have you anything to back it up?"

"As a matter of fact . . ." I dug into the basket and pulled out my notes. They were only a little grease-spotted from the pies. "This shows my new theory of the crime, and my examination of the evidence. You'll also find references to the Police Surgeon's report, and—"

"Hold up, now." The Inspector crossed his arms over his chest, making no move to take my file. "You did a very fine thing, checking up on your neighbor and telling us what you witnessed. But now you've got to let us do our jobs. I can let you in to see the prisoner, because I don't think he's dangerous. But I can only give you ten minutes, and that will have to satisfy you. Understand?"

I nodded warily. I couldn't risk missing this one chance.

"And then I won't feel the need to mention this incident to your father."

Go ahead and tell him, I thought angrily. *He won't care.* Nobody listened to me, anyway.

Evidently feeling we'd settled the matter, Inspector Hardy went on. "It's good you came today," he said. "It might be your last chance. Hamm's going up before the judge next week."

"Already!" Father hadn't said anything. I was running out of time. "Why so soon?"

The Inspector shook his head. "That's your father's department, I'm afraid. Right through here. I'm sure Mr. Hamm'll be that glad to see you."

He left me waiting in a dark little room furnished only with a bare table and two hard chairs. It was infinitely depressing, with unpainted brick walls and a dingy linoleum floor the color of . . . floor. The only light came from one tiny, barred window. Finally, another policeman arrived, herding Mr. Hamm before him into the room.

"Lass!" He balked at the door. "What are tha' doing? Tha' shouldna be here!" His voice was harsh, but I deserved it.

The constable nudged him inside and stationed himself inside the door, obviously intending to listen to our every word.

I stood up and gave Mr. Hamm a curtsy. They'd taken his clothes, the sturdy brown trousers and familiar old coat, the bracers and the floppy felt hat. He now wore ugly, colorless coveralls, like a workhouse uniform. His hands, clutched before him like they still bore the shackles, were the only recognizable thing about him. Prisoners were subjected to a humiliating cold bath and scrub with lye soap and rough brushes when they were arrested, but it hadn't managed to get all the dirt out of Mr. Hamm's fingernails.

Those fingernails did me in. I forgot all about Investigative Objectivity and flung myself at him, wrapping my arms around his middle.

"There, there, I've not ever seen tha' cry. Tha' won't start now." He gave me a firm squeeze.

I sniffed and wiped my nose with my sleeve. "I'm sorry! This is all my fault. I know you didn't kill Miss Wodehouse. Why did you confess?"

Mr. Hamm shot a look at the constable. "Here, let's sit. Tell me what tha's been up to these days. Has tha' found the little kit, then?"

"Peony? Yes, she's fine now, but—" What should I say about the lilies? "She got some nectar on her that made her sick."

"Nectar, aye?" Mr. Hamm's gaze was keen.

Conscious of the guard, I said in a low voice, "We think it came from lilies, from somewhere inside Redgraves."

Here he frowned. "Inside? In the house, you mean?"

I nodded. "Could there be some left—maybe hidden, somewhere?"

Mr. Hamm was shaking his head. "Now, lass, don't go catchin' lily fever. Tha's too sensible for that."

Voice hushed, I said, "The Gilded Slipper lily—is it real?"

He leaned back with a slow smile. "Now, there's a *real* mystery. Nineteen years, I worked as close to that old lady as anyone ever did, and even I don't know if that plant were real, or a rumor, or a fancy. She'd never say."

I took the fleur-de-lis key from the basket. "What does this open?"

He turned it over in his hands. "Never seen that one, I'm afraid. Where'd tha' come by it?" His smile grew as I explained about the lily vase. "Just the sort of thing she'd do, too, innit?"

Mr. Hamm cared about those plants as much as Miss Wodehouse had, I knew. "How could you destroy all the lilies? All your work together, all those years?"

"I told tha' I did what the Mistress bade me do. Made me swear to it, should sommat happen to her."

"She *wanted* you to destroy the specimens in the garden? To burn them? Why?"

"Had her own way, the Mistress did. Couldn't rightly explain the half of what she wanted."

But why would Miss Wodehouse have him destroy the lilies if she'd meant to leave them to him in her will? That didn't make any sense. I wanted to ask Mr. Hamm about it, but I couldn't risk the policeman overhearing. It was motive, and I wasn't about to strengthen their case for them.

Mr. Hamm eased back in his chair, getting comfortable. "I see tha's got a basket, there."

Stalled for the moment, I slid over one of the paper-wrapped pies Cook had sent. "I don't think she baked a file into it."

Chuckling, Mr. Hamm wrapped his hands around the parcel. "Look at that, now. I planted those first onions in yon back garden, you know."

"Mr. Hamm, please talk to me. Why did you lie to the police about what happened? I saw the Police Surgeon's report. Miss Wodehouse died of digitalis poisoning, not arsenic."

"People make mistakes."

"Well, *someone* did," I said softly. "You told me you wouldn't push Miss Wodehouse into the mud. But you'd poison her with arsenic? That's a much more horrible thing to do."

He was silent, but his ruddy hands had gone stiff and white around the circle of pie wrapper.

"Is someone making you lie? Is it Priscilla?"

This finally got some reaction. His eyes snapped to me, clear and narrow. "Now look here. Leave young Priscilla out of it. And if tha' knows what's good for thee, tha'll stay well away from the whole affair!"

"Why in the world would you lie for somebody you just met?" I demanded. "Who is she to you?" The pieces almost clicked into place. "Did you know her before, when she was younger? Before she went to America?"

He grunted assent. "I knew her da', back home in the Dales. The Wodehouses had a few acres of moorland up there. Corey Park, it were called, some of the prettiest country tha' ever did see."

I sat up straighter. "You and Priscilla's father were friends?"

He gave a gruff laugh. "Not Himself and the likes of me. Not at first, anyhow. Ah, the tales I could tell of those days." He sobered. "I run into some trouble, though, and Mr. Ned, he helped me out."

"What sort of trouble? You mean your criminal record? Mr. Hamm, you need to tell somebody."

He sighed. "Well, I reckon it don't matter anymore. The lads I ran with, we had a little sideline, selling game to butchers in town." I stared at him blankly, and he filled me in. "Poaching, lass. I could've gone down for hard labor—three years in the mines. But Ned, he stepped in and cleared it with the Magistrates. Got my sentence cut in half, working his family's land as gamekeeper. That were my first run-in with the Wodehouses, you see."

"After your sentence was up, you came down here?"

"Aye. His cousin were lookin' for somebody good with plants. The Mistress took me on, despite my record."

I pounced. "Then how could you ever have hurt her? I understand you owe Priscilla's father a debt, but you can't take the blame for a murder she committed!"

He jerked back like I'd struck him. "What? Little Priscilla, *kill* somebody? Tha's talkin' madness."

He sounded sincere—but he'd had the newspaper articles in his rooms, so he must have seen "Black

Widow Poisoner," same as I had. "Priscilla told the police that you and Miss Wodehouse had an argument—that you'd stolen something from her."

Mr. Hamm wearily rubbed his face. "Wish we could take that back now." He eyed me over his hand. "Tha'll not let me have any peace till I tell thee, aye? Fine. Mr. Ned's folks disowned him when he ran off with that American opera singer. Couldna stand her. So he brought her down to Redgraves instead. They were happy here, for a few years, Ned, Cissie, and the little 'un." He nodded, remembering. "And the Mistress, she *doted* on the wee lass."

I tried to imagine Priscilla as the daughter of a glamorous opera soprano, but my powers of fancifulness weren't up to the feat. "What happened?"

"Mrs. Ned, she got an offer to sing back in America, but they couldna afford the trip. They asked the Mistress, but she refused. So I took some money—what we kept for the plants and repairs and such—and I gave it to Ned to take his bride and daughter off to America. So, lass, I *did* steal from her. And it's taken me near twenty year to pay it off again. But what really hurt the Mistress was that I went behind her back and sent Priscilla away."

I frowned and swung my legs. I understood how Miss Wodehouse's resentment might have been born, but not why it had lingered. "Why didn't she want to see Priscilla, then, when she came back to England?"

Mr. Hamm's face was lined with regret. "She'd only say too much time had passed. I know she was frightful when the young lady come to call uninvited, but to pretend like she's not even your own flesh and blood . . . It makes no sense."

But it did to me. Miss Wodehouse had taken one look at Mrs. Scharpe and known right away she wasn't her long-lost darling first cousin twice removed. It didn't take many deductive steps to see what happened next. The "heiress" came home to cozy back up to her dear auntie, only to be rebuffed. So she killed her before the truth about her identity could come out. One thing still didn't make sense, though.

"But *you* recognized her?"

"Oh, aye. The spitting image of her da', she is. Down to that cleft in her chin."

It wasn't like Mr. Hamm to be deluded, but it sounded like his friendship with Ned Wodehouse had meant the world to him. "You'd do anything to protect Miss Priscilla, then?"

Mr. Hamm glanced at the guard again, weathered hands gripped together. "Aye, that I would. And tha'self, too, if I had to," he added softly. But I scarcely heard him.

"Even confess to a murder you didn't commit? Is she worth *dying* for?" I leaned across the cold table. "If Priscilla had something to do with it, you've got to tell Mr. Ambrose. He can help—"

He stood up so fast he knocked the chair over. "Lassie, it were that good to see tha'. But I've nowt else to say on the matter." He turned to the constable still lurking silently by the door. "I'll go back now."

"Mr. Hamm, wait. Let me help you!"

"Go home. I've told tha' everything." His face had gone hard again.

Desperately, I tried to think what else I could say, what else to ask, before my one moment slipped away. "Wait—" I had my file of papers, the ones Inspector Hardy hadn't been interested in, and thrust them at him. "Take these. Give them to Mr. Ambrose. Maybe— maybe it will help your defense."

His frown softened. "Thart a goodly lass. But stop askin' questions on this. *Please.*"

He pressed my handful of documents away. A moment later, and he was gone.

22

Ex Parte Communication

Never let your Investigations be hampered by outdated conventions of decorum. The pursuit of justice cannot be fettered by so-called "propriety."

–H. M. Hardcastle, *Principles of Detection*

Inspector Hardy led me back out into the afternoon, whereupon I took an involuntary deep breath of fresh air, which was probably what everyone did when released from jail. I was troubled by my conversation with Mr. Hamm. Why was he sticking to his obviously false confession? He hadn't admitted–in so many words–that he was protecting Priscilla, but his hints and evasions had said enough. I could only think of one other person who might help now. Mr. Ambrose must have realized that his client was innocent, and I was anxious to bring him the new evidence about the footprints. It was Highly Irregular, the Prosecutor's daughter consorting with Defense Counsel—but right now, Mr. Ambrose and I were on the same side: Mr. Hamm's.

Father's old office was just a few streets from the police station, in an older building on the corner. I had been here dozens of times, naturally, but not in a few years. Ambrose & Belgrave* occupied the suite on the top floor of the building—a full five stories up, past a chemist, a stationer's, a secretarial agency, and an insurance brokerage.

It takes an exceptionally long time to climb five flights of stairs in August. I can't recommend it, Dear Reader, even in the pursuit of justice. When I finally reached the pinnacle of the building, panting in a manner hardly befitting a Young Lady of Quality, the office door was propped open and ceiling fans rattled away hopefully overhead. All they seemed to be doing was spreading papers about. One sailed out the open door as I dodged past.

Inside, more files bulged out of overflowing drawers and were piled up on the three desks crammed into the small room, made even smaller by the jumble of books everywhere. Mr. Ambrose shared the office with his legal clerk, a young man training in the law.

---

* Jonas Belgrave, Esq., had died a million years ago, but the firm still bore his name.

There had been a variety of them over the years, and I didn't recognize the one who worked here now, his curly fair head bent over a contract balanced atop a stack of open books.

"Hullo, there," he said when I came in. "Who are you?"

"Myrtle Hardcastle." I pointed to Father's name, still stenciled on the glass pane of the office door.*

"No kidding," he said. "I thought you'd be older. We kept your desk free, in case you ever decided to come back. Have a seat. Plenty of work, Counselor."

I stifled a grin. "I'm here on official business," I said. "It regards *Crown against Hamm*."

"Well, Mr. Ambrose isn't in at the moment, but you're welcome to wait."

I groaned inwardly, feeling as wilted as my damp skirts. What was I to do now? I supposed I could spare a few moments before tackling those stairs again. I sat heavily on the desk, shifting aside a stack of magazines. "Where did you say Mr. Ambrose was?"

"Well, I didn't, Your Honor. Because I don't know. He may be working at home today."

"But you said he'd be back soon." I couldn't make that *not* sound cross. "What am I waiting for, then?"

He pushed his contract aside. "Well, you got me. I've gone and perjured myself. What's the penalty for that?"

---

* Along with the names of Mr. Ambrose, Mr. Belgrave, and a couple of others I'd never met. Clearly they needed to update their signage.

"A contempt violation, and possible jail time," I snapped. "But you can avoid the latter if you answer my questions truthfully from now on."

The clerk sat up straight, a prim and attentive witness.

"State your name for the court," I said.

"Robert Blakeney, Esquire," he said promptly. "Well, almost."

"Almost Robert Blakeney?" I said. He was funny.

He grinned back.

"And what is your current position?"

"I know this one! Legal clerk for the law firm of Ambrose, Belgrave . . . and Hardcastle."

"And how long have you held this position, Mr. Blakeney?"

"It's my third week," he said proudly.

I looked at him sternly. "That was an honest question."

"And an honest answer—on my honor, Your Honor! I started a fortnight ago yesterday."

"August the second?" That was when Miss Wodehouse died. Surely it was only a coincidence that Mr. Ambrose got a new law clerk the morning after his wealthiest client passed away. "What happened to the previous clerk?"

Mr. Blakeney looked serious for the first time. "I've learned not to ask questions like that," he said quietly.

"I was told he was 'unsatisfactory,' and that his services were no longer required. That's all I know."

"Oh." I frowned. The familiar office was feeling stuffy and strange. I set my basket heavily on the desk and tugged at my collar.

"If you don't mind my saying so, you look like a fellow who could use a solicitor's advice," Mr. Blakeney said. "Perhaps I can help. You said it's about one of Mr. Ambrose's cases? Do you have some information?"

For a moment I regarded Mr. Blakeney with stupefaction. Was he really asking me? "As a matter of fact—" I reached into the basket for my file, but when Mr. Blakeney saw the size of it, he shifted uncomfortably in his seat.

"I'm sure I don't have to warn you about the Prosecution consorting with the Defense. Ex parte communication, or something. It's in here somewhere." He waved a hand at his books. "Should you be telling me this?"

I winced. He made that sound like I was betraying Father by being here. "I just want to help Mr. Hamm." Mr. Blakeney was looking at me intently, so I added, "He's my friend."

"He doesn't seem to have very many these days, does he?" said Mr. Blakeney. "All right, then, what do you have?"

"Shouldn't you be writing this down?"

Mr. Blakeney rummaged about and unearthed a notepad and pencil.

"My name is spelled M-Y-R-T-L-E," I began, because he didn't seem to be taking any notes.

"Thank goodness you've said that, because I was going to go with S-T-E-P-H-E-N, and then where would we be?"

"I'm serious. Don't you realize they're going to hang your client if we can't prove he's innocent?" Before giving him a chance for another silly response, I plunged into my findings about the footprints. "So it *wasn't* Mr. Hamm in the gardens that night with Miss Wodehouse, you see?"

He scratched his head. "I'm afraid we're going to need more than that, Stephen. You know he's confessed, right?"

"I know he's *innocent.* But there is more. I think her niece killed her."

Here Mr. Blakeney's head snapped up in surprise. "Miss Priscilla? Why would you say that?"

"Because Miss Wodehouse found out Priscilla is an impostor, and that's why Mr. Ambrose needed us to find the will." Something about that didn't sound *exactly* right, but it must have been the heat.

"Now you've definitely gone over my head. Which will?"

"Miss Wodehouse's missing will—the one you

needed Priscilla to find, because the one you have here isn't signed."

Now he was staring openmouthed. A moment later, he rolled his chair to the bank of filing cabinets in the corner, never standing up. "See this? It's *all* Wodehouse and Redgraves, going back a hundred years at least. Old Man Ambrose's father had the account first, you know. Wodehouse anxiety built this very office. And here"—he dipped his hand into a drawer—"is Miss Wodehouse's last will and testament."

"It's massive!" At least now I knew Priscilla and I weren't looking for a couple of flimsy sheets of paper. The thing must have been more than a hundred pages long.

"Who told you it wasn't signed? Her signature's right here." In bold black letters plain as day, the last page read: *Signed, Cosigned, and Witnessed this 14th day of July, 1893. Minerva Faye Wodehouse, Whitney Rhodes Ambrose, and*—a garbled scrawl from the third, unidentified witness.

But there indeed was Miss Wodehouse's signature—on her will, in her own hand, scarcely a fortnight before her death.

Priscilla had lied to me.

She must have had some other reason for wanting my help. Maybe she'd hoped Clever Myrtle would dig up something else altogether—like the missing lilies. Did this version have the handwritten addendum I'd found in the greenhouse coal chute? "Who inherits the lilies?" I reached for the document again.

"*I'm* barely supposed to be reading this." Mr. Blakeney held it out of reach. "I shudder to imagine what Ambrose would do if I handed it over to a Prosecution spy."

"I'm not!" I cried, then realized he was teasing me again.

"If there's something relevant in here, I'll let you know. This could take a minute; better make yourself comfortable."

I looked around politely as he combed through the pages. Mr. Ambrose's desk was almost neat, compared to the rest of the room. I could see the top of it, at least. His inkwell was dry, and his letter tray had a memo from last May on top. "Does he work at home a lot?" I said.

Mr. Blakeney gave a whistle. "My word, your reputation is well earned. Solicitors of the advanced and respectable age of sixty-four have earned the right to set their own hours."

I sat down in Mr. Ambrose's chair. It had casters and a hard wooden seat that spun, and felt excessively official. Leaning against the far window, perilously in danger of toppling out, should anyone ever manage to reach the orifice to admit the fresh air, was a coatrack, overburdened with several generations of discarded hats and coats, including Mr. Ambrose's muddy old wool overcoat, the one he used to wear before the fancy replacement he'd had on at my house. "Mr. Ambrose left his coat here?"

"Not much call for a Chesterfield in August."

Moments later, my fingers were at work in their practiced game, examining Mr. Ambrose's pockets. I found a box of matches and a crumpled handkerchief with his initial, a swirling green *W.* There was also a small, battered leather case, empty, whose purpose I could not deduce, but which reminded me of Miss Judson's cases for her pens and charcoal.

"It's too bad you weren't here sooner. My predecessor left his coat behind, too, and frankly, it scared the dickens out of me. A sort of mustardy plaid. You could have exorcised that one, too."

"What?" I spoke up sharply. "A ghastly yellow tartan jacket?"

"Well, yes, Your Honor, one might use those words to describe the garment in question."

Mr. Ambrose's old law clerk was *Cousin Giles.* I was such an idiot.

He'd told me that. That first day at Redgraves, looking for the will. *That's why I stopped working there,* he'd said. And yet he'd claimed to be on an errand from Mr. Ambrose last night—getting a new shirt for Mr. Hamm. Who had a prison *uniform.*

My brain was throbbing—it was *very* hot in that little office. Still holding Mr. Ambrose's old handkerchief, I backed into a desk, knocking a stack of papers to the floor in a slow avalanche.

"Stephen?"

"Did Mr. Northcutt give notice, do you know, or was he sacked?"

"No idea. Further Ambrose sayeth not, I'm afraid."

I clambered free of the papers. "I should be going. Thank you for the—thank you, Mr. Blakeney."

"Wait, don't you want to know what the will says about the flowers?"

I turned back. "Actually, can you check something else? Did Giles Northcutt inherit anything?"

Now Mr. Blakeney looked uncomfortable.

"Miss Wodehouse was *murdered*," I said. "And your client is going to hang for it. That will might have the real killer's motive in it!"

"When you put it that way . . ." Mr. Blakeney turned toward a section close to the end. "Miss Wodehouse did leave her nephew a legacy: an antique ceramic elephant from Borneo."

The smashed elephant! "That's it?" I'd be tempted to clobber the thing to smithereens, too. "That's a little miserly, isn't it?"

"That's not for me to say. But I wouldn't exactly call it generous."

Giles must have known about the will, and his inheritance, long before Miss Wodehouse's death. So why had he asked *me* about it? What game were he and Priscilla playing?

"If you don't mind my saying so, you look troubled."

I liked Mr. Blakeney, silly as he was. I wanted to trust him, and he hadn't dismissed me outright—yet I hesitated. I needed more proof. The situation with Mr. Hamm had taught me that.

"Could you do something for me?" I took his notepad—where he had *not* made any notes of our conversation—and jotted down my address at Gravesend Close. "Would you ask downstairs at the chemist's if your predecessor ever purchased any digitalis?"

"I say, now, you'd better tell me what this is about."

I shook my head. "It might help Mr. Hamm. Can you do it?"

He was muttering something about odd jobs and menial labor, but he nodded and reached for the notepad. We were thus engaged, hands holding the paper together, when the stairwell door flew open and somebody's staggering footsteps interrupted us.

"Whitney? Oh, I beg your pard— *Myrtle*?"

I spun round. "Father!"

23
PROSECUTORIAL
DISCRETION

Of course, there are moments when even the greatest
Investigator must bow to powers outside his own control.

— H. M. Hardcastle, *Principles of Detection*

"The plot thickens," said Mr. Blakeney. "An impostor!"

Father sagged against the doorway, his Prosecutor's
robes hanging half off his shoulder. "Myrtle? What
are you doing here?"

"I'm afraid that is a matter of attorney-client privi-
lege, Mr. Prosecutor," Mr. Blakeney said. "Stephen's
business is his own."

Father pressed a pained hand to his sweaty forehead. "I'm sorry, who is Stephen?"

I snatched my hands away from the notepad, upon
which I had just given a strange young man my home

address. I felt a flush creep up my face, but it was so hot in here, maybe nobody would notice. "I came to see Mr. Ambrose, of course. What are *you* doing here?"

"I—the same. Robert?" He turned to Mr. Blakeney with evident relief. "Have you seen him today?"

"Have I seen Mr. Ambrose? I'm not at liberty to disclose that information, but *hypothetically* I might surmise that an employer whose desk has the layer of dust and dead fern that Ambrose's has might very well have chosen to work at home. Frequently." Shielding his mouth with his hand, he added in a stage whisper loud enough to be heard across the street, "It's the stairs, you know. They do you in after a few years."

Father dropped his brief-bag and sat down heavily in the nearest chair. "Dear God, those stairs! I had forgotten."

"Miss Judson keeps telling you to get more exercise," I said, sitting beside him. "You ought to bicycle to work. It's tremendously healthful."

"Stephen showed remarkable fortitude. He wasn't even breathless when he got up here."

"Not to mention *youth*," Father said with a grin. He had finally caught on.

"I'm sorry you missed Mr. Ambrose, sir," said Mr. Blakeney. "Was there something I could help with? If you're looking for a file . . . ?"

"I don't think you're supposed to share your files with the Prosecutor's Office unless your client waives disclosure," I said. Both of them stared at me. "Well, you're not!"

"Stephen, you scare me," Father said. "No, I just wanted to ask his advice."

"That's what I wanted," I said, and for a moment he and I sat in exactly the same position, half sulking, chins in hands.

Mr. Blakeney gave a seal's bark of laughter. "I don't know if you noticed, but this is a solicitor's office. We certainly don't offer *advice*." He rummaged through the heap on the desk and found a small clock. "It's almost teatime. You might find him at his club."

Father thanked him and rose to go. "Come along, Myrtle," he said, breaking the spell. "It *is* nearly teatime. Aren't you due somewhere?" We were to meet Cook at the tram and ride home together.

"Come back any time, sir. Sirs!" Mr. Blakeney called. "We'll keep the stairs waiting for you!"

∾

Three flights down, Father still hadn't scolded me for being alone in public with a strange man. Perhaps he was only breathless, and the lecture would come at the foot of the stairs. Or down the block, after he'd recovered himself. But we passed the insurance brokerage, the secretaries, the stationer, and the chemist without comment.

Perhaps he was too angry with me to speak.

I clutched my basket and scurried after him as he headed up High Street toward the tram stand, long legs clipping over the pavement, brief-bag swinging. We dodged fellow shoppers, shopgirls, and clerks all headed home for their tea. Dear Reader, do not for a moment believe that *knowing* Father's interrogation tricks meant I was immune to them. Halfway to the tram, I couldn't help myself—too many thoughts had bubbled up inside, unspoken, and no more would fit. I blurted out the next one that came to mind.

"Aren't you going to stop at Mr. Ambrose's club?" We'd passed it, about a block ago.

Father whirled around, robes swirling like an Inquisitor's cloak.

"Mr. Blakeney—I mean the clerk—said . . ." I gave it up before I confessed myself into a lifetime's sentence of confinement to the house.

"No," he said with a sigh. He looked even wearier than he had at the top of the stairs. "I'll try to catch him tomorrow. Cook will be waiting for us."

I risked another question. "What did you want to see Mr. Ambrose for? Was it about the case?"

He waved a hand to a passing coachman so we weren't run down in the crossing. "Not exactly. I wanted to talk things over, I suppose."

"Is that allowed? Isn't that ex parte communication?"

He had the opportunity to avoid the subject by

launching into a lecture on legal terminology, but he didn't. He didn't say *anything* else.

I couldn't take it any longer. "If Mr. Hamm is innocent, you can't put him on trial. You just can't."

Father gave another heavy sigh. "It isn't up to me, I'm afraid." I knew that; it was the Magistrate's decision whether to proceed with the trial.

"Perhaps Mr. Ambrose could convince Mr. Hamm to recant his confession."

"If we could find him. But no, that wouldn't help, either."

I knew that, too. "What if there were someone else—another suspect? If somebody else confessed, or there were more compelling evidence, you'd have to let him go then?"

"Oh, if only we had another suspect!"

I stopped short in the middle of the street, fingertips caught between my teeth. Father was blinking at me, one hand frozen in his ginger hair. The tram clanged in the distance.

"Dear God Almighty," he said. "I actually just said that, didn't I?"

❧

The three of us arrived home to find Miss Judson and Peony in a State. They were engaged in a standoff in the kitchen, a deep basin of water between them on the table. One of them was soaking wet—not, I'd wager, the one intended by the enterprise.

Peony crouched behind the bowl, back arched, eyes deadly narrow, and fur erect—the penny dreadful version of herself: *The Fiendish Feline of Redgraves!* Miss Judson looked fit to murder someone. Her tweed skirt and once-ivory blouse were drenched (a scandalous quantity of bronze skin and white corset cover visible through the wet fabric—which Miss Judson doubtless found both mortifying and irrelevant), and she bore a towel and brush in her hands like weapons.

"No one move," she said, voice severe. "I almost have her."

"Miss Judson?" Father spoke carefully. "Is there something we could help you with? Myrtle, could you . . . get the cat?"

One did not simply "get" Peony. Despite Modern Science's claims to the contrary, Peony had a mind of her own, and just now she was speaking it, in downright demonic tones. The sound issued from deep in her throat, a low, guttural warning that set the hairs on my arms on end.

I stayed where I was.

Cook came to our rescue, swooping in and seizing Peony firmly behind the shoulders. In one practiced motion, she plunged the possessed, growling Peony into the water, whereupon Miss Judson set upon her with the scrub brush.

At which point I *finally* remembered. "She got into the lilies again?" My stomach sank. I had left Peony at Redgraves with Father and Priscilla after she had vanished into Miss Wodehouse's bathroom.

"She will be fine," Miss Judson declared, adding darkly, "I Took Precautions."

Father blanched noticeably at this, which suggested the details of Peony's previous treatment for lily toxicity had been shared with him. And which explained Peony's present pleasant mood. "Poor kitty," I cooed, and she hissed at me.

I heard the odd, snuffling sound of Father trying to stifle a laugh.

"You might help," Miss Judson snapped, and Father sprang to—doffing his robes and dropping them right on the floor. He thrust his hands into the basin and bravely caught hold of some part of the squirming cat. Peony thus restrained, Miss Judson was able to proceed with the operation. Soap was rubbed into fur, the cat dunked beneath the water like so much laundry and swept out again in Father's arms. I passed him the towel, and he wrapped it around her, cradling her to his chest and whispering to her in Latin. Peony clung to her rescuer, and her deep angry growls softened to piteous meows. She rubbed her head in Father's beard—and he nibbled on one of her ears.

What in the name of sanity had happened to my household?

⤲

Miss Judson's mood had not improved when it came time to acquit myself of my afternoon's activities. Peony recovered sooner, sprawled before the schoolroom fire, painstakingly redoing the bath we'd just given her, front paw splayed out like a lioness's after a kill, licking her claws. I did not find it especially reassuring.

Miss Judson sat in the one comfortable chair in the room, knees primly crossed, a book upon her lap, like a statue of *Governess Awaiting Tardy Charge*. I crept in warily.

"I brought tea?" I held the tray before me like a shield. Cook had piled on Miss Judson's favorites, in part to pacify, in part to thank her on behalf of Peony, who in fact *had* been saved from near disaster by Miss Judson's underappreciated ministrations.

Miss Judson lifted one neat eyebrow and indicated the corner of the bench, where I began unloading toast, tea, and leftover trifle. Wordlessly, I handed her a plate, and she nodded her thanks. "And what did you get up to this afternoon?"

There was something ominous in that question, and I decided not to test her. I clambered down to the floor with my own plate, sloshing tea on my skirt. "I went to see Mr. Ambrose," I began.

"Ah."

"I think it was Priscilla's footprints we saw in the garden, not Mr. Hamm's." I explained about my discovery, but instead of a look of enlightenment, a little crease formed between Miss Judson's brows. "What's the matter?"

"As much as I enjoyed the notion of her guilt, I think we should move on to other suspects."

"But the footprints! And she staged that break-in. I know it."

She shook her head sadly. "Myrtle, your father's not a fool. It's one thing not to like the girl your father fancies. It's another to accuse her of murder."

"She's duped other men before!" I jumped up and retrieved my file from the basket. Triumphantly, I brandished "Black Widow Poisoner" at her, but to my disappointment she did not pounce on it as Cook and I had.

"Where did you get this?"

"It was in Mr. Hamm's house," I said, before I remembered that she didn't know I'd been over there last night.

"It was *where*?" Suddenly, she sounded quite a bit like Peony had before her bath.

One does not lie to Miss Judson. That is to say, there'd never been a need to, and this was probably not the moment to launch my maiden efforts. Scotland Yard should hire her: with three simple words, Miss Judson had extracted my full confession. She listened silently as I described my nocturnal adventure, in as unemotional tones as I could—I was a constable reporting on my nightly beat, nothing more. But that silence was dangerous, like steam building up in a boiler.

"Stop. Just stop. I've heard enough." She stood, skirts falling into place as she rose.

"But the newspapers—"

"Can wait. I don't even know where to begin. She's our neighbor—you can't simply barge about her property, especially while she's at your home, dining with your father. And *at night*?"

"When *else* was I supposed to do it?" I stamped my foot, like a baby. "Are you forgetting that we're trying to solve a murder here? I put an innocent man in jail, and nobody is helping me get him out! Not you, not Father, not Mr. Ambrose. Even Mr. Hamm won't help me!" My voice got louder with every sentence, and my face felt hot—and I realized with horror that I was about to cry.

Miss Judson had no sympathy. Her keen ear had caught another incriminating word. "Mr. Hamm?" she said. She turned her head slightly, like a snake scenting prey.

I kicked my toe against the floorboards. "Um. I might have gone to see him, too."

There was a pause.

Followed by an explosion.

"To the *prison*?" Miss Judson's voice hit an impossible octave and echoed from the rafters.

"I went to the police station!" I cried. "Why isn't that allowed?"

"You know perfectly well why! Aside from the fact that you lied to your father *and* to me, you are going to get me sacked and yourself killed."

I scowled. "Who would kill me at the police station?"

"I wouldn't rule out your governess."

"I don't understand!"

Miss Judson's face had turned a shade I'd never seen before. "Because you don't *want* to understand! You are the cleverest girl I've ever met, but you are *deliberately* obtuse about the simplest things. Young Ladies of Quality do not break into their neighbors' houses or frequent jailhouses and lawyers' offices! Or sneak about and play detective and—"

"And get innocent men arrested?" There was a sting in my chest, poking into my throat, and I couldn't choke it back. We had never quarreled.

But we weren't quarreling.

She was *scolding* me.

Like a regular girl. And a regular governess. Heat flooded my cheeks. I gave my teacup a savage kick, smashing it to pieces against the brickwork, grabbed my papers about Priscilla, and got out of there as fast as I could.

Before I really did cry.

24

SUMMARY JUDGMENT

An Investigator must work alone, in silence and in secret, with no applause or appreciation or thanks. His only care is the pursuit of Truth and Justice.

–H. M. Hardcastle, *Principles of Detection*

It turned out that I couldn't actually stay in my room forever. My sulk was interrupted toward the end of breakfast the next morning, when a rap at my door requested and required my presence in the dining room. Still in my dressing gown, I trudged down as slowly as I could, Peony dragging her feet as well. Miss Judson was in her habitual place, as though nothing had occurred. I glared at her and was about to sit when Father forestalled me.

"Ah. Myrtle, this came for you." He passed over a thick parcel.

"You opened it?" Peony gave a tinny, disapproving meow.

He looked genuinely apologetic. "I saw the letterhead and assumed it was for me."

The thick envelope stamped AMBROSE & BELGRAVE was addressed to Stephen Hardcastle. Mr. Blakeney! As much as I'd have liked to peruse its contents away from the prying eyes of Father and Miss Judson, my impatience got the better of me. I tore off the wrapping and found a bundle of magazines and a folded note:

Dear Stephen: Dead end at the chemist's, I'm afraid, and nothing in the will about the lilies. But these were in the office when I joined the firm. I can't make heads or tails of them, but maybe they'll mean something to you, given your keen interest in flowers.

VTY, R. Blakeney, Esq.--almost

The magazines turned out to be garden journals, plant catalogues, and issues of *Cottage Garden Weekly*. Keen interest? What did he mean? All I'd done was ask who inherited Miss Wodehouse's lilies.

"I understand that I'm not entitled to the details of your private correspondence with your legal counsel," said Father, "but I *am* dying of curiosity. Take pity on a fellow?"

"It's just some garden catalogues." I set the magazines on the table, willing them to produce some profound Investigatory Insight, whereupon everyone helped him- or herself to a copy. I gave Miss Judson a nasty scowl, which she entirely ignored.

Planting myself in my seat, I browsed articles titled "New Methods in Irrigation," "Aspidistras for All!" and "Beware the Slug"; adverts for Celebrated Acme Weed Killer and Edwards' Invincible Lawn Mower; and page after page of exuberant illustrations showing the newest and brightest trends in ornamental plants. Why had Mr. Blakeney sent these to me?

"Oh, look," Father said. "Delphiniums are in for spring."

"Mmm," said Miss Judson, flipping a page.

I glared at them both, and to emphasize, this time my stomach growled. Where was Cook? Where was *toast*?

And then, it seemed, we all stopped browsing at once.

"Wait," said Father.

"What's this?" said Miss Judson.

"Meow?" said Peony.

"That's impossible." I'd taken a new approach, examining the magazines themselves for clues: dog-eared pages, a broken spine, a coffee stain. And there, in a paid notice from the May issue of *Amateur Gardening*, I found it.

LEGENDARY
REDGRAVES SPECIMENS
RARE & ONE OF A KIND.
SERIOUS COLLECTORS & PRIVATE BUYERS ONLY.
INQUIRE AT: 44 HIGH STREET, SUITE B, SWINBURNE

Father peered over the edge of *Floral Treasures 1893*. "Are we all looking at advertisements for flowers from Redgraves?"

Miss Judson opened *Hyde's Horticultural Almanac* so we could see the tantalizing drawing of an exotic lily, sweeping petals spotted and frilled.

"I was under the impression Miss Wodehouse wouldn't sell her specimens," Father said.

"She wouldn't," I said fiercely.

"Then who placed these notices?" Miss Judson met my eyes and I knew what she was thinking. Mr. Hamm? Priscilla? Or someone else?

"Quick, look for more." Father's voice was keen with excitement. Hands darted across the table, tearing through pages and spilling magazines everywhere. Within moments, the whole collection was splayed open on the tabletop, every last issue displaying another advertisement with the name REDGRAVES in big, bold letters.

"Mr. Ambrose must have been looking into these illicit sales," I said. I raised my eyes to Father's. "Wouldn't this be another motive? Enough to find another suspect?"

"Myrtle." Miss Judson sounded weary.

"It would be *a* motive," Father said carefully. "A Prosecutor might say that the accused himself placed these adverts, then killed Miss Wodehouse to prevent her from discovering them."

"Arthur Hardcastle, you *wouldn't!*" Miss Judson cried, eyes blazing.

"Well, I'm not saying I believe it," he said. Peony bounded onto the tabletop, one white paw atop the magazine before him. "Don't *all* of you gang up on me!"

I tried to be rational. "Either Mr. Hamm placed these or someone else did." I combed through the collection. "They all go to the same address, Forty-four High Street, Suite B."

"There you go," Father said. "Easy to find out more. It says inquire at that address. So, inquire."

I seized upon this. "It's just downtown. We could be there and back by lunchtime."

"Well, now, I meant you could *write*," Father said.

"No time like the present, Counselor," Miss Judson said cheerily. "Writing will take days. Myrtle and I will ride down and *inquire* right after breakfast."

I hadn't *got* any breakfast, but before Father could change his mind, I leaped from my chair, magazines in hand, and did my very best to sweep out of the dining room on Miss Judson's trail, brisk and composed and purposeful.

つめ

We did not, in fact, set out to Inquire Within straightaway.

"Don't bother getting dressed yet." Miss Judson steered me into the schoolroom. "We have business to attend to."

"What *sort* of business?" So far the Apology did not appear to be forthcoming.

"Your father forgot to mention this in the excitement just now, but he would like you to do something for him." She pointed me toward the fireplace-end of the room. "You won't like it."

"*You* don't seem to like it. Wait—it's about Priscilla, isn't it?"

"I'm afraid so, yes. Your father would like you to invite her to tea."

I groaned. That was worse than the Tedious Girls! I had a sudden image of Priscilla and her pink frills invading my schoolroom, exclaiming over our toast in her ridiculous American accent.

Miss Judson just carried on as if it weren't a disaster. "This will be your first Event, so we'll want to make a good showing of it."

"I don't want to plan Events!" I was ninety-nine percent certain Billy Garrett had never caught a murderer at a tea party. "She *poisoned* five people!"

"Well," Miss Judson said, "this would be just the chance to catch her out at it, don't you think?"

I regarded her, eyes Peony-narrow. "A trap?"

"If you wish to think of it that way." She turned to the desk behind her, where her skirts had concealed a large white carton. She withdrew the lid with a flourish. *"Et voilà!"*

"What in the world is that?" I beheld the contents with the expression most people give viscera. It was an atrocity of pale blue silk and lace, afflicted with bows and buttons and writhing tentacles of ribbon. I backed up lest the thing spring from the box to attack me.

Miss Judson shook it out. It was, if possible, even worse in life-sized three dimensions. Peony hissed at it. "This is a tea gown," Miss Judson said—voice betraying a disturbing lack of horror. "This is what the hostess wears to receive friends for tea."

I struggled for something tactful to say. "I'm sure it will look very . . . lacy on you."

She suppressed a smile. "Oh, no, my dear. This is what *you* will be wearing."

"No."

The smile grew wider. "Oh, yes."

"It's not my size," I said hopefully.

"Easily fixed." She produced her sewing basket—that dastardly weapon. "Your father gave permission to alter one of your mother's gowns. I found this in the attic."

"My mother *never* wore such a thing."

She rummaged through the tissue in the carton. "Perhaps not. It appears to have been a gift from Aunt Helena."

Better and better. "*Why* must I do this?"

Miss Judson sounded gleefully sinister. "Remember yesterday's debacle? This is your penance."

⁓

Twenty minutes later, after a hot, itchy, and hazardous ordeal called a "fitting," I pedaled furiously after Miss Judson into town, where we pulled our bicycles up to 44 High Street. The summer air was thick and humid, and the smell of the nearby brewery had settled over the day in a yeasty fug. "You might have been more careful with the pins," I grumbled, rubbing my arm.

But Miss Judson was distracted by the matter at hand. "Myrtle, look!" She pointed to the round green awning above the doorway, and eagerly pawed through her sketchbook.

"Your sketch!" I cried, recognizing it. "Ghastly yellow tartan jacket!" This is where she'd drawn Cousin Giles arguing with someone the morning of the flower show.

"And Bowler Hat." She frowned as we chained the bicycles to a stair rail. "What do you suppose it means?"

The bell on a shop door jangled. "Maybe Mr. Bowler Hat works here."

"Is he our nefarious flower seller?" She quirked a smile. "I wonder if anyone's ever said *that* before."

"He could have placed the notices for Priscilla. I saw him with her that night, remember?"

"Good thinking. When was the first advertisement dated?"

The earliest of the magazines Mr. Blakeney had sent was from May. "*Before* Priscilla came back to England." I sighed. "While she was still busy poisoning widowers in Boston."

Miss Judson eyed me sidelong, and we edged over to let a man and his dog pass by. "I need a better look at that article you found," she admitted. "But I see no reason an enterprising young woman couldn't have managed both crimes."

"Exactly! She started selling flowers even before her aunt died." Bowler Hat must be a local agent—an Accessory—to handle affairs here in town while Priscilla was still overseas poisoning Boston businessmen.

"And *there* is your motive. Just as your father said this morning. Miss Wodehouse discovered the duplicity, and Priscilla had to silence her."

"Perfect! Let's go prove it." The quicker Priscilla

was in jail, the quicker we could forget about this tea party nonsense.

Number 44 housed a shipping firm called Garrow & Sons (Suite A) and New Century Press (Suite B). Miss Judson cracked the door, which gave a tremendous unhappy squeal, and a quantity of dust showered down on her hat.

"That," she said, brushing off the brim, "does not inspire confidence."

Neither did the interior. Despite its High Street address, the building was dim and dingy inside, with a shade pulled down over Garrow & Sons' window, and a dark, narrow staircase leading upstairs. There was a burnt-out electric bulb at the top of the stairs and what looked to be a month's worth of newspaper bundles stacked up on the landing outside the office door.

"Is this what the black market looks like, do you suppose?" Miss Judson whispered. "I was expecting, I'm not sure . . . armed ruffians guarding the place."

"You're enjoying this!"

"Well, it's not a morning teaching geography."

A peeling card pasted on the door identified the offices of New Century Press, Est. 1878. Why did that sound so familiar? We squeezed through, into a little anteroom clad entirely in unpolished wood paneling. I sneezed, waking a cloud of dust, as Miss Judson strode to the counter and gave the bell a sound slap.

In the corner was another untidy stack of what I presumed were the publisher's wares. "I knew it!" I cried. "They publish the Billy Garrett stories!"

"You don't say." Miss Judson drew out a few samples. "*Terror o' the Main, The Lady Highwayman* . . . Refined literature, indeed. Why are they placing personal notices about flowers? It *is* a front!"

"I don't think so." From the pile of penny dreadfuls, I'd unearthed a copy of *Hyde's Horticultural Almanac.* "They do these, too, I guess."

"Is there one in there?" She meant another Redgraves advert. We leafed through a page or two, but our search was interrupted by the answer to our bell. A bespectacled man with a crabbed walk sidled through the inner door and blinked at us in surprise.

"We gave at Christmas," he snapped, and turned back, waving us away.

"No, wait!" I cried—but Miss Judson was quicker, lunging across the counter and grabbing the man by his shirtsleeve. I stared at her in wonder.

"My good man," she said smoothly, as if she hadn't just accosted a perfect stranger in public, "we are here about the advertisements for Redgraves lilies."

"What's that, now?"

I produced one of the magazines Mr. Blakeney had sent. "It says inquire here if we're interested. We're *very* interested."

He took the magazine and frowned at it. At us. "I can see that," he said. "Most people *write*. But I suppose I could take a message if he comes in again."

"Oh, that won't do at all," Miss Judson said, voice sunny. "We want to know who placed the notices."

"No idea," Crab said. We waited and he reluctantly added, "They come by post, with payment. Do you want to leave that message or not?"

I started to shake my head, but Miss Judson's sunny smile grew. "Better than that, we'll order some." She took the paper and pen from Crab's hand and waggled her fingers expectantly at me. I handed her the magazine, and she tore the advertisement right out.

"Miss," I hissed, "those are *expensive*."

She ignored me, swiftly filling out the order form. "Envelope?" Her voice was commanding, and Crab hastened to find one for her. She produced her reticule and withdrew a startling sum of money, which she sealed safely inside with her order. "You'll be *sure* he gets this?"

"Yes, ma'am. We're a respectable operation." He seemed concerned Miss Judson might return should he fail to follow her instructions to the letter.

"Very good," she said. "And I'd appreciate it if you didn't tell him who was inquiring."

"I don't know who's inquiring," he grumbled. "But suit yourself." He shoved the envelope into a cubby in the counter and turned back, about to disappear into the print shop once more.

"Wait!" I called. "When does the next Billy Garrett story come out?"

Here he softened just a little. "Oh, a fan, are you? Well, I'm sorry to tell you, we've seen the last of our intrepid boy detective."

I felt like he'd slapped the breath right out of me. "What?"

"The author died."

I wanted to sit down. "What? When?"

"About a year ago. We had somebody take over for him, but it's not working out. The last few numbers..." He shrugged.

"Oh," I said, deflated. "I liked them." They'd been cleverer than usual, twisting round to ingenious solutions relying more on plot and character than brash action. And they'd featured Billy's sweetheart Violetta in some quite daring adventures of her own as well.

He was nodding. "Well, there you go," he said, as if that explained everything. "Oh–" He came back into the office and dug through a stack of papers piled high behind the desk. "The author sent us another story. We can't use it, but maybe you'll like it."

He handed me a stained and rumpled manuscript, with a cover page that read:

MABEL CASTLETON,
GIRL DETECTIVE
by Edgar Corey

25

QUESTIONED
DOCUMENTS

> Although a crime like murder may have many motives,
> the motive behind forgery is almost always greed.
>
> —H. M. Hardcastle, *Principles of Detection*

"I cannot believe you fail to see the resemblance." Miss Judson wheeled her bicycle along as we walked back up High Street. There was entirely too much glee in the way she skipped past puddles in the roadway.

"I don't know what you mean," I muttered. The manuscript the printing agent had given me was balanced against my handlebars, and I was relying on Miss Judson to navigate as I read it aloud. I tugged my straw boater lower on my head, though it didn't come close to shielding my face from passersby.

"*Mabel Castleton?* Girl detective? Daughter of a Magistrate in the charming hamlet of Swinebridge?" Miss Judson gave a flourish with her arm to encompass the charming hamlet of Swinburne. "With her faithful feline sidekick Petunia?"

"Don't forget her nanny, Miss Goodson, the stuffy schoolmarm!" I snapped.

She let out a whoop, startling a flock of pigeons. "She was the best part!"

"Are you quite finished?"

"Oh, my word. I hope I end up being the murderer. Are you sure you didn't write this? It's frightfully clever."

"How can you say that? And *frightful* is the right word! The thing is mortifying. Maybe *you* wrote it."

"You can't think *I'd* do something like this," Miss Judson said. "For one thing, I haven't the time. For another, I'd give you a much nobler name. Like . . . Laurel . . ."

I liked that. It was subtler, for one. I stood a little straighter. "Thank you."

". . . Softcastle," she concluded, before collapsing in snickers once more.

"This isn't funny!" I steered my bicycle to a stop under an eave. "For one thing, it's libel. Secondly, just because the first publisher wouldn't print this, it doesn't mean someone else won't. Do you think Father will find it so amusing?"

She finally sobered. "I suppose you have a point. But we have bigger issues at hand, remember. The–"

"Don't say tea party!" I'd had my fill of that subject this morning.

"Adverts for Redgraves flowers, and who wrote *those*." Jauntily, Miss Judson propped a booted foot against the brick building. "What did we learn?"

"Not much." The entire errand to Inquire Within at the print shop had been an unqualified disaster, if you asked me.

"Stop sulking. Of course we did. We know that the notices were placed by post, and that there have been several orders already."

"None of which helps us prove Priscilla is involved." As I said that, realization struck me. "Oh, we're idiots! Where's that letter I pulled from Priscilla's wastebasket?" I thrust the manuscript into Miss Judson's hands and dived into my satchel.

"Do you care to explain that, or do I even want to know?"

"This!" I resurfaced, brandishing the crumpled paper in one hand, my magnifier in the other. I spread the letter flat against the brick wall. "Look!"

Miss Judson squeezed beside me so we could both see through the lens. "You're comparing the type! Well done, Mabel." Ignoring my scowl, she pulled out the first page of *Mabel Castleton* and held it up for comparison.

"Look at the name, here." I pointed to the typed *Mrs. Evalina Scharpe* on the letter begging forgiveness from her (shortly-to-be-poisoned) paramour. Larger-than-life letters leaped up at us, grainy and bold against the fibrous texture of the paper. "The lowercase *a*'s are squashed, see?" The serif of the *a* was too close to the rest of the letter. "And here, in the story . . ." There on the front page, three squashed lowercase *a*'s.

"Wait, I don't see anything." Miss Judson peered in closer. I also pointed out how the period at the end of each sentence was slightly elevated above its line of text, as if punctuating the writer's guilt. She breathed in sharply. "My word."

"Not so funny now, is it?"

A smartly dressed older couple strolled past on the pavement, and Miss Judson pulled me closer to the wall. "Don't be cheeky." Her voice was a stern whisper. "What are we going to do?"

"Tell Father, of course!"*

"I see," said Miss Judson. "How do you foresee that playing out, exactly?"

"We will ride straight over to his office and present our evidence."

"And our case is what?"

I glared at her. "What do you mean? Priscilla's written a horrible story about us and tried to sell it to

---

* I was *not* whispering.

a publisher, while she's also placing adverts for stolen Redgraves flowers in magazines all over town, and she poisoned four people in America!" My voice hit a strident pitch—I saw the older couple turn back with disapproving frowns—and I struggled to restrain myself.

Miss Judson raised a single eyebrow as if to indicate I should continue. But I'd given her everything I had on our culprit. "Oh, and she murdered Miss Wodehouse."

"Aha."

"What does that mean?"

"It means I'd like you to take a moment to hear yourself. You sound hysterical and ridiculous."

"I do not! I am *never* hysterical!" I stamped my foot.

She stepped forward with a neat swish of skirt. "Let us keep walking. You have just made four quite disparate accusations against a woman to whom your father has grown rather attached. Your own reputation of late is not at its most unimpeachable. Kindly imagine, for a moment, how your father may receive this news."

"You kept saying to wait until we had more evidence," I said. "Now we do." I waved the manuscript at her.

"But evidence of what? A fertile imagination?"

"Miss Judson!" I wailed. "Language!"

She gave me a mild smile.

"Fine. What do *you* suggest?"

Miss Judson gave her bicycle bell a cheery jangle. "I suppose we shall just have to wait and see what comes of Inquiring Within."

We didn't have to wait long (although the brief delay tried everyone's patience. I had to write lines again. In Greek.*). Monday evening, Miss Judson sallied into the kitchen, bearing a lumpy parcel bound in green-striped twine, a gold seal proclaiming its importance. I was helping Cook peel potatoes but had been distracted by one that had started to sprout.

"No dissection at my table." Cook swatted me lightly on the back of my head, barely more than a friendly Peony-tap.

Father was just as eager to see what the post had brought as we were, and soon we were all assembled around Cook's worktable.

"If this is going to be regular," Cook said, "I'd appreciate a warning."

Father looked around with approval. "It's not half cozy in here," he remarked. "We may well make it a tradition, Cook. Prepare yourself for a weekly onslaught of Hardcastles."

"Get on with you," she said, settling herself into a corner by her archnemesis (the hob) to Observe. Peony sat against Cook's skirts like her miniature, right down to their matching white bib-aprons.

* Οὔτε γελοῖα ἔσομαι οὔτε μανοῦμαι

"So," said Father in his deep, resonant Prosecutor's Voice. "These are the Notorious Lilies of Redgraves."

"The Gilded Slipper lilies," Miss Judson corrected. "Go on," she urged me. "Unwrap them."

"They're yours," I offered generously. "You ordered them."

"Well, if we're arguing technicalities, then *technically* they belong to your father. He paid for them."

"How *much* did I pay?" he inquired.

Miss Judson smiled her secretive smile. "Let's just call it an investment in Myrtle's study of jurisprudence." She handed him the letter knife. "Mr. Prosecutor?"

"In that case," he said, "it seems only right for Myrtle to do the honors."

I fairly snatched the letter knife from him; this was getting out of hand. I realized they were engaged in a sort of ritual flirtation, but we had Evidence waiting! Carefully, I first examined the parcel. "Miss Judson, will you please take notes?"

"An honor indeed," I heard her say, but it sounded a bit muttery.

Father watched, chin in hand and elbows on the table like a little boy.

"The parcel is approximately nine inches by twelve inches by an inch and three-quarters deep. The post-mark is from Swinburne, so that doesn't help. Too many people have handled the item for finger marks to be of any value—"

"If indeed they *are* of any value," Father said. "The jury would think I was barmy if I started talking to them about fingerprints on the post."

I glared at him. "What about on knives?"

"Back to the evidence at hand," Miss Judson interjected. "And for what it's worth, I am of a mind with Myrtle on this. The literature from India and Japan on the subject of fingerprints is fascinating."

"Is it?" Father regarded Miss Judson curiously. I focused on my parcel. The address was in plain block capitals, making the handwriting all but useless. I carefully wriggled the string free, and the paper wrapping sprang open like petals blooming before our eyes, revealing the Famous Redgraves Specimens.

They were bulbs, of course; a mature plant would not fit or keep well scrunched up inside a parcel and shoved through a postbox. For a moment I just looked at them.

Father broke the silence. "Is that what you expected?"

"I'm not sure." With the tip of the letter knife, I prodded the clump of bulbs apart. They *were* lily bulbs—they had the interesting cabbagey shape of cloves clustered together, a tendril of roots twisted up below. And there was a distinct yellowish hue to their flesh, as one might expect (for no scientific reason, mind you) of *Lilium wodehouseia* 'Gilded Slipper.'

"There's no way to say whether these came from

Redgraves, let alone what they'll be when they bloom. But they're so—"

"Unimpressive?" Father offered.

"Shriveled?" suggested Miss Judson.

"Hmph," said Cook. "What rubbish. Redgraves lilies my foot! Minerva Wodehouse never grew those spindly little spuds, her."

We all turned to stare at her.

"Well, look at 'em!" She quit her post in the corner to come scold the poor things further. "All limp and scrawny. I'd be ashamed if those came out of my garden, and I'm not a patch on Miss W. You mark my words. That's a fraud."

There was something to what Cook was saying. The product advertised on the label—the huge white lily in all its gilded glory—certainly did not *look* as though it stood a chance of emerging from the lumpy, waxen knobs spread in their dusty mulchy bag. "But bulbs do look like this," I said tentatively. "You can't always tell what they'll be when they're grown."

"Hear, hear," said Father, for some reason. Miss Judson coughed politely.

"Not these," Cook insisted. She seized one from the table, brushing the remaining dirt from its skin. "Oh, it's all right, I suppose," she said. "And it'll probably give off *a* lily or two—with some work. But not a prizewinner. What did you pay for these, Mr. H?"

"I—uh, Miss Judson?"

"Five guineas ten," she said, and we all turned and gaped at her. Father may have choked a little. That was almost as much as a new microscope! That was more than Cook's *wages*. Cook clapped a hand to her throat.

"Well, it's not my place to say, Mr. Hardcastle," she said, her tone suggesting she felt entirely free to say it anyway, "but you've been taken in. You being the Law and all, I think you should march back to whoever sold you this rubbish and demand your money back. Five guineas," she muttered. "I'll give you five guineas' worth of roots and onions from the compost heap, and have my retirement!" She was still shaking her head as she stalked back to the hob and savagely attacked it with her spanner.

I held the dry little lump of bulb in my hand. It suddenly felt strangely heavy—heavier than its own weight would suggest. Dimly I was aware of Miss Judson and Father still discussing the price, but all I could hear was Cook muttering, "Five guineas, my retirement."

"That's it!" I said, but nobody heard me. I stared at the bulb, realization spreading like a pool of blood. Miss Wodehouse's killer had planned this all along—a fraud. The fabled Gilded Slipper had never been found after all. But someone wanted the world to *think* it had and was selling fake bulbs with Miss Wodehouse's name on them. Until they were caught.

"She found out," I said, softly, amid the hubbub of the kitchen sounds and chatter. "She found out they were selling fake Redgraves flowers, and they killed her."

Father was still talking about fingerprints, but Miss Judson put up a forestalling hand. "She was attacked among the *real* lilies," she reminded me.

My mind chewed on this. "Maybe they planned to steal real Redgraves bulbs to sell. But she caught them at it."

"There are still adverts out," said Miss Judson. "And orders coming in."

"And going out, evidently," Father muttered.

"But no real Redgraves lilies to fill them," I said.

"Hence the fakes."

"Which *someone* is still selling." I looked up at them. "Someone who's *not* in jail right now. This proves it's not Mr. Hamm!"

Father sat back heavily and looked at me. Then at the Decidedly Not Redgraves Lilies (per our very own household flower judge). "And we have no idea who sent these."

"No," I admitted. "But they must come from Redgraves." This *had* to be the work of Priscilla and Giles!

Father was shaking his head. "You've just convincingly proven to me that they certainly do not."

"But—" My voice broke off. He was right. Fake Redgraves bulbs had no logical reason to have been sent from Redgraves.

"And you weren't able to learn the identity of the advertiser from the publishing house?"

"No," I said. "The notices come by post, with payment already."

"It's probably the same at every other publication, too," Miss Judson put in.

"But someone collected your inquiries. There must be some way to get in touch with the advertiser."

I noted the way Father avoided saying "culprit" or "suspect." Next he'd start saying "alleged," and we'd be done for. I had to do something before this whole summation fell apart.

"We paid a guinea apiece for those bulbs," I said. "How many orders would they have to fill before making enough of a fortune?"

"Before they were satisfied?" Miss Judson looked thoughtful. "Probably never. They'll keep at it until somebody catches them."

"Or till those scrawny lilies start sproutin' up in the spring," Cook grunted from the hob.

"They've already killed to protect the scheme," I added. "We have to stop them!"

"Hold on now," Father said, holding up a hand. He stood up and collected the parcel—wrapping, twine, scrawny bulbs, and all. "You've all done enough. I will take it from here."

"*We* found those!" I cried. "That's *our* evidence!"

"Myrtle." Miss Judson's voice was gentle but final. "Your father's right. If those bulbs are the motive for murder, it's time to hand them over to the authorities. But I am *certain* your father *will* keep you apprised of *any* further developments in the case. *Right*, Mr. Hardcastle?"

"Hmm? Oh, right. Of course." He gave me a faint half smile, but I could tell his thoughts had gone far away from me again. "Good show, girls." He patted me on the head—but this time I didn't feel proud.

I felt thwarted.

I kicked my way back up to the schoolroom. Peony followed. She sprang up beside me on the workbench with a worried *mrrow?* and butted me in the hand with her head. Distracted, I scratched under her chin.

Something else was still amiss, aside from Father's seizing control of things at the most inopportune moment possible. The purchase from Inquire Within had produced counterfeit lily bulbs. Which meant that Miss Wodehouse's famed Gilded Slipper lily probably didn't exist after all, and we were chasing around in circles after nothing.

"*No*," said Peony.

I looked at her, heart thumping.

"You know, don't you?" I said. "You *know* where the lilies are." Oh, "Clever Myrtle" indeed. The answer had been staring us in the face—literally—for a week now. Peony knew the truth. She'd shown us already. There *were* still lilies growing somewhere at Redgraves.

I bent down, face-to-face with my faithful feline sidekick. "You know where the Gilded Slippers are, don't you?"

Peony purred and purred.

"And you're not telling, are you?"

Peony looked smug. *"No."*

26

DISPUTE PENDING ELSEWHERE

Corpus delicti, Latin for "body of the crime," refers to the fundamental indications that any crime has been committed, such as a dead body with a knife in its back or a missing person and a ransom note.

–H. M. Hardcastle, *Principles of Detection*

This wasn't the time to announce Peony's discovery to Father. Who knew what his next move would be? Seizing possession of all of Redgraves and making sure I never managed to get over there ever again? The knowledge that the lilies were right next door and I couldn't get to them was more than tantalizing. It was agonizing.

Don't go catchin' lily fever, lass.

Mr. Hamm's advice. I clutched Peony tight and tried to take it to heart. But what if those same lilies could help free Mr. Hamm? I *had* to find them. At least before Priscilla did.

The next morning, I ran into Father on his way to work. He was examining his reflection in the secretary mirror, scrutinizing his whiskers and his eyes. It looked like he was preening, which was impossible—so he must have been checking for signs of poison. He seemed fine to me, except for the obvious delirium surrounding Priscilla.

He spotted me. "What's that you have?" Miss Judson had sent me to fetch the hateful tea gown, which had been pressed by Cook.

I showed him a tentacle of ribbon. "I think it was Mum's?" His frown deepened, only confirming my suspicions. "I knew it," I muttered. Miss Judson had made up that story about Mum to get me into this stupid dress. Then I recalled that it was all Father's idea. "I'm wearing it when Miss Wodehouse comes to tea."

"Miss Judson said you were planning the menu. It's all finger sandwiches and clotted cream, then?"

I tried hard not to scowl. "In parts of China they eat fried cockroaches as a delicacy."

Father nodded solemnly. "Good luck finding roaches *here*. Cook wouldn't allow it."

He was in a good mood, so I braved a legal consultation. "Have you decided what to do about the lily bulbs?" I felt my brow furrow, preparing for counter-arguments even before he'd spoken.

He straightened his already straight tie. "I want a look at this newspaper office. They may be more forthcoming when a fellow shows up with the might of the whole Magistrate's Office behind him."

"Could I come with you?" I'd abandon my lily quest in a heartbeat for the chance to accompany Father to question a suspect.

With a fond smile, he said, "I wish you could, but the might of the Magistrate's Office would be somewhat diminished by that lacy blue thing, I'm afraid." He reached for the tea gown with tentative fingers, a look of horror on his face that made me giggle.

He grew sober first. "And then I need to have a little chat with my Opposing Counsel about any knowledge his client might have had of this scheme."

"Mr. Ambrose?" I said. "Do you think he knew anything about it?"

"Let's hope he can shed some light on this. The Magistrate's Trial is in a few days, and I need to be sure I know everything before I stroll in and accuse Mr. Hamm of murder."

I felt a desperate pang. I *had* to let him know about Priscilla! I fidgeted, shifting my weight from one foot to the other. "I need to tell you something else," I said finally.

"What's that?" Father consulted his pocket watch with a little frown. "Tonight. When I get back. We'll talk then."

"I'll wait up."

❧

As soon as Father left, I raced upstairs, tossed the tea gown onto my bed, and rejoined my cohort in the schoolroom. Miss Judson was at her desk, jotting notes under the dubious supervision of Peony. Eager to get to Redgraves, I breathlessly explained my deduction to Miss Judson, outlining my plan to resume our search of the property, this time with feline assistance.

Miss Judson looked unconvinced. And, in fairness, so did Peony.

"She's not a truffle pig," Miss Judson said. "How will she know what you're looking for? She might just as easily lead you to her secret stash of *Rodentia*."

"*Mrow!*"

"She's already found them at least twice. Cats are creatures of habit," I added, with more confidence than was scientifically warranted. "We'll simply follow her."

"Didn't you try that before?"

"I didn't know where she was going then. Now we do. Come on," I urged. "You'll need your gloves and your measuring tape—and don't we have a spade somewhere?"

She lifted her hands. "Oh, no. You're on your own this time."

I dropped my satchel, dumbfounded. "Don't you want to find the lilies?"

"Naturally, I'm curious," she said. "And I do think you have a sound argument for Peony having discovered them."

"So?"

"So, I think you stand a better chance of finding them without me."

I stared at her. "How can you say that?"

"You and Priscilla already have a rapport. She'll let you look. I don't think she'd be as kindly disposed to 'the help' coming along for the party."

"It's not a *rapport*." I sputtered like it was the name of some contagion. "And you're not 'the help'!"

Miss Judson would not be moved. "You go ahead," she said with finality. "I have work here."

"You're just doing tea party things," I scoffed.

"The toils of the martyr." She gave an elaborate sigh and shooed me away.

She had at least provided a believable pretense for my visit. I did have to issue Priscilla an invitation to tea tomorrow, and paying calls on the neighbors was a time-honored pastime for Young Ladies of Quality. Miss Judson had detailed this social ritual thusly: I would call at Priscilla's house, at an hour I would be hopeful she was not at home, at which point I could leave my card (the invitation, rather) with her maid, so that Priscilla could return the call at an hour *I* would not be home, and thereby we could avoid seeing each other altogether.

"There's a knack to it," she'd explained.

Today, however, what Peony and I really needed was an invitation *inside* the house, so I had to hope against hope* that she would, in fact, be home.

She was not. Or, just as likely, she was pretending and had merely instructed Trudy to say she was out (a variation on the tradition). At any rate, Trudy was a frustratingly responsible housemaid and would not let me inside while her mistress was out. Even my excuse of fetching things for Peony met with no success.

Peony rubbed against Trudy's skirts, letting out piteous meows upon which Trudy took no pity whatsoever. "There's bowls out back," she said firmly. "You can have those."

Undaunted, I wandered round to the conservatory side of the house, frowning up at Miss Wodehouse's rooms. Holding my hands before me, I gazed through the window of my spread fingers, urging the shape of her balcony or the number of windows to suggest some clue to the lilies' whereabouts. But if there was

---

* a phrase whose meaning becomes clear only in such circumstances

anything up there, wouldn't I have seen it already, in my many hours of Observation of this precise location? No, the Gilded Slipper lilies were somewhere *inside* Redgraves, and no amount of studying the exterior would produce them.

"Where did she hide them?" I said. "Do you know, Peony?"

Peony claimed she did *not* know by focusing intently on a sprig of privet.

"Liar." With an all-too-familiar thwarted sigh, I stooped for Peony's bowls, which Trudy had thoughtfully filled with cream and kippers, when I spotted something strange. The climbing rose that sprawled up the side of the house was dying, all blackened leaves and skeletal thorns surrounding withered buds that had never bloomed. It hadn't been like that a few days ago. I gave it a closer examination but found no evidence of aphids, black spot, powdery mildew, or any of the other problems Mr. Hamm had warned me about. Maybe something was wrong with the roots. I followed the dead stem to the ground.

The earth at the base of the plant was broken up and soft, as if recently worked. I frowned. There was no reason for anybody to be digging around the rosebush—particularly in the absence of the gardener. Using the tiny spade from my collection kit, I scraped at the soil. The metal blade clinked against something hard. Eagerly, I dug deeper and unearthed—not bone, alas, but something nearly as interesting—a cold cylinder of glass and metal. I sat back on my heels with a gasp.

It was a syringe. The type to give injections with, like digitalis. And it was buried right outside Miss Wodehouse's back door, with enough haste and carelessness to break the roots on her rosebush.

I should leave it here.

I should leave it here and fetch the police and let them see the evidence in situ.

But Priscilla could be back at any moment, and Trudy knew I was out here. Priscilla might see the disturbed earth and instantly realize I'd discovered where she'd hidden the syringe after dispatching her aunt. I withdrew my hankie from my sleeve, gingerly wrapped the syringe in it, and carefully but hastily ferried it right back home to Miss Judson, Peony springing like a shot ahead of me.

"What is it?" Miss Judson asked, after I'd rattled off the explanation of how we'd gone to Redgraves to invite Priscilla to tea and/or search for the lilies and accidentally come home with the murder weapon instead. "I mean, besides *not* being the Gilded Slipper lily?"

"It's a syringe," I said.

"Well, I can see that." She gave it a grave look. "I can't think of a respectable reason to bury a syringe outside your back door."

"Why bury it at all?" I said. "And why so close to the house? Why not throw it into the compost heap, or the sewer, or just put it back where you got it, no one the wiser?"

"Are you being Socratic?"

"This is Priscilla's doing," I said. "This proves it. She's probably disposed of dozens of murder weapons and just got careless."

"She wasn't expecting Myrtle Hardcastle, Girl Detective." Miss Judson turned the syringe over thoughtfully. "Why digitalis, though? The other cases were arsenic, right?"

"Maybe it's easier to get arsenic in America." In England, arsenic sold for household use was dyed blue to avoid confusion with innocent white powders like flour and sugar. "Or maybe her other victims were younger—people unlikely to have heart attacks out of the blue."

"Maybe," Miss Judson said. "Where did she get the digitalis, though?"

"You can grow it in your backyard. She wouldn't even need a chemist's. Can we tell Father *now*?" I said. "We don't have equipment to test this for digitalis." But I was already uncovering the microscope to see if there were traces of anything suspicious (like blood) on the needle.

Miss Judson paused a long moment. "Yes, I think we should," she finally said.

⁓

Father hadn't returned by dinner, by which time I was feeling Exceptionally Irrepressible. Who knew that being an Investigator involved so much intolerable *waiting*? Preliminary tests on the syringe had been disappointing; it was caked with too much dirt to make out anything useful, which left me nothing at all to do except sulk.

"Can't we go down to his office in town?" I pleaded.

Miss Judson took an entry from Peony's lexicon. "No."

"But—"

"No."

I ground my peas into my plate with the back of my spoon. "Should we take the syringe to the police?"

Miss Judson eyed me over the edge of her glass. "Is that a serious question? Or an excuse to have me escort you into town?"

I gave her a hopeful look. "Can't it be both?"

She rubbed the bridge of her nose. "It's been a trying day," she said. "Perhaps we ought to have an early night." Which was just about the *worst* suggestion Miss Judson had ever made.

I sat at my window for hours that night, face pressed against the glass, watching for Father's return.

It never came.

I strained into the darkness, hoping to catch the ringing bell of a late tram or footsteps clipping down the street, but the only sound out there was an unconcerned trill of crickets. Father sometimes worked late and slept at the club (if we had a *telephone*, he could *call* and let us *know* he wouldn't be returning), but he'd picked an inconvenient night for it. This waiting was like an itch all over the *inside* of my body, and I'd have to claw my own skin off if he didn't get back soon.

Perhaps something had gone wrong. I tugged the quilt closer to my chin, remembering when Mum was sick–the clutch of fear in my belly every time she coughed or rustled in her sleep or didn't get up on time in the morning. She'd always laugh when I came running to check, and tell me nothing was going to happen to her.

She'd been wrong. People got sick, poisoned, run down by coaches, knocked senseless and thrown into ditches–the newspapers and Father's caseloads were full of such events, all the time. I pulled my knees up to my chest, uprooting Peony, who gave a sleepy protest and stalked away. Why was he so late?

At last! Hoofbeats clattered into Gravesend Close, and a closed carriage pulled up to the streetlamp outside. I was starting to climb out of bed when the carriage door opened.

And Priscilla climbed out.

My heart lurched. Without so much as a word to the driver, Priscilla hastened right past my window, never looking up, and disappeared into the dark clutches of Redgraves. The carriage rolled away again, rattling into the night.

༄

The next morning, Father still wasn't back. I checked his bedroom for the usual untidy rumpling of his bedclothes (even when he tried to make the bed), but it was Cook-neat from yesterday.

"He must have slept at the club and gone straight to the office," Miss Judson conjectured. I was not reassured, despite having come to the same conclusion. "Come along. You've work to do. Priscilla arrives at four."

"Don't remind me," I grumbled, following her down to breakfast in a cross stupor. Cook had already laid out the newspaper at Father's place, and I caught a glimpse of the headlines. Hand shaking, I picked up the paper to show Miss Judson.

"Does that say break-in?" Miss Judson leaned over me. "At Garrow and Sons? Isn't that—"

"Forty-four High Street, Suite A." My voice wobbled. "Downstairs from Priscilla's publisher." I met her eyes. "Where Father went yesterday."

She considered this. "That's an awfully big coincidence, don't you think?"

"No," I said, crushing the edges of the paper. "I don't think it's a coincidence at all."

"Nor do I. Get your things. We're going downtown."

27

IN ABSENTIA

> Missing persons cases are among the most challenging
> to Investigate. Under what circumstances did the subject
> disappear, and did he do so of or against his own will?
>
> –H. M. Hardcastle, *Principles of Detection*

We abandoned our bicycles at the cab stand across
from the courthouse, where an ordinary morning
bustle of people congregated on the wide steps. I was
halfway through the crowd, Miss Judson close behind,
when a familiar voice hailed me.

"Stephen!" Mr. Blakeney, Mr. Ambrose's clerk,
jogged down the steps, juggling an armload of files.
"Did you get my package?"

"Yes, thank you." I glanced anxiously toward the
courthouse doors, but made myself take a moment for
Mr. Blakeney. "Father's investigating now," I said, trying to keep any doubt from my voice.

"On the trail of notorious garden cataloguers!" Mr. Blakeney caught my nervous gaze. "If you don't mind my saying so, Stephen, you look out of sorts this morning."

"I have to talk to my father," I said. "Have you seen him today?"

"He's not in," he said, showing me his armload of files. "I was supposed to drop all this off at the Prosecutor's office, but the door's locked and his clerk hasn't seen him all morning."

The knot of worry I'd shoved down my throat became a cold pit in my belly. "He left for work yesterday morning and never came home."

Mr. Blakeney's cheery face grew sober. "That is odd. Have you checked his club?"

"He was planning to talk to Mr. Ambrose," I said. "Didn't he come by your office?"

"Not yesterday. And I've been in court all morning. One of Mr. Ambrose's clients was arrested for robbery, and I stood in for the old man."

A spark fired in my cold belly. "What robbery? At Garrow and Sons?"

"I don't know why Ambrose doesn't employ *you*. You're more on top of his cases than we are."

Miss Judson finally elbowed her way through the crowd. "Myrtle, look!" She'd bought a newspaper extra, and on the front page was a "mug shot" of the man arrested in the Garrow & Sons robbery.

She flattened the paper, holding it steady against the wind.

"Bowler Hat!" I cried.

"I see you know our illustrious client," Mr. Blakeney said. "He's just going by Donnelly these days."

I'd forgotten that Miss Judson hadn't met Mr. Ambrose's clerk yet. I made the introductions, then explained our previous encounters with this Donnelly fellow, the late-night meeting with Priscilla and his argument with Mr. Northcutt outside Number 44 High Street.

"It explains how he and Cousin Giles know each other," Miss Judson said, "if Giles worked at Bowler Hat's solicitor's office."

Distracted, I nodded. I was looking up the steps again, waiting to see Father emerge. Just because Mr. Blakeney hadn't seen him didn't mean he wasn't in there, safely at work, where he was supposed to be.

But Miss Judson said aloud what I hadn't even let myself think. "This Mr. Donnelly. Does he have any . . . *violent* crimes on his record?"

Mr. Blakeney started. "Wait. You mean, you really *don't* know where Mr. Hardcastle is?"

"It's highly unusual for him to be gone so long without word," Miss Judson said. "If there's *any* light you can shed on the matter, Mr. Blakeney, we would appreciate it."

Mr. Blakeney looked as though he'd like to shove a hand through his hair, but he couldn't reach it with his arms full. "Have you been to the police?"

"I don't think it's that serious!" Miss Judson's voice rang with alarm.

"Come with me," Mr. Blakeney said. "I need to bring these files to Mr. Ambrose at the club. We'll get to the bottom of this."

Gratefully, we followed Mr. Blakeney down two blocks and across the street to the Monarch Club, a handsome brick building with brass fixtures that made it look very grand and gentlemanly. The invisible green door swung open, and someone I did not expect came trotting down the steps, slicking back his oiled hair.

"Cousin Giles!" I cried. "I mean, Mr. Northcutt."

"Well, if it isn't the curious little girl next door." He nodded to my companions. "Blakeney. Miss Governess." They nodded back politely.

"You're a member of this club?" I asked.

"It *is* the only club in town," Mr. Blakeney said under his breath.

Cousin Giles gave a lazy shrug. "The rent's cheap. At least until something better comes along." The way he said that made it plain that "something better" ought to be Redgraves.

"You must have seen her father, Northcutt," Mr. Blakeney put in. "He stayed here last night."

"Mr. Prosecutor? Here last night? I don't think so."
He patted absently at his jacket pockets.

"Oh," I said, unable to keep my disappointment in
check. If he wasn't at work, and he wasn't at the club,
where on earth was he?

"Big day in court, Blakeney?" Giles said. "Defending
Swinburne's criminal element?"

"You would know," Mr. Blakeney said easily.

I wondered what Giles *did* know, and despite my
worry for Father, managed to blurt out, "Do you know
anything about the break-in at the shipping agent's
last night?"

"Only what I read in the papers. Now, let's go see
about your father, eh?" He hooked Miss Judson and
me by the arm and escorted us inside Swinburne's
gentleman's club.

I wasn't sure what to expect. Although Father came
here regularly, I had the vaguest sense of its being—if
not *disreputable*, exactly, at least the sort of place Young
Ladies of Quality should not frequent. Inside, though,
it turned out to be just a sort of grand house, with an
ancient butler who answered the door, a big foyer full
of velvet furniture, and—I shot Miss Judson a Look—a
telephone unit mounted in the front hall.

"Just where are you taking us?" Miss Judson
inquired.

"Yes, that's what I'd like to know."

That booming voice had all of us spin round. "Mr. Ambrose!" Not even trying to be restrained, I flung myself right into his arms.

Or his chest, rather. He just stood there like a block and did not embrace me back. "I say, what is the meaning of this?"

I pulled back. Had I somehow mistaken someone else for my Mr. Ambrose? But no, that was the same familiar whiskered face I'd known all my life—and it was looking thunder at Cousin Giles.

"Ambrose, old boy, the poor kid's looking for her dad. Have you seen him about?"

"What kind of question is that? Are you out of your mind bringing them in here? Get them out of here at once!" Mr. Ambrose turned on his heel, ready to stalk off, and ran right into Mr. Blakeney. "Blakeney! What are *you* doing here?"

"We're all looking for Mr. Hardcastle, sir."

"Mr. Ambrose!" I wailed. "Father's *missing.* He didn't come home last night, and he never made it to work this morning." My voice was shaking like a child's. I bit my lip so hard I tasted blood.

Miss Judson squeezed close to me. "It will be all right," she murmured.

"Listen to your nanny," Giles said. "Mr. Ambrose will sort everything out. Just like he always does. Isn't that right, Mr. Ambrose?"

"That's enough!" Mr. Ambrose rubbed his ruddy face. Why was he so cross today? "Blakeney, fetch my bag, would you? And see that Mr. Northcutt finds his way out."

He nodded. "Stephen, let me know if there's anything else I can do." I gave him a grateful smile. "Northcutt, you heard the man."

Giles gave an exaggerated bow. "Oh, yes, sir. Whatever you say, sir. Right away, sir, Mr. Ambrose, sir."

Miss Judson watched them go with a little frown. "He's rather an unpleasant fellow, isn't he?"

"You have no idea," said Mr. Ambrose. "Such a disgrace. And after everything his aunt did for him." Then he brightened perceptibly. "Now, my girl, what's this about Arthur missing? Nonsense. I just saw him this morning."

All my breath rushed out, and I felt light-headed with relief. "Did he have a chance to speak to you?" I asked. "About Mr. Hamm and the lily bulbs?"

"Hold on, now. You've lost me. Come and sit down. Miss Ada, it's good to see you."

Miss Judson gave her neat nod. "You as well, sir."

Mr. Ambrose led us to a private parlor with walls covered by portraits of important, stern-faced gentlemen, and ushered us into a trio of tufted leather armchairs. The room was dark and gloomy, despite the sickly yellow glow of the gas. I fought the urge to pull my knees up to my chest, and mimicked Miss Judson's straight-backed poise as best I could.

Mr. Ambrose stretched his leg out before him, rubbing his knee. "You'd better start at the beginning. Lily bulbs?"

It all poured out, every bit of it. The adverts and Inquire Within, the order of fake Redgraves bulbs, Father's errand to 44 High Street, the robbery, even Priscilla's stories, culminating (rather accidentally, but I'd got Carried Away at last) in Peony's discovery of the real Gilded Slipper lilies. Mr. Ambrose made me stop and explain things several times, and the very action of giving my testimony calmed me. Even my posture started to feel less strained.

At the end, he sat back in his chair and took off his eyeglasses. "Extraordinary, my dear. Just extraordinary. And you have all of this recorded somewhere?"

"Of course," I said. "And Father knows everything, too." I wasn't sure why I added that, except that someone finally appreciated all the work I'd done, and I didn't want to look like I'd been wildly irresponsible during all of my *extraordinary* deductions. "Is it enough to free Mr. Hamm?"

He was nodding thoughtfully. "Well, it's certainly worth a look, my girl. Have your father send everything to me."

"Whenever I find him," I grumbled. "Is he still

here?" I'd give him a piece of my mind about making Miss Judson and me worry so.

"Here?" Mr. Ambrose frowned.

"You said you saw him this morning."

"At the courthouse, my dear."

I felt suddenly cold despite the stuffy room. "Mr. Blakeney said he didn't show up for Mr. Donnelly's hearing. And neither did you," I added.

He gave a little chuckle. "You've caught me out. Let the lad have a little practice before the Bench. Didn't need an old lawyer getting in his way."

I swung my feet, trying to make sense of this. Why would Father leave the courthouse without going to his hearing? And where had he gone? At least Mr. Ambrose had a good excuse for missing a court date. He might not be worried, but I still was.

"Perhaps we *should* go to the police," I said. "Priscilla might have got to him."

"Now wait a moment, there," Mr. Ambrose said. "You girls are overreacting! Call the police because a man misses an appointment? I thought you had more sense than that." He heaved himself from the chair. "But if it makes you feel any better, I can put out a few calls. You'll have your father home safe and sound tonight. Mark my words."

I wanted to believe him. But in my heart, I knew something was wrong. Father wouldn't simply not come home. Frowning uncertainly, I rose, too. "Thank you, sir." Miss Judson and I said our goodbyes and let ourselves out.

To my surprise, outside the parlor door lurked Cousin Giles, fiddling with his cigarillo case. "The old man help you out?" he said.

"Yes, thank you," I said, though I was more uncertain than ever.

"No problem. You take care, now."

Outside, Miss Judson and I regarded each other. "Do you believe Mr. Ambrose?" I said.

"Which part? The part where your father is safe and sound, or the part where we're overreacting?" She sounded cross, and lines of worry creased her forehead.

I looked out at the street, scowling. My thoughts were tangled round Mr. Ambrose's robust reassurances and the vision of Priscilla slinking home after midnight. Something wasn't right here. "Father wouldn't miss a court date. He just wouldn't."

Miss Judson smoothed the hem of her jacket and smartened her hat a bit more than was necessary. "Well," she said, brisk voice sounding forced. "Where to now?"

There was only one more place I could think to look. "Forty-four High Street," I said.

ल

We headed toward the now familiar green awning. Outside, the building looked just as it had the other day, a narrow stone edifice squeezed between two bigger buildings like the last book crammed onto a shelf. It was painfully quiet, and you could hardly tell there'd been any trouble, except for the CLOSED sign on the front door and the scratches left on the doorjamb by the pry bar.

"They've already replaced the lock," Miss Judson Observed. She tugged on the door, but the new lock held fast. I edged in beside her and pressed my face to the glass, but couldn't see anything beyond Garrow & Sons' shaded door.

I pulled back and looked around. "Maybe there's a back entrance."

"Let's go see."

We walked our bicycles round the corner into a grim, narrow alley, bordered by brick walls on both sides that blotted out the grey sky. Skinny number 44 was easy to pick out from its looming neighbors, and we approached its shallow loading dock. Carriage doors were bound shut with a massive chain that looked undisturbed at any time in the past *century*, let alone last night. I gave it a frustrated yank. It groaned and rattled as it fell back against the wood.

"Nothing," I said, giving in to a groan and rattle myself. "There's nothing here."

"All right," Miss Judson finally said. "We tried."

I scuffed my boots wearily against the dock's wooden planks, feeling the seams clunk through my soles. An out-of-place glint caught my eye—a brass button jammed between the boards.

"What are you doing?"

"Wait." I pried out the button with trembling finger-tips. There was still a bit of gold thread attached. "He was here!" I cried. "Father was right here."

28

SELF-INCRIMINATION

The Latin maxim *nemo gratis mendax* contends "no man lies for free," which asserts that a person with no reason to lie must be telling the truth. However, the converse is also true: someone who lies always has a reason.

–H. M. Hardcastle, *Principles of Detection*

We stared at the button in my hand like it was the last trace of Father. I had to stop my mind from whirring, kicking out all the calamitous ways he might have lost it. "It was loose," I said to reassure myself. "It could have fallen off at any time."

Miss Judson gave me a long look as if to ask whom I was trying to convince. But finally she said, "You're right, of course. I've been threatening to mend that for weeks. But, just for the sake of argument, why might he have lost it *here*? If there was some sort of—

of confrontation, perhaps we ought to speak to the police after all."

"No, Mr. Ambrose is right," I said wretchedly. "Going to the police over a lost button and a missed appointment? They'll think we're hysterical women."

Miss Judson's lips pursed. "I don't think we should wait much longer. If he doesn't turn up by supper, we're calling Inspector Hardy."

We rode home in a furor, faster surely than I've ever pedaled up High Street, past the courthouse and the tramway and the park-that-used-to-be-a-grave-yard and up into Gravesend Close. The name rang oddly at me today, and I tried to ignore its backward clanging: *The end, the graves, are close.* Father was not at work. Father was not at home. Father was not at his club or the office or the courthouse, or at Redgraves. I clamped down my jaw, slammed my bicycle inside the carriage house, and marched into our house. Miss Judson followed worriedly behind.

⁂

Priscilla was late.

We stood in the foyer, both of us dressed for battle. "It's four-oh-two," I said darkly, hands folded against the beribboned skirts of the tea gown.

"You are exceptionally punctual," Miss Judson reminded me. "Priscilla's clocks may be in disagree-ment." Her costume for this affair was a sleek blue skirt and crisp white shirtwaist that set off her deep complexion and made her look unusually stern. She gave no sign that her composure was close to cracking, although I was certain she felt just like I did.

Finally, there came a timorous knock on our front door, and on our stoop stood a wilted-looking Priscilla, wearing a limp white frock nearly as vile as my own.

"Myrtle, dearest!" She thrust an armload of flowers at me. I recoiled.

"Foxgloves?" I choked. "You know they're poisonous."

Priscilla looked wounded. "You weren't planning on eating them, I hope." She smiled uncertainly. "Don't you look . . . um . . . that color suits you."

I resisted the urge to tug on the tea gown's itchy lace collar. "Won't you come into the parlor?"

"Said the spider to the fly!" she twittered.

Bewildered, I looked to Miss Judson for clarification. "A poem," she murmured, relieving Priscilla of the flowers and laying them discreetly on a side table. "About a murderer."*

I gave Miss Judson a Significant Look and fairly shoved them both into the parlor. In the Billy Garrett stories—no. I could no longer take my cues from Billy, now that I knew *she* was behind him. I was on my own now.

* Mary Howitt's 1829 verse "The Spider and the Fly," about a spider who lures a fly to her death at the center of his [*sic*] web

My stomach was a tense knot as I took my seat. Fortunately, I had no intention of consuming anything in Priscilla's vicinity. I dropped a crustless finger sandwich onto her plate. "Did you inherit your mother's talent for the stage?" That was supposed to sound sweet, but it came out rather bilious.

Priscilla blinked at me. "Me? Oh, no. I'd be a hopeless actress."

"You're too modest," Miss Judson said. She stirred her tea with slow, ominous strokes.

Perched on the edge of the hard sofa, the blue silk foaming about my ankles like spittle from a cyanide victim's mouth, I clutched my saucer in a death grip. "Then you must take after your father," I said. "He was a writer?"

"I'm afraid I'm a disappointment to them both," Priscilla said. "I'm not clever like you two."

"But you must have had such an interesting life in America," said Miss Judson. Reaching for the sugar, she had shifted almost imperceptibly closer to Priscilla, and we now had her pinned between us. Our quarry did not seem to notice. She was peering beneath the top layer of bread at the filling on her sandwich. She was wise to be cautious.

"Everyone always thinks that," she said, mouth tight. "But we weren't as glamorous as Mother made us out to be. It took everything I had left, and then some, to scrape together the transatlantic fare to come back home. But no more about that." She plastered her smile on her face once more. "How is Mr. Hardcastle this afternoon?"

I felt the specter of Miss Judson's restraining hand on my arm, although she could not physically reach me. "We were wondering the same thing, Miss Wodehouse."

Priscilla frowned. "I don't understand."

"Hmm," I said. "I'm sure." I reached behind a needle-point cushion and withdrew "Black Widow Poisoner" and *Mabel Castleton*. Like a barrister handing evidence to a witness, I passed the newspaper article to her.

She took it and blanched. "Where did you get this?" she whispered. "Has your father seen it? That's such a dreadful picture! Both of them. I can't believe they talked me into using it."

I handed her Mrs. Scharpe's letter. "Do you deny writing this?"

Priscilla looked between us as if silently pleading Miss Judson for aid. Miss Judson merely lifted an eyebrow. "Well, no," Priscilla said. "You're so frightfully clever, it's impossible to hide anything from you."

"Then you *admit* to poisoning these people?"

Priscilla stared at me. "What?"

"Where is my father?"

"Ada, what is she talking about?"

"Did you poison my father, like you poisoned your husbands in America?" I was on my feet now, brandishing the manuscript like a weapon.

Now Priscilla's jaw dropped open. She tossed back her head and a gay little sound bubbled out of her throat. "Oh, dear. Oh, my. Myrtle, surely—I mean, you didn't *believe* that story, did you?"

"You deny the accusations against you? Someone else poisoned those American widowers and made away with my father?" My voice cracked dangerously on those last words.

"No one poisoned anybody!" Priscilla cried.

"Well, *someone* poisoned your aunt."

A little furrow appeared on her brow. "You're right," she said. "Someone did kill Auntie. But *I* didn't do it. And what do you mean, made away with your father? Has something happened to Arthur?"

My Investigatorial Restraint cracked, and I might have kicked the leg of the tea table, sloshing the tea and sending biscuits scattering. "You know very well what's happened!"

Miss Judson spoke up. "Wait, Myrtle—I don't think she does." She reached for me and tugged me back down.

"Where did you find that newspaper?" Priscilla asked. "I've been looking all over for it. I was surprised Auntie had it. It's so new, after all."

I was scarcely listening. I was staring instead at the grainy wedding portrait of Mrs. Scharpe and one of her unfortunate husbands, "the American soldier." Who was wearing a *British* army uniform, the khaki kind Our Boys wore in India—and a round pith helmet, belatedly reminiscent of another piece of headgear. I shoved the article at Priscilla once more. "Priscilla, who is this man?"

Now her furrow became a downright scowl. "Frank Donnelly." She fairly spat the name.

"Let me see that." Miss Judson craned in. "Bowler Hat *again*! Who is he?"

"He works for my publisher. Why?"

And then, at last, it started to make sense. "You *wrote* this article?" I waved "Black Widow Poisoner" at Priscilla.

"I'd hardly credit it with the term 'article'—"

"And this letter from Mrs. Scharpe was going to the newspaper as well?"

"Again, you're rather generous with your terminology," Priscilla said. "The *Daily Questioner* isn't exactly the London *Times*."

Miss Judson was shaking her head. "None of it's true, then. It's just a silly, made-up tabloid story."

Priscilla clasped her hands around her knees. "You've found me out! My deep, dark secret. I'm a Sensation Writer. I also do quite a good Gallows Confession, but the market for those is drying up."

"And Billy Garrett?" I said.

Now she smiled rather fondly. "Daddy's greatest creation! I did my best after he died, but that loathsome little Mr. Creech has no literary discrimination."

Her eyes fell at last on the *other* manuscript in my possession, *Mabel Castleton*, and she turned pink. "Oh. Did you like that?"

And, Dear Reader, she might not have kidnapped Father or poisoned four people in America—or Miss Wodehouse—but that didn't mean I wanted our lives made into a laughingstock. I met her eyes and lied right through my teeth. "I didn't read it."

"Oh."

"But *I* did!" Miss Judson said—with far more enthusiasm than politeness called for. "And I thought it was *splendid*. Really clever—you have such a knack for dialogue!"

Priscilla squeezed Miss Judson's knee. "Thank you, Ada. But what's this you're saying about Mr. Hardcastle? What's happened?"

I slumped back onto the sofa, deflated. Peony, supervising from the hearth, gave her querulous chirrup. "We don't know," Miss Judson said. "He left for work yesterday morning and he hasn't been seen since."

Priscilla started. "Dear heavens. Did you check—no, of course you did. And then you thought—well, of course you did. Oh, dear. Well. I *haven't* done anything despicable to your father, Myrtle. But it's a good thing I'm here now," she declared. "I am *rather* good at mysteries."

At this claim, Miss Judson gave *me* a Significant Look, this one toward upstairs. I shook my head emphatically. It was one thing having Priscilla not be a murderess, one thing to have her in my parlor—I did not want her in the schoolroom, too. She'd think we were all *friends* now!

Priscilla seemed baffled. "Perhaps more tea?" she suggested.

"Good idea." I glared at her.

Miss Judson threw up her hands. "Oh, fine. I'll fetch it," she said. "And I'll bring it to the schoolroom. Myrtle, why don't you show our guest what we've been working on."

It's a good thing Miss Judson wasn't our culprit. I'd never have caught her. She was always a step ahead of me.

"What made you think I had something to do with Auntie's death?" Priscilla wanted to know.

But we had arrived at the schoolroom, and I slid the blackboard open. "Oh," she said, taking in our lists and charts about the murder. "I see."

She recovered swiftly, seizing the chalk. "Right. Well, the man you call Bowler Hat, his name is Frank Donnelly. He works for New Century Press." She wrote those down.

"Is he a writer?"

At this she barked out a most unladylike laugh. "Quite."

"What did he want that night when you met him out by the streetlight?"

She pinched her lips. "Money. He lent me fifty pounds to pay for my ticket to come home. I'm supposed to work it off with stories, but Mr. Creech stopped buying them. And that Ambrose won't release Auntie's estate until I find that will, so I can't pay him back fairly. That's why I came to see your father. I really was hoping he could help me."

Fifty pounds was a fortune. It would take years to pay off that much money. "You didn't have to go first class," I pointed out.

She quirked a smile. "Fair enough," she said. "But what's all this about the Gilded Slipper lily? You know that's just a myth."

Miss Judson had returned with the tea, along with second helpings of cream cakes for everyone. "Well, Myrtle's working on a theory," she said, "that the lilies might be real."

Priscilla turned to stare at us. I scooped Peony up from where she was trying to reach the cakes. "When I found Peony, she was in your aunt's bedroom, and she was covered in lily nectar."

"So?"

"There are no lilies in the garden anymore," I said. "Mr. Hamm destroyed them, according to your aunt's last wishes."

Priscilla's blue eyes grew wide. "Who else knows about this?"

I scowled. "Nobody. And it's just a theory, anyway."

My shoulders slumped. "None of this tells us who really killed Miss Wodehouse!"

Or what in the world had become of Father.

Priscilla, chalk in hand, still studied the blackboard. She put a finger on the list of suspects. "Alibis!" she said abruptly. "Who could have been in that garden with Auntie? Who moved her to the bathtub?"

"We thought it was Bowler Hat," I said. "And you."

"Or Giles and you," Miss Judson said.

"It wasn't Donnelly," Priscilla said. "He and I were having a very public quarrel about my loan, in the parlor of my boardinghouse. The landlady thought–" She gave a shudder but did not elaborate. It didn't matter. I had taken the other chalk and marked lines through her name and Bowler Hat's. We'd cleared Mr. Hamm. That left but one name on our dwindling list.

"Giles," I breathed.

We were all silent for the longest moment, even Peony. Staring at the list, it seemed both impossible and inevitable.

"It's true, isn't it?" Priscilla's fingers were at her mouth. "He really killed her–because of this counterfeit lilies scheme?"

"It's certainly starting to seem that way," said Miss Judson.

"But we don't have any concrete evidence," I said. "All of this is circumstantial." I waved a frustrated arm at the blackboard.

No one had a chance to reply, for at that moment, footsteps thundered up the stairs—too heavy to be Father's—and Cook burst into the schoolroom.

"This came for you, Young Miss," she said, shoving past Priscilla to hand me an envelope, *MH* scribbled on the back in grease pencil. "And before you ask, I didn't see who left it. It was under the back door when I went to fetch some veg for supper. No footprints outside, either."

Other than my monogram, the envelope was blank and unsealed. Spine prickling, I withdrew the contents. It was a single sheet of ordinary office paper, but somebody had had a field day with magazines making it up. It was assembled of different cut-out letters, pasted together to form a message:

We HAVE YouR faTheR
BrinG EviDENCE
GREEnhOUSE
NiGhtFaLL
CoME aLoNE OR ELse

29

PERICULUM
IN MORA

Act with care, but not hesitation. There may be mortal peril in delay.

—H. M. Hardcastle, *Principles of Detection*

I dropped the ransom note like it had bitten me. It lay where it landed on the bench, nobody knowing how to react. Cook decided first: she let out a bloodcurdling shriek.

"Himself, kidnapped!" she cried. "What are we going to do?"

Miss Judson put a hand on Cook's arm. "We're going to remain calm, Mrs. Stansberry," she said, but her voice wavered.

"Very well, Miss," Cook said, composing herself. "You're quite right. I'll see to my post." And she bustled out of the room again. I heard this only distantly, a murmur of faraway, meaningless sounds. I kept staring at the note. The *T* in "Father" was from the letterhead of the *Swinburne Tribune*. I'd seen that sturdy gothic typeface every morning of my life. But everything about it now was choppy and wrong. I felt like that cut-up newspaper.

"Myrtle?" This was Priscilla.

Slowly I turned on her.

"What do you want?" I said, my voice full of venom.

"What?"

I picked up the note and fairly shoved it into her chest. "What do you *want?* 'Bring evidence.' *What* evidence? Why are you doing this?"

She stumbled backward, hands catching at the paper. "Myrtle, please. This wasn't me."

"You had plenty of time!" I shouted. "You were late! This note wasn't there when we came home." The fastest way from Redgraves was through our adjoining gardens. Priscilla could easily have slipped this note under the back door, *and* gone through the entire charade of the tea party and our chummy investigation before Cook ever had the slightest reason to go outside. "Why are you pretending?"

Priscilla's hands grew firm on my wrists. "I'm not. I've written hundreds of ransom notes for the penny dreadfuls," she said. "And this one is rubbish."

Miss Judson, frowning, came forward. "Explain."

Priscilla took a breath. "First, why go to the effort to paste all these letters together? The only reason to do that is so that you wouldn't recognize the handwriting."

Or if the kidnapper had only ever seen ransom notes in stories, I thought.

"And ransom demands are *specific*," she continued. "This one is too vague—what evidence do they mean? Why not ask for money, or the syringe, or that page from the will? This was written by an amateur." She waved a hand at the blackboard, where we'd circled our final remaining suspect. "If Giles killed Auntie, he could be capable of anything."

"But why kidnap Father? What purpose could that possibly serve?" I hugged my arms to my chest.

"He's trying to scare us," Miss Judson said.

"It's working!"

"You two must have figured something out." Priscilla was scowling at the blackboard. "Something that implicates Giles. Something he thinks you told your father, maybe."

My heart took a sickening jolt. "Oh, no."

"Myrtle, what is it?"

"At the club, Giles was right outside the room when I told Mr. Ambrose that I'd told Father we knew where the real lilies were. He must have been eavesdropping!"

"That's it, then," Priscilla said. "That's what he's been after all along. Tell him where the lilies are, and he'll let your father go."

"It might not be so simple." Miss Judson sagged against the workbench. "We might have . . . exaggerated our knowledge about the lilies' location."

Priscilla's expression grew pained. "What do we do, then?"

I clamped my jaw tight. "We just have to find the lilies."

"It's so easy, is it?" said Priscilla. "People have only been looking for fifty years."

"But we have someone here who knows where they are." I looked to Peony, who gazed back solemnly.

Priscilla stared at Peony. At me. "This is madness! You're mad—the both of you! In here, playing Girl Detective, when Arthur's being held for ransom by a murderer. And you're hoping for help from a *cat*?"

"Hmm," said Miss Judson. "You two, come with me. You *three*," she amended, to include Peony.

We crossed the hall to Miss Judson's room, whereupon I halted in the doorway with surprise. Drying-strings now crisscrossed the walls, clipped with dozens of sketches and watercolors, every one of them of Redgraves. More sketchbooks lay open on the bed. Evidently Miss Judson had Observed Redgraves just as much as I had, capturing the building and grounds from all angles in every season. Now she turned all those casual drawings to a purpose.

"You've been looking for the lilies!" I said. "I'll bet nobody's tried it this way before."

Priscilla looked dubious. "How does this help us?"

I plucked a picture from the strings. "This is your aunt's bedroom." I pointed to the balcony above the conservatory. "Peony got to the lilies somehow. Where could she have gone, from your aunt's rooms?"

"Well, *I* don't know," Priscilla said. "I'm not a cat, am I?"

I was starting to dislike her again.

"Wait, wait." Miss Judson broke in. "I've found something. Does anyone care to hear it?" Priscilla and I turned to her, a pair of guilty schoolgirls. "Thank you. Observe." Miss Judson walked from picture to picture. "What do you see?"

"Miss Judson! This is no time to be Socratic!" But the question had already begun to work on me. Drawing to drawing, vista to vista, gable to rooftop and—"What's behind all these peaky bits?" I held up my page. "You don't ever get an unobstructed view of the roof, because there are gables hiding it from every angle."

Miss Judson looked triumphant. "On the roof?" I whispered.

"Dear heavens, how could I have forgotten?" Priscilla was lost in the pictures. "When I was little . . .

322}

There was a courtyard, with a little room, like a tower. Auntie used to say it was my secret castle, for a princess. Auntie and I—we planted *flowers* up there." A surprised little laugh escaped her.

"What kind of flowers?" Miss Judson sounded breathless. But we all knew the answer.

"What was the view?" I couldn't help it; they'd engaged me. "When you played princess, you looked out the window, didn't you? What did you see?"

Eyes wide, Priscilla said, "Gravestones. It faced the cemetery."

A thrill went through me. Priscilla's secret room overlooked this very house.

"We need a better view," declared Miss Judson. "Myrtle, do you still have your spyglass?"

"Of course." It had been a gift from Mr. Ambrose when I was younger.

"All right, then," Miss Judson said. "To the garden! I have a Plan."

The four of us tromped down to the back garden. The doors to our carriage house were open, and thence emerged Cook, a shotgun propped against her shoulder. The scene was so improbable, for a moment I could scarcely take it in.

"We own a gun?" I said stupidly.

"It were Mrs. Hardcastle's father's," she said. "Himself kept it for sentimental reasons. And emergencies."

"Cook, love, what do you intend to *do* with that?" Miss Judson's voice was mild, but I caught a hint of admiration in her tone.

But a sturdy *harrumph* was all Cook would give us. "And what are you lot about, then?"

"Miss Judson has a Plan to find the Gilded Slipper lilies," I explained. "But she hasn't told us what it is yet."

"If you'll come with me." Miss Judson led us to the base of the beech tree in our garden. Its shivery leaves were a deep golden green against the late-afternoon sky, and the nearly full moon sat atop Redgraves like a beacon, already bright as a gaslamp.

"Spyglass," she commanded, and I handed it over. She stuck it into the waistband of her skirt, like her own weapon. A moment later, she had folded up her shirtsleeves and experimentally grasped a branch. "Haven't done this since my Boswell days,"* she huffed, "but I think I remember–" *Et voilà,* Dear Reader, before I could say *Fagus sylvatica,* Miss Judson had hauled herself, hand over slipping boot, into the limbs of the tree.

There was a burst of applause. "Ada, how splendid!"

I tried to climb up after her, but my height and the tea gown conspired to foil my best efforts. "Can you see anything?" I finally called, defeated. But before she had a chance to answer, there came another voice.

---

* the Boswell School for Young Ladies of Quality, in Leicestershire

"Er, don't shoot, ma'am!" Mr. Blakeney stood in the drive, hands raised like a criminal.

"Mr. Blakeney!" I exclaimed. "What are you doing here?"

"I was going to ask the same question," he said. "Madam, if you please, you don't want to shoot a solicitor-in-training on a Wednesday. It causes all sorts of paperwork." He peered into the tree. "Is that Miss Judson up there?"

"Good evening, Mr. Blakeney," she called back. "We are *rather* busy at the moment."

"Yes, I see that," he said. "Er—Stephen, I was rather troubled by what happened earlier, and I wanted to check on you. Can I presume whatever . . . this is, means your father still hasn't turned up?"

"He's been kidnapped!" Cook roared. I presented the ransom note, and all the details came tumbling out. I realized halfway through our explanation that I was shivering, and Priscilla unexpectedly put a sisterly arm around me.

Mr. Blakeney bore up well. "All right," he said, after taking it all in. "And we're not going to the police because . . . ?"

"Haven't you ever read a crime story?" Priscilla said. "They always get in the way!"

"It says come alone," I added in a small voice. "Or *else.*"

Mr. Blakeney winced and rubbed his forehead.

{325

"And does Miss J. being in that tree have something to do with the ransom? Please say yes."

"We're looking for Miss Wodehouse's lilies," I said. "We think they're on the roof somewhere."

"I think I see it!" Miss Judson called down. A moment later, amid an alarming rustle and creak of leaves and branches, she came skidding back down the tree trunk. "There's an iron fence up there, or what looks like one, anyway. It could be Priscilla's courtyard."

"But how do you get there?" I turned to Priscilla. "Can you remember?"

Priscilla shook her head. "It's all changed since then," she said. "And did you ever see any roof access? You've been over every inch of the place, too."

"We're running out of time," I said. "We can't go hunt down a way to the roof *and* get to the greenhouse by nightfall!"

Priscilla looked glumly at the drawing. "*This* will have to be enough for Giles, then. Not that anything ever was."

Miss Judson, rebuttoning her sleeves, hesitated. "I don't know. This is getting too dangerous. Is this information really enough to trade for Arthur's life? What's to stop Giles from killing both your father *and* you?"

I stared at her in anguish. "What else can we do? We can't leave him in the clutches of a murderer!"

"And I cannot send you in there alone. Your father would never forgive me if I let anything happen to you. Nor would I."

I paced round the tree, Peony so close at my heels I nearly tripped over her. I scooped her up, and she wriggled onto my shoulder, as the plan banged around in my mind. There had to be something we could do. "The boiler room!" I cried. "Giles probably doesn't know about the back room at the greenhouse. One of you could wait in there with Mum's shotgun and make sure I'm safe. *Please?*"

After an interminable moment, a stone-faced Miss Judson gave a cautious nod. "That *might* work. Mr. Blakeney, do you know how to handle a shotgun?"

"Not entirely," he admitted. "Madam Cook?"

"Then I'll do it." Miss Judson recovered the weapon from Cook. Somehow, no one seemed surprised.

Priscilla still looked doubtful. "He's already killed once for these lilies. We're just going to let him get away with it?"

"Do you have a better idea?" I demanded. "Do *you*?" I turned to Miss Judson. To Cook. They said nothing. "All right, then. Let's get ready."

Back inside, we assembled round the evidence once more. While I cinched up my courage to face Cousin Giles, Miss Judson reviewed the functionality of the old shotgun, and Priscilla picked anxiously at the ruffles on her dress. Studying our collection, Mr. Blakeney poked at the syringe with a wary finger. "Stephen," he said slowly, "what is this?"

"The murder weapon. A syringe for digitalis. We think."

"That's what really killed Miss Wodehouse? Digitalis?" He looked stricken. "*That's* why you wanted to know if Northcutt had ever bought digitalis from the chemist's downstairs?"

"Of course," I said. "What's the matter? Giles must have got it somewhere else, is all."

"That's not it," he said. "If only you'd told me what it was about! Stephen, *I've* picked up digitalis from that chemist's shop before. With syringes just like this one." He held it up, its copper-and-glass surface glinting in the lamplight. "They're for Mr. Ambrose's heart condition."

30

LET THE MASTER ANSWER

An Investigator must be prepared for any endeavor. Physical fitness, skill with various weapons, and ingenuity are recommended.

—H. M. Hardcastle, *Principles of Detection*

My blood grew cold at Mr. Blakeney's words. "Mr. Ambrose is sick?" I managed, even though I knew, right now, that was the wrong question. "How sick?" I turned on him, suddenly, unaccountably, *angry*. "He can't be sick!"

Mr. Blakeney looked helpless. "I assumed you knew. But, Stephen, this could mean—"

I snatched the syringe from him. "It doesn't mean anything! Giles killed Miss Wodehouse. *Giles.* And Giles has my father." But as I said that, the day came rushing back: how angry Mr. Ambrose had been when we'd shown up at the club, his obvious annoyance with Giles, his efforts to reassure me—*to keep me away from the police.* His lies about Father.

Giles's partner wasn't Priscilla. Or Bowler Hat Donnelly. It was Mr. Ambrose. *My* Mr. Ambrose.

I clutched the syringe until my fingernails bit into my palms, picturing the events of that awful night three weeks ago roll out like the haunting flicker of a zoetrope. Miss Wodehouse dropping the key into the vase as she rushed outside to hide the will in the coal chute, to keep Mr. Ambrose and Giles from discovering that she'd left her lilies to Mr. Hamm. She'd confronted them in the lily garden, and—*Oh.* "Mr. Blakeney, does Mr. Ambrose smoke cigars?"

"Well, he's not supposed to, with his heart like it is," he said gently, but nodded.

And Mr. Ambrose had lost his silver cigar cutter in the scuffle. I closed my eyes and passed the syringe to Priscilla before I could talk myself out of it. "Take this to the police. Mr. Ambrose's cigar cutter is there as well, and drawings Miss Judson took of the bootprints. Have them send a constable to the Monarch Club. He's likely to be there, not at—at his home, and someone will need to search the law office as well."

"I'll go with her," Cook volunteered.

The others were silent, watching me with grim faces. I didn't want to meet any of their eyes. *What happened to Miss Wodehouse makes sense to you?* Father had asked me that, and I'd said yes. It would, once we had all the pieces and the people responsible for her murder.

I'd been wrong. Now that I knew the truth, it made less sense than ever.

The hall clock chimed, and Miss Judson put a hand on my shoulder. "It's time. Are you ready?"

With a firm tug at my lacy bodice, I said in my most professional voice, "Let's go."

✺

The greenhouse felt like a massive cage. I could look straight up and see through the glass ceiling, but the steel bars arched ominously overhead, like a jail cell. The dry tile floors were spick-and-span, as though Mr. Hamm had swept thoroughly just before being arrested. Clay pots were arranged in tidy stacks, and along the walls hung racks of trowels and rakes, bags of manure and bone ash below, all awaiting Mr. Hamm's return.

Miss Judson and Mr. Blakeney had taken up positions in the boiler room, the cracked door concealed behind the smocks and aprons. Now I gazed at that shelf of fertilizer, lost in thought. Mr. Hamm kept a few bags of quicklime on hand as well. I chewed on my thumb, a dreadful idea brewing.

Perhaps, even, a *penny* dreadful idea.

I had to work fast. It took all my strength to haul one of the bags of quicklime from the shelf, since it was almost as large as I was. I'd show Miss Judson what good our chemistry lessons had done.

Quicklime is more properly calcium oxide, a by-product of limestone. It's called "quick" because of the energy trapped within. Energy released, quite invigoratingly, by *water*. Mr. Hamm had demonstrated this once, to my delight, but I had been strictly forbidden to experiment with the stuff on my own. I said a silent apology to my tutor.

Using some pruning shears, I jabbed a hole in the sturdy waxed sacking, then, like a villain in a story with a barrel of gunpowder, dragged it through the greenhouse, leaving a trail of coarse, chalky powder in my wake. Water clanked through the pipes overhead. I dropped the half-full bag under a leaky sprinkler and forced a bigger opening with the shears. Finally, standing on tiptoe, I reached up and nudged open the water valve.

There was nothing to do now but wait. I had worn a hole in the sole of these stupid shoes, and my hem had given up its cyanotic hue for ashy grey. I put the shears aside and posted myself near the door. I could see the boiler room, the dripping pipe, and the bag of lime. I was ready.

I wasn't ready at all.

But Giles came anyway.

The greenhouse door flung wide, slamming into the glass wall. "After you, Counselor."

A figure in tweed pants and a torn waistcoat, a white pillowcase over his head, stumbled across the threshold. Giles followed, as ugly as an old bruise in his ghastly jacket, prodding him in the back with a pistol.

"Father!" I cried and leaped toward him, but Giles yanked him out of reach. I yanked myself to a halt, breathing hard.

"Myrtle?" Father's voice was muffled. His hands were tied behind his back with twine, green-striped, just like the string on the package of counterfeit bulbs.

In a situation like this, Billy Garrett would be full of swagger. Miss Judson would harness a preternatural calm and let it settle over her like a cloak. Even Peony, perched on the beam above Giles's head, appeared calm but ready, eyes keen and tail flicking languidly.

"Come in," I croaked. So much for my languid, swaggery calm. "I have what you want. Father, are you unharmed?"

"Myrtle? What in the world— Young man, you have no idea what sort of trouble you're bringing upon yourself. You haven't hurt anyone yet; if you let me go now—"

"Save your breath, Hardcastle." Giles pushed Father farther into the greenhouse.

"Father, he killed Miss Wodehouse!" I blurted. Then, because of the blindfold, added, "It's Mr. Northcutt, Priscilla's cousin."

"Aren't you the clever one." Giles had enough swagger for all of us, and he aimed it right in my direction. It took every ounce of my forbearance not to flinch away from him. Behind me, I could hear the slow *drip, drip, drip* of the leaky mister.

Father's voice came again. "*What* are you doing here, Myrtle?"

"I'm rescuing you, Father. Please be still." My voice wavered only a little. "Mr. Northcutt, I brought what you asked for." I stretched my arm out as far as my four-feet-ten-inches' height would permit, and Giles snatched Miss Judson's drawing from me.

"What the devil is this?" he spat.

"It—it's the lilies," I said. "The Gilded Slipper lilies. See, they're in that little courtyard on the roof, there—"

"And what exactly am I to do with them? Are they going to fetch me a train out of town? Pay off the coppers? Save my neck from the noose? They're *flowers*, you stupid girl!"

I was stunned. Nobody had ever accused me of stupidity, so this was an utter novelty that left me momentarily speechless. "What *do* you want, then?"

"Shut up," Giles barked. "I have to think." Pushing Father ahead of him with the pistol, he paced before the racks, muttering to himself. His oiled hair flopped in his face, and his other hand, with Miss Judson's drawing, fumbled nervously against his jacket pocket.

Overhead, the pipes rattled, and a sour, rocky smell left an acrid taste in my mouth.

"You haven't hurt anyone tonight," Father said. "If you explain everything to me, I can probably help you. I'm sure it was all just a misunderstanding."

Giles gave a bitter laugh. "Right. A misunderstanding."

"Tell him," I urged. "Father's famous for being fair-minded. What were you doing in the garden that night? You were just claiming what was yours, right? Your inheritance?" Off to my right, the leaky pipe had dripped enough to make a puddle on the bag of lime. The chalky powder began to steam and fizz. I edged closer to Giles. "And when your aunt found you, you just wanted her to be reasonable, right?"

"But she wasn't reasonable, was she?" Father put in. "She was a bitter, quarrelsome, miserly old woman who never had a penny to spare for anyone, not even a beloved nephew."

"Shut up!" Giles gave Father a furious push—right into me. I caught him, more or less, on my way to the floor. We landed in a painful heap, and before we could sort ourselves out, Giles trained the gun on us.

I grabbed Father by the shoulders, like a shield. He was kneeling practically in my lap, and I could smell his lemony moustache wax and stale coffee. I pulled the pillowcase off, revealing his bewhiskered ginger head, blue eyes blinking against the dim light.

"That's my girl," he murmured, and I thought my heart might burst.

"I need to think," Giles muttered again.

"Then *think*!" I cried. "What was your plan, anyway? Kill the old woman, kidnap the Prosecutor? Then what? Kill his daughter, too?"

"Myrtle!"

A sharp glint at my knee caught my attention—I'd landed on the pruning shears. I had to keep Giles distracted. "If he *accidentally* killed his aunt, is that still murder?" I said. Father blinked at me. I knew the answer as well as he did, and he knew I knew. "If he didn't *mean* to kill her, then that's *manslaughter*," I continued, inching my hand through a heap of skirts for the shears. "You don't hang people for manslaughter, do you?"

"Er," Father said—and then he caught on. "Certainly not. Young man, if there are mitigating circumstances, I'm sure the courts will be understanding."

Giles's eyes narrowed. "Like what?"

"She attacked you first," I improvised. "She was a madwoman—it was self-defense!" Behind us, the lime gave a startling crack, which seemed to me as loud as a gunshot, and I took the moment to snip through the twine binding Father's hands together and press the shears into his hands.

"You'd have to confess, you know," he said. "You'd have to genuinely show remorse for what you've done."

"Remorse?" Giles spat out the word. "Hardly. You're not as clever as you think, Mr. Prosecutor. Don't think I can't tell what you two are doing. You're stalling."

"Stalling?" Father looked at me. "Myrtle?"

"We'd have to have a plan, and I'm afraid I just don't," I said. "I think Mr. Northcutt's stalling."

"Enough!" Giles shouted. "Both of you, get over here now. We're ending this. This picture shows where the Gilded Slipper lilies are, you say?"

I nodded warily.

"Good," he said. "The three of us are going to take a walk. You can show me."

Giles waved us toward the greenhouse door with the pistol, but we didn't get far. The glass door swung open, and there stood Priscilla like a ghost in the moonlight.

"I'm sorry," she whispered, tripping inside. "I ran into trouble on the way to the police."

"My dear girl." Mr. Ambrose's bulk filled up the doorway. "I've delivered you safely back home, and what do I find but your wicked cousin, engaged as always in some folly." Priscilla was eyeing me desperately, and I saw that she was empty-handed. Where was Cook?

"Arthur, my lad, you're safe!" Mr. Ambrose made for Father—but I blocked his path.

"I know what you did," I said softly. "You won't get away with it."

Mr. Ambrose caught me around the shoulders like he had done all my life, but it no longer felt safe in his arms. Giles was staring venomously at us, apparently unsure whom he wanted to point his gun at. Priscilla sank down onto a stack of pots, and Peony jumped onto her lap.

"Whitney?" Father's voice had a dark edge to it. "What is this?"

"Yes, *Whitney*," mocked Giles. "Why don't you explain it?"

"You ungrateful, worthless imbecile! Can you do nothing right?"

Giles decided what to do with the gun. Pointing it at Mr. Ambrose, he said, "Don't try to pin this on me, old man. You're the one who killed her."

Father gasped, face ashen.

"It's true, Father," I said. "It was Mr. Ambrose's dig-italis. For his heart condition. We found the syringe."

Priscilla put her head in her hands, looking wretched.

"This syringe?" Mr. Ambrose lifted his free hand and held it up to the light: the only evidence we had linking him to Miss Wodehouse's murder. He dropped it to the floor, where it bounced against the hard tiles. I tried to kick it away with my slippered foot, but he was faster. His great black shoe came smashing down, splintering the glass and crushing the metal. I let out a little cry.

Priscilla said, "I'm so sorry, Myrtle. He grabbed me before I could do anything."

"I don't understand," said Father. But he did. I could see the gears of his mind clicking into rhythm, against the clanking pipes in the background. Sweat beaded above his collar.

"It was all about the money," I said. "Miss Wodehouse wrote a new will, leaving nothing to Giles or Mr. Ambrose, her loyal friend who'd worked tirelessly, thanklessly for her for decades."

"You have no idea," Mr. Ambrose muttered.

"So Giles and Ambrose hatched a scheme," I continued. "To use the Redgraves name to sell counterfeit flowers. They knew it couldn't last—Miss Wodehouse would discover them eventually, or the customers they'd bilked would figure it out when their flowers bloomed—but she was an old lady. She couldn't live forever, could she?"

"Enough!" Giles cried.

"Let the girl finish," Mr. Ambrose said. "She's worked awfully hard on this, you know."

It made me sick to hear him say that now, but I forged on. "Giles got impatient. He went to the gardens to get what he thought was his due: real Redgraves lily bulbs. But Miss Wodehouse caught him looting her gardens, and confronted him. He attacked her—"

"She attacked *me*! You were right about that. The old lady was crazy—came after me with a rake, screaming like a banshee! I had to defend myself."

Mr. Ambrose gave a guffaw. "You're pleading self-defense? Can't wait to see that go before the jury." I squirmed in his grip, but he just hugged me harder.

"What happened next?" Father said.

"You know what happened," Giles whined. "I had to fight back—but she was just an old lady. I—I hit her too hard, and she fell. I thought I'd killed her."

"So he called in old Ambrose for help, just like he's done his whole life," Mr. Ambrose said with a snarl. "Who else would come clean up his mess?"

"Don't pretend this is the first time you've done something like this," Giles said.

Frowning, Father took a step toward us. "What does he mean?"

It came flying back to me in a ghastly, belated recollection. The file in Dr. Munjal's morgue. How in the world could I have forgotten DECAPITATED? "There was another case," I said. "In the Police Surgeon's files. One of your elderly clients died from an overdose of digitalis."

"An *accidental* overdose," Mr. Ambrose said.

"I remember that," Father said slowly. "The Cartwright case. Whitney, what did you do?"

"He was a sick old man, suffering a horrible death. I did his family a favor."

Father looked horrified, but his voice was calm. "What do you intend to do with us? You'll never get away with killing three more people."

"Oh, I think I might," Mr. Ambrose said. "I rushed to Redgraves to rescue the kidnapped Prosecutor, only to discover that Miss Wodehouse's nephew had already killed my dear friend and his daughter."

The remaining color drained from Father's face.

Giles looked wary. "What's going to stop me from killing you, too?"

"You stupid boy, I'm your insurance. Don't worry; you'll be committed to Broadmoor with the rest of the criminal lunatics. I won't let you hang."

"How about I just shoot you instead?" Giles took two swift steps, gave me a shove that sent me reeling into Priscilla, and put the pistol right into Mr. Ambrose's face.

Mr. Ambrose didn't even blink. "As if you had the guts."

After that, everything happened at once. I heard a shout from the back of the greenhouse—"Mr. Blakeney, NOW!"—and with a hideous metallic shriek, all the sprinklers burst open and we were hit with a sudden drenching rainstorm. Priscilla let out a glorious squeal, and Peony, in a panic, jumped straight for Giles. I heard the pistol go off—but could not tell where the shot went, for at the same moment, my little chemistry experiment finally worked.

The bag of lime, now sufficiently waterlogged by the sprinklers, exploded.

There was a blast of rock and powder and acrid gas, metal racks crashing under shattered glass. Everyone screamed, and someone flung me to the floor in a confusion of dust and chaos and debris.

"Don't move." That crisp voice I would recognize anywhere. "I will shoot you without hesitation." Miss Judson stepped into the fog of lime gas, even now dissipating with the rain from the sprinklers. She held the shotgun as easily as her sketchbook, and it was trained on Mr. Ambrose. Priscilla scrambled around in the debris and found Giles's pistol.

"Who got shot?" I cried. "Peony?"

"*No*," said a surly little feline voice, and the sodden and bedraggled cat stalked out the open greenhouse door.

Giles was doubled over, coughing. Mr. Blakeney materialized out of the dust and herded him into the path of Miss Judson's shotgun.

"Miss Judson?" Father looked dazzled, his beard and hair dust-coated. He struggled to his feet. "Miss Judson!" He was beaming, like he'd just found the prize in a Christmas pudding.

"Mr. Hardcastle," she said briskly, but she was hiding a smile. "Can you find something to secure this fellow?"

"Yes, ma'am," he said, and produced a roll of gardening twine. As they bound the dazed and choking Giles, I scoured through the mess on the floor, trying to find the bits of syringe. My eyes were streaming, my throat raw. Somewhere, surely–it wasn't *all* lost!

"Myrtle." That soft voice belonged to Priscilla, and I felt a tug on my sleeve. I turned and saw her kneeling beside Mr. Ambrose, who was slumped on the floor.

For a moment I could neither think nor move. Mr. Ambrose had fallen against a planter. His usually ruddy face was pale; one hand clutched his chest. "Mr. Blakeney!" I screamed. "He needs his medicine!"

"On it, Stephen!" And like Billy Garrett himself, Mr. Blakeney came sliding on his knees through the muck, right next to Mr. Ambrose. He ripped open Mr. Ambrose's jacket and found the battered leather case of syringes, the vial of digitalis. "Get his sleeve." Mr. Blakeney tapped the vial with the syringe and withdrew a dose, like he'd done this before. He grabbed Mr. Ambrose by the wrist–Priscilla had wrestled him from his jacket and rolled up his shirtsleeve–and jabbed him in the arm with the needle.

31

SUMMATIONS AND CLOSING ARGUMENTS

There is no more honorable pursuit than the search for Truth and Justice.

–H. M. Hardcastle, *Principles of Detection*

It was a few days before we made it over to Redgraves to search for the Gilded Slipper lilies. A lot more happened on Wednesday night, and on into Thursday morning, and indeed the rest of the week. Priscilla would not budge until all the loose ends were tied up.

"The story must end properly," she insisted, and there was no arguing with her.

After the explosion in the greenhouse—fair enough, after *I* blew up half the Redgraves greenhouse—the police arrived, summoned not by Cook (who *had* made it to the station after all, and was waiting impatiently, having no idea what had transpired back at home) but by Dr. Munjal.

"I heard the explosion from across the park," he explained, after rushing through the dark gardens with his doctor's bag. "Was anyone hurt?"

Mr. Blakeney swiftly put him onto Mr. Ambrose, who recovered with plenty of time for him and Giles to start pointing fingers at each other. Again. Not that I got to watch for very long. Father ordered me home as soon as the first police wagon rattled up the street.

"You're soaked through to the skin," he said, smoothing my limewashed hair from my face. "I don't want you catching pneumonia on top of all the excitement."

"You don't get pneumonia from being wet. *Or* from excitement.* Besides, you're soaked, too, *and* probably concussed, and did Giles even *feed* you—"

"And I'm *fine*." Father squeezed me hard. "Thanks to you. And Miss Judson."

One final player in the narrative had also run for help. We found Trudy with Peony at our house, sitting on the back stoop, looking thoroughly overset. Miss Judson brought them inside and deposited them by the kitchen fire with tea, while she and I went to change out of our wet things.

* no matter what texts on "female hysteria" might say

"Well, I'd say this has done its duty." Miss Judson held up the ragged carcass of the tea gown, hopelessly soaked, stained, burnt, blown up, hem-trodden, and reeking of lime and gunpowder.

"Let's give it a noble funeral," I said, and stuffed it into the hearth.

The full story gradually came to light over the next several hours. Father had turned up at 44 High Street after work on Tuesday night and had the unfortunate timing to run into Giles and Bowler Hat Donnelly as they were breaking into Garrow & Sons to retrieve the proceeds and evidence of the counterfeit lily scheme. Giles had hired Bowler Hat as a lookout, and he'd taken his job a little too seriously, giving Father quite the blow to the back of his head when he stumbled upon the scene. Now with an unconscious Prosecuting Solicitor on his already dirty hands, Giles could think of nothing else to do but carry on with the abduction and ransom.

All the ugly details of their plot, and the murder it had led to, likewise poured forth as the week drew on. Giles confessed and agreed to testify against Mr. Ambrose, if you could call blaming him for everything "testimony." Mr. Ambrose, on the other hand, refused to say anything. Indeed, he had refused to speak to anyone at all, including Mr. Blakeney (who was now, sadly, out of a job), and was evidently planning to represent himself at his trial.

"What's going to happen to him?" I asked at breakfast Saturday morning. I was afraid I knew the answer.

Father gave a little sigh and shuffled his papers about. "He's an old man with health problems. There's a good chance the judge will show mercy."

"But why did he do it?" I pressed. "Was he in debt? Or was it for revenge, somehow, for how she'd treated him? Because she left him out of her will?"

Father shook his head, as downhearted as I was. "All of those things, it seems. His embezzlement from Redgraves had gone on for years. He must have hoped Miss Wodehouse would pass away without discovering his deception."

I listlessly stirred my eggs. It seemed such a small, senseless reason to kill someone. "I still don't understand."

"I don't either," agreed Father sadly. "I wish I did."

At this point, a harried but cheerful Cook interrupted our breakfast. "Herself is here!"

"Send her in," Miss Judson called back. "And please bring some more of those little tarts, you know the ones."

Priscilla flitted in, in pink lace and creamy ribbons, and bent to give Miss Judson and me each a kiss. "Arthur." She gave him a neighborly nod. "Are we ready?"

I hopped right up, but Miss Judson and Father did not immediately spring to their feet with me.

"You two go on ahead," Miss Judson said.

"We'll be along shortly," Father added. But neither of them was really paying us any attention at all.

Priscilla had a look of wicked pleasure on her face as we strode out of the dining room and on toward Redgraves. "Well," she said, "I could see *that* coming practically from Boston."

"What do you mean?" I said innocently.

Redgraves's colors glowed in the morning sun—every shade of green and red and yellow, rose and daisy and lavender. Even a hedge of myrtle had broken out in white, starlike flowers. And then I saw the damaged greenhouse, like a great blackened arrow pointing to the Irrepressible Neighbor Girl, and I couldn't help wincing. Particularly when I saw the figure *beside* it, taking in the bare metal beams, the broken glass everywhere, the overturned racks and pots and planters. But my wince couldn't last long this morning.

"Mr. Hamm!" I cried, and flung myself the last few yards between us.

"Lassie!" He caught me up and swung me around like a toddler, and I didn't even care. "It's that good to see tha'."

"I'm so sorry about your greenhouse!" In a soft voice, I added, "And for sending you away in the first place."

"Ach," he said, waving away my apology. "Tha' can help by cleaning up this mess. And giving me a full report on how the plants've fared since I've been gone."

We set off across the Redgraves grounds, following Priscilla and Peony. Father and Miss Judson had finally brought up the rear. They might have been in another *county*, the way they were dawdling. I Observed Father offering his arm to Miss Judson, and diving to catch her hat when it somehow (very suspiciously) went flying from her head.

Mr. Hamm seemed in even less of a hurry, stopping to deadhead the petunias or brushing a ladybird out of harm's way. It was as though he'd been gone for years, not just a few weeks. Watching him now, my chest felt tight.

"Why did you confess?" I couldn't help that. It just tumbled out.

Mr. Hamm crouched beside a hosta just starting to put out pale purple blossoms. "Does tha' know, these are also called 'August lilies'? Almost missed them this year, did I." But he was looking into the distance, where Priscilla knelt in the grass in serious conversation with Peony about a sunbeam.

I followed his gaze and almost understood. "Did Mr. Ambrose threaten her?" That was a despicable abuse of an attorney's power.

Mr. Hamm stood up and brushed off his knees. "Don't worrit tha'self, lass." His eyes lingered so long on me I felt a stab of fear. Old fear, *expired* fear now, and just a tiny pinprick, but there nonetheless.

"Did he threaten *me*?"

"I'd never let tha' come to harm," he said gently. It was a better promise than I'd been able to make him.

I had one last question for Mr. Hamm, although I thought I'd figured it out. "When you destroyed the lilies—that was about Giles, right? Miss Wodehouse didn't want him to get his hands on them." With her secret will hidden, there'd be no other way to protect them from Giles and Mr. Ambrose.

He looked off into the distance again. "She never said *why*. But, aye, I reckon so." Each of us lost in thought, we rejoined the procession.

We caught up to Priscilla outside the house. She was frowning up at the roof, shielding her eyes from the sun. I dug out Miss Judson's best drawing (not the one I'd tried to give Giles; the police had confiscated that), and we clustered round it together.

"Do you have any idea how to reach this spot?" Priscilla asked him. "I can't find any way to the roof at all."

Mr. Hamm's eyes narrowed. We watched clouds shifting overhead, casting the gabled rooftop in and out of shadow. "I haven't been up to the roof since she had the bath put in. I did wonder, then . . ." He shook his head at Miss Wodehouse's eccentricity.

"It *must* be in the bathroom," I said. "That's how Peony's been getting there."

"What are we waiting for, then?" Priscilla said.

Trudy was in the kitchen, scrubbing down the table. "Mr. Hamm!" She stood straighter, trying to dry her hands and smooth her apron and smarten up her cap all at the same time. Her wide eyes were as bright as the sky outside.

"Ah, Trudy," he said with a warm wink. "We're goin' on up to the Mistress—the old Miss Wodehouse's rooms, if it's all right with tha'."

She stared at us and nodded, eyes huge. I thought the odds were good she'd start to cry again, but she dived back to her scrubbing with renewed vigor, and I heard her whistling as we moved on.

And so, finally, the entire lot of us—Priscilla, Peony, Mr. Hamm, Father, Miss Judson, and I—crowded into Miss Wodehouse's Famous Modern Bathroom. Commodious as the room was, it probably was never intended to admit four and a half adults and a cat all at the same time. At least without someone in the bathtub, which is exactly where Miss Judson was at that moment, perched with one boot on the edge, like a sea captain scouting for land. Father's face was nearly the same shade as his hair, and he was making a focused study of the ceiling. Everyone else swarmed about, looking for whatever passageway Peony had used.

"Drafty in here," Priscilla remarked, hugging her arms.

"Mmm," concurred Miss Judson.

Mr. Hamm was cleverer than the rest of us. He set Peony down on the floor and gave her a little nudge. "There now, kit," he said. "Show us thy spot?"

Peony gazed back at him, jade green eyes narrowed to slits. It would have been a prime moment for one of her *no*s. But instead, she leaped onto the rim of the tub, and thence to the top of the boiler.

"Oh, she'll burn herself!" cried Priscilla.

"No, it's not lit," I said, putting a hand to the cold copper.

Priscilla's head quirked to the side. "Really?" She nudged her way through. The boiler was like a giant copper coffeepot set into a half-round recess in the tile wall. Priscilla peered around it. "Where's the coal?"

For a heartbeat, we all looked at her. Then, "Oh, I'm an idiot," I said. "Of course! How did she heat the water, then?"

"Could we idiots move this along?" mumbled Father. "All this talk of bathroom boilers is making me feel rather faint."

Priscilla searched the tank with her fingers, seeking a crack or a secret opening, and then simply pushed it aside. It slid out of the way far more readily than you'd expect a Famous Modern Boiler to do–"There's no *water* in here!"–and behind it, tucked neatly into the tile recess, was a little iron gate. Just exactly Miss Wodehouse–sized, with bars far enough apart to admit one small, determined cat.

The iron bars twined round an escutcheon in the shape of a lily. "Lass," said Mr. Hamm, "does tha' still have that key?"

I was already fishing for it in my satchel. As the rest of us watched eagerly, Mr. Hamm unlocked Miss Wodehouse's gate, revealing a tight, twisting metal staircase. A little breeze whistled down like steam from a teakettle, carrying the ghost of a sweet, mysterious fragrance.

Mr. Hamm went up first. I was on Priscilla's heels, with a faceful of ruffly backside, the staircase creaking under our weight. We emerged into sunlight, dazzlingly bright after the secret stairwell. Mr. Hamm was silent, and so was Peony, but Priscilla let out the softest breath of a word. *"Oh."*

Oh, indeed. We stood in a private courtyard, ringed by an iron fence and surrounded so closely by gables and chimney pots there was scarcely anywhere to stand. Everywhere, the summer sun shone on green and white and gold. It wasn't merely a garden–it was a miniature *forest* of lilies, nearly as tall as I was, cascading with masses of creamy white blossoms as large as my two hands. From the glowing, sunlight-colored heart of each flower sprang a long yellow stamen, dripping the scone-scented nectar, anthers caked with shimmering pollen, like gold dust. I put out a finger, and it came away glittering. *Gilded.*

"My word," said Miss Judson. "How could I forget my sketchbook?"

Mr. Hamm stumbled in a daze across the rooftop, and then with a laugh like a little boy's, plunged right into the flowers. He knelt among them, head bowed. Peony reached her white paws up his knee and gave a happy meow. "Tha' did it, Mistress," he murmured, cradling a huge white lily in his strong hand. "Tha' surely did."

"They don't look much like slippers," Priscilla said judiciously. "Why did she call them that?"

"She didn't," I said. "That was what they were called in that old story where she first read about them." I pulled the carefully hand-lettered marker from the earth and handed it to her. "*She* called them *Lilium wodehouseia* . . . 'Priscilla.'"

Priscilla buried her face in a gilded blossom so we wouldn't see the tears spring up in her eyes.

A warm arm snaked round my shoulders. "Well done, Myrtle," Father said, squeezing firmly. "Very well done, indeed."

☙

We returned home that afternoon to find we'd had callers while we were gone. As I riffled through the post, Miss Judson set up her sketchbook and pastels. Father commandeered the sofa, Peony in his lap, administering a rather severe lecture on the neglect of his ginger whiskers. A contented clinking from downstairs let us know Cook was tinkering with the hob.

"Caroline Munjal wants to know if I can come to tea tomorrow. Her father has a new Marsh apparatus he'd like to demonstrate."

"Mmph," came Father's approval.

"And Aunt Helena called again." I held up her card. "She's left a brochure from some sort of excursion service." I handed that off to Miss Judson and settled happily between them with the *Police Gazette*. Perhaps there'd be a new feature: PROSECUTOR'S IRREPRESSIBLE DAUGHTER FOILS FRAUDULENT FLOWER RING, SOLVES LOCAL MURDER.

"A holiday's not a bad idea," Father said. "It would be a nice change from all this murder business."

"Railway crimes are up again," I said absently. But a headline had caught my eye. I bent closer and read:

TRAGIC "ACCIDENT" IN ARGYLL!
THREE GO IN, TWO COME OUT—
HEIR TO BANKING FORTUNE
MYSTERIOUSLY SHOT DEAD WHILE HUNTING.
IS THE "WITNESS" TELLING THE TRUTH?

I glanced up. "Does that excursion service go to Scotland?"

Finis

(Then again . . .)

A NOTE FROM THE AUTHOR

The 1890s were an exciting time in criminal science and police work, including the development of many scientific and investigative techniques we rely on today. Although DNA analysis was nearly a century away, the value of fingerprints was still being debated (although they'd been used for identification in India and China for centuries), and blood analysis was rudimentary, pioneers in toxicology (the effects of poisons), forensic medicine (using medical knowledge to determine the facts of a crime), and crime scene analysis added new tools to the police arsenal seemingly by the day.

England's criminal justice system of the 1890s was also growing into its modern form, undergoing rapid and expansive changes that confused even the English public! In Myrtle's day, the prosecution of crimes was handled by a jumble of different local offices, depending on where you lived—even, at times, by the victims themselves. With advances in police methods came the realization that a modern system of prosecution was necessary, as well, and some courts, police departments, and local councils began to employ their own full-time prosecutors—solicitors like Myrtle's father. After a series of initial proceedings at the local level (like the magistrate's trial Myrtle interrupts), cases for serious crimes like murder were escalated to higher courts, such as London's Central Criminal Court, more commonly called the Old Bailey. The system continued to evolve over the next century, becoming more and more centralized and consistent, until the establishment of the Crown Prosecution Service in the 1980s.

Readers interested in exploring the real-life stories behind this fascinating period of crime history can find more resources online at www.elizabethcbunce.com.

ACKNOWLEDGMENTS

> A good Investigator is generous in recognizing the contributions of his–of *her*–compatriots and fellows.
>
> –H. M. Hardcastle, *Principles of Detection*

My first and biggest thanks go to the Wednesday Morning Group, who sat through weekly chapters of this book, and whose keen ears and even keener enthusiasm kept me on track (and feeling more than a little like Charles Dickens, with an audience eager for each new installment!): Roz Bethke, Sherry Bushue, Victoria Lynn Catt, Victoria Dixon, Michele Helsel, Bridget Heos, Elizabeth Niedt, Anola Pickett, Judy Schuler, Katie Speck, Roderick Townley, Wyatt Townley, and Marilyn Underwood. Special thanks to Laura Moore, who also reviewed the complete manuscript. And Exceptional Thanks to Judy Hyde, our fearless leader, for reading every single word *aloud*. Even the Latin, French, and Greek. *In omnibus gratias.*

Thanks also to Barbara Stuber and Carmella Van Vleet, for toast, coffee, and commiseration; and to Diane Bailey, who truly appreciates skirts with pockets. Thanks to Jennette Boone Sylvanus for regular infusions of music and curiosities, and for spirited eleventh-hour greenhouse brainstorming.

Thanks to Special Agent Erin Murphy and the whole EMLA force, and to Elise Howard and the amazing team at Algonquin Young Readers: Sarah Alpert, Ashley Mason, Susan Wilkins, Laura Williams, Carla Weise, Brett Helquist, Leah Palmer Preiss, Megan Harley, Caitlin Rubinstein, and Kristen Bianco.

For research assistance on thorny nineteenth-century questions: Bryan Voell at Johnson County Library, J. Anderson Coats (yes, *that* J. Anderson Coats), Kimberly Carter at the Linda Hall Library of Science and Technology, Nancy Pope and Baasil Wilder at the Smithsonian Libraries, and English legal archivist Richard Wilson. Thanks and kudos go to Dr. Pamela Gordon at the University of Kansas, for her brilliant rendering of "I will not be hysterical and ridiculous" in ancient Greek.

To the many librarians, booksellers, teachers, families, and kids who offered generous insights about representation and inclusion, particularly Christine Noria and Diego Noria, Scott McKuen and Gina Thompson McKuen, Debbi Michiko Florence, Paula Yoo, and the rest of the EMLA retreat crowd.

To Sophie, the real-life Peony, a little black cat who showed up one night in the rain and brought a big adventure with her. We miss you, Kitcat.

And to my irrepressible side-partner, Christopher. Everything. Always.

MYRTLE HARDCASTLE'S INVESTIGATIONS WILL CONTINUE IN . . .

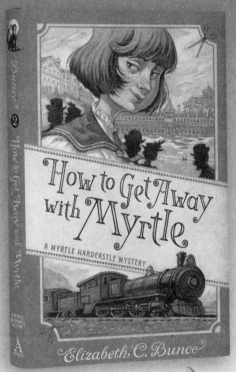